Out of Splinters and Ashes

by

Colleen L. Donnelly

Out of Splinters and Ashes

Cover Art by *Diana Carlile*

The Wild Rose Press, Inc.
PO Box 708
Adams Basin, NY 14410-0708
Visit us at www.thewildrosepress.com

Publishing History
First Vintage Rose Edition, 2018
Print ISBN 978-1-5092-1778-6
Digital ISBN 978-1-5092-1779-3

Published in the United States of America

Grandma was impossible to stop. She charged around me, into the room, flipping on a light as she did.

"You can go now," she barked at the soldier still holding the door. "This won't take long."

He nodded at Grandpa, then shut us in, us and the mirror.

I saw Amabile's story all over again as Grandpa spotted the mirror, the deep-down flicker I'd noticed before, but brighter now. Grandma and I disappeared as time took him backwards, his face transforming from old and haggard to young and alive—then to terrified, and lastly to nothing, except guilt. Grandma didn't raise the mirror as I expected her to, and shake it in his face. She let it hang in front of her, between them, the charred frame and lone lily all he could see.

I stared at the trembling finger that stretched and touched the blackened wood, scars this man probably deserved exposed at the cuff of his sleeve.

"I believe this is yours." Grandma's voice was low. I'd never seen them this close together before, never seen them face each other. But I'd seen the mirror between them forever without knowing it was there.

Praise for Colleen L. Donnelly

"Colleen has a unique style of writing that pulls you right into the story. Her books are refreshing and intriguing! Once I start to read them I can't put them down—she is an amazing author!"

~Julie Daniels, Pastor's Wife

~*~

"What do you see as you gaze into the mirror? Generations, mysteries, intrigue, and all those untold stories? That's what Cate saw as she pursued her family's path to find the source of her grandparents' unhappiness. Her desire to perhaps correct a wrong set Cate on an incredible journey to find so much more than she was looking for."

~Kacee Everhart

~*~

Colleen's awards and accomplishments:
Amazon #1 Author
RomCon Reader's Crown Finalist
1st Place Jim Richardson Memorial Award
for short story in 2010
1st Place Ozarks Writers League Award for short story

Dedication

To my mom,
my eternal sounding board for story ideas;
to my readers, who fill me with encouragement
when I'm lost in the forest and its trees.
And to my editor, Nan—
forever patient and wise to a fault.

Chapter 1

The book was small with a hard, plain cover, dark and dusty green with an embossed flower barely visible on its front. Dietrich held it on his open palm, stretched his other arm upward, and twisted the ridged plastic casing of the airplane's reading light. A soft glow lit a circle around the name pressed beneath the flower: *Amabile*. A name and a book that had meant nothing when Monika, the woman claiming to be Dietrich's aunt, had handed it to him.

"The author is the same on both books." Monika pointed to the paper booklet she'd first given him, explaining her natural mother had wrapped that one in Monika's blanket with her when Monika was given up for adoption at birth. "They are the same name and the same story. I found the hardcover book after my adoptive mother gave me the first. This story is all I have to find my real mother."

"You still haven't found her. I'm sorry." Dietrich made no mistake declaring Monika was mistaken. It was what he did; he was a journalist of all that was pure and the truth of and for his country. And now for his family, his Oma, his grandmother who couldn't be Monika's mother. Erika Müller, his grandmother's name at that time, could never have given birth here in Berlin, right before the Second World War, before she'd even met his grandfather.

"My real father is in there, too, if that's my mother's story. He was American. You're a journalist, one of the top in Germany. You write for the government, so you would want to know the truth about me…about us…wouldn't you?"

Dietrich looked at Monika then, tall and slender, light hair, and narrow features. She almost resembled Germany's old Aryan ideal from that war, just like he did, he being Oma's true descendant. But Monika wasn't claiming to be from Dietrich's Opa, his grandfather. She was claiming to be half American, from another man, from before the war. It couldn't be. Oma would never have loved an enemy or allowed herself to be taken advantage of by one. What this stranger—Monika—was saying would destroy their family, not to mention his integrity and reputation as the author of all that was right for his country.

"Erika Müller was surely my mother. Erika Schmidt now, I realize, since she married your grandfather. She was an author before she married him. And I understand that the story types between hers and this one are different, but if you…"

"My Oma is not your mother. Again, I'm sorry, but you couldn't be more wrong. About everything, including about me if you think with my reputation I would trust fiction as a reliable source." He asked her to leave and she agreed, but she refused to take the hardcover book with her.

"Read it. I know it's a story, but it has to be true. Show it to your Oma and ask her. I'll come back soon…sometime soon. Maybe then I can meet her."

He wouldn't, and Monika wouldn't either. He would never read it or show it to Oma, and Monika would never be allowed back. He kept the book so she'd go, intending to mail it to her with a letter warning her to never return. He would have burned the book if it hadn't been for the determination on Monika's face, the threat her desperation posed. This book and her silly theory meant too much to her, though it meant nothing to him.

Until he found another. Also plain, its size and coloring barely noticeable amongst the other books in Oma's attic. Those books were her romantic tales, their covers exploding with lovers entangled in intimate poses—books she'd written and was well known for, stories that had kept at least Germany's women warm before and into the Second World War. *Erika Müller* was slanted across the bottoms of each of those covers in delicate script, appropriately alluring for such stories.

But the book he'd found near them was like what Monika had left behind. Ordinary, with *THE MIRROR* embossed in simple block lettering at the top, and *Amabile* at the bottom, beneath the same sort of flower.

It couldn't mean anything. It was surely a coincidence. But he'd done his research then—on Monika, on Amabile, even on Erika Müller. But he'd asked Erika Schmidt in person, not about Monika, or Amabile, or about loving an American enemy, but about being a writer, something the two of them had shared in common even though she hadn't written since before he was born. He'd also asked again about her injuries, the burns and scars she kept covered by clothing even in the summer. "Furnace explosion." That was all Oma ever said. But he knew it was a tremendous explosion that had nearly killed her not long before the war. Making it impossible for her to have had an American lover and deliver a child at that time.

Dietrich set Monika's book on his lap and opened *The Mirror* again, ancient and yellowed, but without the noisy protests that come with age and from being hidden in an attic for so long since he had opened it many times recently. The faded print stared up at him. He'd always known. He'd always closed his eyes to what was but wasn't there with Oma even before these books and Monika had come to his door—his door instead of Oma's, thankfully. His journalistic instinct, the inner eye that turned impressions into words, had always sensed something. He'd been aware of an occupied vacancy at Oma's side, an absence so powerful it was palpable. It was in the way she stood, the way she moved, so much a part of her it had become a part of their family, all of them allowing space for a presence that wasn't there. He'd excused it as sorrow. She'd lost her parents, given up her writing, and then her husband had passed, his Opa. But the manifestation of what was missing had been missing much longer than at least his grandfather.

That absence, that invisible presence, had a form, according to Monika. The form of a man, and he was American. A runner in Hitler's Olympics, tall and lanky and blond. And cruel. According to the stories, he'd run fast, run away with Amabile's heart, and then run away for good.

Dietrich stared at the sort of book he'd never bothered to read, this one in particular being one he wished he hadn't. If the journals he wrote for knew— knew that such a relationship might be in his background, knew their top government research journalist was using fiction to find the truth—he'd be fired.

He leaned back in his seat. Time and secrecy were of the essence. He would read this and the other book one more time each on the flight from Berlin to New York, sifting out every detail about "him" that he could—the American who had stolen Amabile's heart and left her with nothing but scars...and, God help them all, possibly a baby. Dietrich stared at the black print, so deeply absorbed into the pages it could never be erased. He'd told Monika to stay away, that he'd contact her in two weeks when he returned. Oma had been told he was on assignment for the main journal he wrote for, and they had been told he was doing research on a tip he'd received. None of them would be patient. But by the time this flight landed, he would know, he would have discovered enough about this man to be able to find him if he existed. But of course he didn't exist, and Dietrich would carry home the truth.

The Mirror
To See What Really Is

The mirror—it was a beautiful gift. From him. One she stared into when she longed to see the two of them again, one she stared at today as she waited for him to come.

The mirror had been hers for several days now, yet she still thrilled at the thoughtfulness that had gone into his choice—the size that nicely framed her shoulders and face...her reflection fitting within its rectangular shape with enough room beneath the slight arch at the top for a hat if she chose to wear one. Enough breadth the two of them could be seen together, pressed close, him so very tall and she with her head hardly reaching

5

his shoulder. But most of all, beyond the mirror's perfect size and shape, she admired the beauty of its beveled glass encased by the dark wooden frame, and the six handcarved lilies rounding its top, three at each of its curved upper corners.

He'd brought the mirror the first time he visited her. "When I saw this, I saw us...saw you," he claimed. He brought the lilies afterward, one at a time, each one uniquely carved by his own hand, symbols of what he'd seen when they'd stood alongside each other and smiled into the mirror. "Each represents a visage of us," he would explain as he attached each lily, describing how he'd seen her and him. Then he would turn the mirror toward her—toward both of them as he squeezed close—and ask if she didn't see the same. She stood rapt with each vision he shared, admired each lily as his shoulder pressed against hers. Then whatever she hadn't understood of his English, or he of her German, they both understood as they gazed at their reflections side by side in the glass.

Six. Six wooden lilies. Six different thoughts since their first meeting on that rainy evening at the start of Berlin's Summer Games. Now, near the end of the games, she stared into his mirror as she waited. For on this day he was bringing the seventh. His final reflection, the one he would attach to the peak, the crown of the mirror.

She turned from the mirror where it hung above her desk and looked to the nearby window, through it and into the street below. Volksoper Street. A mere alleyway recently, instead of the broad thoroughfare it normally was, crowded on both sides with colorful banners hailing the games amidst Germany's red national flags. She imagined him there on the street, how he would look as he came—tall and lean, blond, a champion bursting between the flags and running her way, the seventh lily like their own Olympic torch in his hand.

He was right about the mirror. Each of those moments he'd marked by a carved flower was there, each visage of the two of them evident when she looked deep into its glass. Every juncture, every emotion, every experience from the past to the future—all visible to her, and surely leading to one thing. Her hand quivered, the nakedness of her ring finger conspicuous, ready for his seventh lily's promise. The seal for the vows they'd made privately in the mirror and informally before God.

Cars, carriages, and even horses' hooves marked time on the cobbled street outside. She watched the gaiety, the whole of her neighborhood with its tiny shops and clutter of artisans doing their part to welcome foreigners here for the games. Local artisans like her. Foreigners like him.

She studied the passersby below, imagined again how he'd look racing along the stones, the grin on his face, his blond hair glistening like the treasure he was to be carrying with that last carving. She pressed her fingertips alongside the sheaves of paper she'd left to dry on the desktop, stretched, and leaned nearer the window as she watched for him. Pages and pages of words rested near her hands, words he liked to hear. Her words. New words. Stories that had changed since meeting him, stories she now wrote as his Amabile...his lily.

Suddenly he was there, tall and rushing through

the crowd, running. Just as she'd hoped, just as his medal—bronze—had proved he could. But faster than she'd thought. And harder. She caught the lift of his chin, the thrust of his chest, the pumping of his fists and elbows that brought his face her way. A face lacking the smile she'd expected to see—fixed, instead, in desperate lines as he raced closer.

The visage burst into a thousand fragments. She saw and felt the blast before she heard it. The pages of her work launched upward—a spray of leaflets obscuring the window and the anguish that exploded on his face. Stories she'd created for him showered the room. Everything around her collapsed, then blew outward, out of proportion, hurled under a great light and deafening noise. Her heart. His face. Her thoughts. Everything. She grabbed for his mirror and the lilies...she grabbed at the glass, at the wood, at what he was coming to say. At what was supposed to be hers.

At what she'd hold on to. Until it was.

~Amabile

Dietrich reached upward and twisted the reading light with his fingertips, narrowing its cone of brightness to a pinpoint and then to nothing, Amabile's book left in shadowy darkness.

Other passengers, men and women, were leaving their seats, unaware of Amabile's words. Stewardesses bent around him, retrieving plastic glasses and trays that were disposable, like this woman had been. "Oma, it couldn't have been you that loved an enemy." It couldn't have been her on the pages on his lap. This was fiction. How could any of it be real? At least his grandfather had died before Monika appeared asking about Opa's wife, Dietrich's father's mother, Dietrich's own grandmother.

"A pillow, sir?" A stewardess, German like Dietrich, spoke English to the American passenger beside him as Dietrich closed the small book. "*Kissen?*" she offered Dietrich as the man next to him took one for the long flight to New York. The soft light highlighted the wave in her hair, brown hair like his Oma's had been. Dietrich nodded as she smiled. He tucked both books into the inner pocket of his corduroy jacket and accepted the pillow she held. "*Danke*," he said as the American said, "Thank you." The stewardess moved away, and the two of them settled back in their seats.

"*Gute Nacht.*" Dietrich nodded to the man next to him, noting the expensive but finely comfortable attire. A business man? It wouldn't be difficult for a man like this to crush some impressionable young German girl and leave her behind. Even Dietrich could likely enjoy his sort of company, the passenger looking cultured and intelligent enough they could talk the whole night, condense the lengthy flight to mere minutes. The man might have thought the same if Dietrich had said goodnight in English instead of his native German. Not this time. The man nodded and burrowed deep into the hard pillow.

Dietrich settled farther back. A different American man needed his attention. "He"—the man in the stories—noticeably tall, lean, and blond. Dietrich fished a charred lump from the pocket of his trousers and turned it over in his fingers. He rubbed his thumb over the rough and splintering wood he'd found in his grandmother's attic with the books.

Passengers rustled around him, settling into sleep. He looked toward the window—a mirror now, with night outside and soft lights illuminating the plane's interior. His grandmother was easy to imagine in the reflection, her face alongside his own, the way they'd always been as he grew up. Dietrich stared at the glass, then leaned close and searched for that other face, "his" face next to hers instead of Dietrich's, that presence that had never been. The face that had never returned in the stories, not even to see if Amabile had survived.

Dietrich sat back in his seat. He stuffed the lump of burnt wood back into his pocket and stared straight ahead. No wonder he dealt in facts instead of obscurities. Vagaries were terrifying, the fodder of hacks and menial reporters to stir up alarm. He would find the facts to Amabile if there were any, find "him" if he existed, find the American who had destroyed her heart, or prove it all fiction, especially fiction Erika Müller hadn't written but merely been fascinated with, and rid his family of Monika forever.

Chapter 2

My grandfather's eyes were strangely alert.

"Cate?" He gazed through his screen door, first at me on his front porch, then at the large envelopes tucked under my arm, and lastly to the yard behind me. He seemed even thinner and taller than usual as he stood peering over my head.

Grandma's at her bookstore. She's not coming back. I looked at Grandpa Crawley's lean face through the screen. Grandma had done this before, started to move out of the back of Non Bookends where she'd set up a little home-away-from-home, to return to living with the man her parents had insisted she marry. But she had yet to make it all the way.

I could tell him I was sorry for all of it—sorry Grandma'd broken their engagement when he returned home to New York from overseas right before the beginning of World War II. Sorry she'd said he wasn't the same man she'd become engaged to before he was sent off months before. Sorry I was standing here telling him his wife wasn't coming back home. Again.

Grandpa continued to gaze through the screen, his quiet blue eyes focused over the top of my head. I really was sorry for this man who'd spent his life here and alone but never complaining. My mother called his house the eye of the storm and Grandma the gale that blustered around it. Grandpa's quiet seemed more than relief the storm had momentarily blown past. He likely longed for her. There was an absence around him, an empty space so evident it took the form of a presence. A place she belonged that hadn't been filled by the long hours he bent over sticks and pieces of wood, carving and whittling each one to nothing. Grandma probably longed for him, too, otherwise her store, Non Bookends, its authors and their platitudes, would have filled her emptiness and kept her from occasionally blowing back his direction.

"Is this a good time?" I lifted the envelopes I held, fanned them like a wing under my arm. He would know these were books Grandma had ordered to read—or have me read—before she allowed them on Non Bookends' shelves, careful to choose only books that suited her crusade…something that involved weapons and war more than love. I'd snatched them from Grandma's table after her march from here back into Non Bookends, announcing she refused to move anything else to their house. *He's expecting someone*, she'd thundered as she stormed past. *But it's someone else, not me*. I didn't bother to argue or tell her she was wrong…again. I'd grabbed these three new arrivals and run the same two blocks I'd always been running between the two of them, ignoring her shouts of *leave things be* as I left.

I couldn't leave them be, no matter what Grandma said. I battled my grandparents' mayhem instead of escaping it like my mother had, moving herself and my father to the other side of New York City. I was going to fix my grandparents and my mother, fix all of us so we could live like a normal family and not look like spectacles to everyone else. Especially to the public

Emerson Cosnik, the attorney I'd been dating, hoped to win the approval of as he ran for the New York Senate.

I fanned the packages again, catching Grandpa's attention, his gaze traveling from them to my forehead and the evidence I'd run. I swiped the sweat with my forearm and waited for the *You shouldn't run, Cate,* he always said.

But he didn't. He looked again to the street and yard behind me. He was supposed to acknowledge the envelopes, assume I had books to read, and let me in so I could say Grandma wasn't coming back in a way that wouldn't feel like a hammer crashing down on a heart and face normally so expressionless I could only guess what was there. But he wasn't expressionless. I glanced over my shoulder where he was looking. Maybe this morning had been different for him and Grandma. Maybe the two bags of her belongings she'd moved here from her little home-away-from-home ignited something. I turned back to the screen, leaned to the side, and peered into the dark of their living room. Those bags should be somewhere behind Grandpa. Maybe he was waiting. Maybe in spite of what she'd told me, he was expecting her to bring more and move back home like she'd started to.

I peered again through the screen at the empty living room while he looked over my head at the empty sidewalk and street. Grandma was wrong. There was no "someone else" in his house. And if it was her he was expecting, he was wrong too. There was no "someone else" in their yard, no repentant wife behind me, coming home.

"Kind of early to be reading." He glanced down at the envelopes, and I could hear the *Kind of early to be running* that he wasn't saying. My running bothered him, probably because I'd worn thin the two blocks of sidewalk between Non Bookends and here over the years, first with a small pair of girls' tennis shoes and now with a women's size seven, relaying messages back and forth between them, fictitious messages so they would each think the other one cared. I'd reinterpreted Grandma's snarls when I ran to his house, and brought back from him what I imagined I saw in his face as he sat whittling nothing. I'd played Cupid, set up dinners for the two of them, made up warm notes and passed them from one to the other, laughed and smiled alone during family nights no one wanted except me.

"I told Grandma I'd look these over for her." I prayed the screen masked my lie. "I thought I'd read them here where it's quiet instead of at the store. Maybe you and I could have a glass of tea and talk a little first."

He frowned. I studied one of my mother's two parents she loved so much she hated them. "I'm coming in, Grandpa." I opened the screen door and walked through it.

He looked past the envelopes, at me, then behind me when the screen door closed. I planted myself in front of him, warding off any chance he'd say what Grandma had said—just leave things be. Leave him be the same way he always let Non Bookends be, never entering her store.

And leave the two bags she'd moved here from Non Bookends be, not because she'd change her mind and decide to move back into her real home after all, but because that "someone else" she thought he expected had upset her. It upset her, but what she'd said was an explosion—*It's not who I expected…*

Grandpa continued to peer over the top of me, a good two heads taller than I was, staring into the empty sidewalk and street with blue eyes dulled by the reflection of the gray weathered screen, white hair that used to be blond hanging in limp strands over his forehead. "Maybe you should just go on and read them at your place," he said. "It's quieter there."

I listened to the silence that had done nothing but grow since Grandma first moved out ages ago, felt the fragile alarm in his gaze that warned me he could stop watching for her and slip back into accepting she was never coming if I left him be. "I want to sit here with you, Grandpa."

His eyes passed to me for a moment, then back to the outdoors.

"You sit. I'll get us some tea." I laid a hand on his arm and glanced around their living room at décor straight from the 1940s—floral wallpaper, tufted sofas, and chintz drapes that other couples their age had left behind for newer furniture and more modern designs. I loved this house, but it was a victim in Grandma's war, a casualty of her reluctant "I do." Grandpa had done his part for the two of them, buying Non Bookends for Grandma right after they were married. "He had to appease your grandma," Mama had told me, waving her arms about the engagement Grandma had broken, and her insistence Grandpa wasn't the same fiancé she'd seen off, and that if Grandma's parents hadn't forced Grandma because of the shortage of available men if the US ended up in a war, neither Mama nor I would ever have come to be. But we had come to be. My grandparents had made a family, somehow, and they'd made this home. It had been a constant, instead of the progress most couples made, but it was a cozy constant that suited them and me.

I squeezed Grandpa's arm and let go, catching then what I hadn't through the screen or in my quick scan. Something was different. Grandpa had changed their cozy constant. He'd straightened what never was messy by squaring everything, aligning each object or stack as if he and Grandma decorated on a grid. The normally comfortable area looked sterile, as if someone had died, personal items stripped away, even the two bags she had brought here, until signs of life were completely gone. *He's expecting someone all right, just not me.* Grandma had paused in her march past me this morning, pivoted a half turn to the left at the last tier of books hiding the way to her room. Her simple belted dress and gray hair had made her deceptively matronly above the fierceness that exploded from her lips, capped the knuckles of her fists with white, and bleached her usually hale complexion. I glanced again around the living room that had changed, something about it having changed her to the point her fierceness had faltered. *It's not who I expected, but the truth is, it's not me.*

But Grandpa never expected anyone. He had spent most of their marriage alone. Even as a younger man, when not at work packaging and delivering meat for the local butcher, he was at home, either in his favorite chair in the living room or in his rocker on the front porch, whittling sticks to splinters.

But what I saw in their living room, this change, this sterile rearrangement Grandpa had done, didn't look at all like the woman I hoped he was expecting. It looked nothing like Grandma's little home-away-from-home in Non Bookends, the cot she slept on, her overstuffed chair and lamp nearby, and the tiny kitchenette across the room. That room was a miniature of what this house had been, the way she left it and Grandpa had always kept it.

"Grandpa?"

He looked toward the door. I followed his gaze to where three US military officials stood, their green, brass, and stripes staring back at us from his porch. "Grandpa?" I gave what I could see of them through the tiny squares of the screen a long stare. A hard stare that tried to penetrate their bulletproof exteriors.

There was no answer as my grandfather opened the door. He didn't welcome them, but he ushered them in. As if he had been expecting them.

"I came here to work." The lie popped out, surprising me more than it did the looks on their faces as they stood in a line staring at me. Grandpa's face joined them. Not alongside and not as cold, but with the same command—I should leave. I wouldn't. I wouldn't leave him be. I wasn't expected, just like Grandma said she wasn't. But to me, neither were they. The military, the war, or anything pertaining to either had never been spoken well of in this house, and I wouldn't let it start now. "I'll be in that room if you need me. Working." I waved the envelopes that felt twice what they'd weighed before, nodded toward and disappeared into what had once been my grandparents' bedroom—just my grandfather's now—across a small hallway from where they stood, leaving the door ajar enough I could hear, but ignored, my name followed by my grandfather's protest.

I staggered across the bedroom and dropped onto his bed. Sentence fragments I took for military formalities spouted from the living room. The officers hadn't expected me, but they were going to ignore me, and they wanted Grandpa to do the same. I tossed the envelopes from Non Bookends to the side, then snatched one back and stared at it, listening to the stilted conversation in the background. They shouldn't be here. Grandma should. I ripped the package open and yanked out a booklet while formal and informal words filled the other room. Those officials might be there because Grandpa expected them to come, but I expected them to go. Soon.

The officers and Grandpa settled into chairs and the sofa in the next room. I could tell by the sounds—by the shuffling, the creaking, and the intermittent blocks of silence—that they were preparing to really talk. The sooner they did, the sooner they could get this visit over. Grandpa shouldn't expect men like that; he should expect my grandmother. And she should be here instead of me, to shoo them out.

I held what looked like a short story on my lap as I imagined Grandpa in his favorite chair staring at the men, wishing them away so Grandma could join him later—expected, and sitting in her nearby chair so she could turn her nose up at this too-brief tale. Grandma chose novels or full-length plays for her crusade, and Grandpa never entertained or expected anyone.

I gazed at yellowed pages of words I cared nothing about as voices rose from the living room, men's voices, forming more distinctive words I did care about.

I sat straighter on my grandparents' bed, perched

nearer its edge, and listened, the scent of my grandfather wafting up from his pillow—from my grandmother's pillow, nothing. The voices lowered, became too muffled to understand. Masculine mumbling I could only guess at as I gazed at the story.

The Forever Meeting

After the rain comes clarity—that moment when thousands of tiny, reflecting droplets finally go away, and color emerges, vibrant in its new sodden state.

So it was the first time she saw him, and he her in return. The shower pelted around them, blinding them to what was there, and what they should have seen—his shoulders, too square and sharp as if at attention, the lean strength of a man built to compete and then leave, and the simple style of dress she wore that was unlike what he was used to but typical of young women in Berlin.

His look split the torrent enough their imaginations took over, allowing them to see what they'd always dreamed they'd someday see. His hair was blond, although it hung in icicles of dripping brown. Hers was dark with curls, but it lay flat and heavy under the wet. The colors of her dress exploded into a life it never really had, emboldened as the fabric melded to her skin. And the insignia that gave him the right to be there shimmered against a soaked jacket different from others in her city.

His accent silenced the assailing drops as he led her to shelter where they'd be safe. She understood his words, though not perfectly. They were foreign, but the language of his eyes was the same as hers, speaking exactly what she'd always imagined she would someday hear. "This way," he said. "Ja," she said in return and nodded. His smile had no accent, and with it he took her by the elbow and steered her to shelter.

My grandfather's voice broke above the story and through its rain, his words turning the ones on these pages back to nothing. "Lieutenant McCoy led our unit with all diligence. He was a solid force that never wavered." Grandpa's normally soft-spoken tone rose, each word deliberate, as if fired from a gun. I'd never heard him speak that way. I closed the booklet. The silence following his statement was long, leaving his mark feeling unsteady.

"Mr. Crawley, it's Lieutenant McCoy's communications before and during the war that we're investigating. Where they originated, and in whose hands they ended."

My grandfather remained silent, as quiet as I was. I ran a finger along the frayed edges of the heavy parchment that made up the small book's cover as I listened, traced its faded frame that was tied with a golden cord binding everything at a creased center.

They spoke again. Louder now, saying names I couldn't understand, a string of them, to which Grandpa said nothing in return. I stared at the thin booklet on my lap as the list was repeated like a ceremony outside the door. I fingered its cover and pages as I listened for Grandpa's response, this story a contrast to their cold conversation, and far too romantic for Grandma's usual preferences. She'd told me once romance had its place, just as all genres of fiction did—a place in time through which we all had to pass, and a place on Non Bookends' shelves only as it pertained to her crusade. I glanced at the trashcan not far from their bed. If Grandma had passed through a time of romance, it was as gone as yesterday's rubbish. Like this booklet was going to be. This one would never make it to her shelves.

"I don't recall any of those names." My grandfather's voice came through the wall and around the edge of the door. *Way to go, Grandpa.* Grandpa never talked about the Second World War or his time in the army, not even to me in the sixth grade when I wrote a report on it. He'd been a soldier before the war began, and dismissed any questions about his part in it by saying he never fought in any of the battles, being sent back home with injuries before the US ever joined in. In spite of Grandma's claims Grandpa wasn't the same man she'd seen off, my mother had seen old newspaper articles proving he was, the community welcoming Grandpa home and hailing him as a hero, especially because of his injuries. Grandpa had been shipped back with scars I'd never seen except for what showed below the long sleeves he always wore and the limp he managed well for his height. Mama believed Grandma resented being with a man who walked a little bit different. I asked Grandma about that and she told me it wasn't the gimp in a man's gait that made him crippled, it was the gimp in his eye.

Grandma always created a ruckus whenever the subject of those military days came up, making so much noise with whatever she was doing it was impossible to hear what little Grandpa said. I never knew if it was his stubborn silence on the subject she was trying to drown out, or whatever he might have said had he been given the chance. Whichever it was, she capped each of his brief dismissals about his part before the war by reminding me that far more truth was told in fiction than anywhere else, and if I wanted to know anything about that era, then Non Bookends was where I'd find it—stories being the truth a man would otherwise deny.

The men in Grandpa's living room didn't look like the sort of men who'd thank me and leave if I suggested they go sift through Grandma's bookshelves for whatever they needed to know about Lieutenant McCoy. I tapped Grandma's little booklet on my hand, then stood, swung the bedroom door open, and marched into the living room.

"Coffee?" I said to my grandfather's ashen face, waving the book as a hopeful conversation starter. Grandpa sat alone on one side of the room in his favorite chair, the leg he favored sticking out in front of him like a long, thin pole. The other three men sat in perfect order on the sofa, shoulder to shoulder, stripe to stripe, *What are you doing here?* written across their faces.

"Cate." My grandfather struggled to his feet with far more effort than usual. He rose until his head towered above mine, white hair, straight and fine, falling over his forehead. If they would leave and Grandma would actually come, maybe he'd struggle less and get his color back. "Why don't you go on now." He paused. "You can read your grandmother's books better somewhere else."

"I'm almost finished with this one. I'll leave them here when I'm done. For her." It was a bigger lie. I smacked the booklet on the palm of one hand as I surveyed the three stolid figures who looked like they'd never read fiction in their lives. They were watching my grandfather instead of me. I glanced his way as he reached for a nearby cane he rarely used. The slow and easy manner he'd always maneuvered with looked different with them in the room. Each movement seemed more pronounced, his deliberate ease telling me Grandma was right—he'd been expecting these men. I stared at my grandfather. Maybe what had always seemed like relaxed behavior had been waiting, instead. Braced...just like he was now as he leaned into his cane. "If you decide you want something..." I forced a smile at him and the three faces that didn't smile back. "I'll be right in there." I nodded to the bedroom doorway, wishing for even a half smile on my grandfather's face. A look that didn't come.

"Best if you just went on." Grandpa's knuckles were white like Grandma's had been. Even the scars striping the hand that gripped the cane were whiter than usual.

"I'll be in there." I nodded toward the bedroom again. If I'd come with my camera, I could go to the basement, to the small developing lab Grandpa had built for me so I'd take pictures instead of running. But the basement was too far away to hear. I pointed the book in the direction of the bedroom. "In there."

"Then close the door. So you can concentrate better." Grandpa tipped his head toward Grandma's booklet.

I walked straight to their room and closed the door behind me, staying close as the latch clicked, close enough to hear my grandfather settle himself back into his chair. I laid the booklet on the highboy dresser nearby and folded my arms on its top, resting my chin on them so that my ear was close to the door. There would be an ending to this discussion in my grandparents' living room, and I would stand here until

I heard it. I wanted McCoy out of the air and these expected men to go away.

Discussion revived in the living room following throats being cleared and my grandfather's apology for the interruption. I could hear it in his tone, even if they couldn't, the chance he was giving them to leave. An opportunity to say my disruption was no problem, that time was short and they needed to go anyway. But they didn't say those things. Instead, one asked Grandpa where he kept his military memorabilia.

"I kept nothing from the service," my grandfather replied. I straightened from the highboy and pressed my ear to the door. The men argued that most veterans kept everything—uniforms, orders, photos, awards, and souvenirs. "I didn't. It bothered my wife."

I covered a gasp with my hand, holding in the shock at Grandpa's claim, which was tantamount to saying, "I love my wife." I stared at the door, unable to believe what I'd heard. That's what love sounded like...and it had been here all along. The war and everything military pertaining to Grandpa did bother Grandma. She'd told me when men go overseas they leave their women behind—wondering. Wondering what some had already suspected, others had denied, and a few had realized before their men's enlistments even began. I never understood what she meant, but the "bother" was there. The "bother" that had silenced the uniformed men's interrogation of my grandfather and fueled Grandma's refusal to have anything to do with this man.

I stared down at the booklet on the dresser top. Grandma's and Grandpa's had never seemed like the love story Mama wished it were, yet there he was, telling these men he'd willingly forgone everything from the service, everything that bothered his wife. Not at all what I'd expect from a man who'd watched his wife march away from him again today. I opened the booklet and peered at a love story like Mama had dreamed of for her parents. One that was natural, not nearly so much work, steady and stable, fixed in black ink, forever dissolved onto a soft and quiet background.

It occurred to her as they ducked into a tiny café away from the rain that the evidence of his lithe power, along with the foreign style of clothing, the marshaled posture, and the accent, all indicated he could be torn away from her. Could, but her heart knew he wouldn't. No matter where he went, her heart would always be his, and his hers. He knew it, too. They dropped into seats at a small table against the wall. And there they sat and spoke without accents, without words.

"Pre-trial" shot from the other room. It jarred me from Mama's dream, silencing the gentler words in black ink. The lieutenant's name was said again, followed by my grandfather's assent, the sort of assent that said, "Yes, sir," while at the same time saying, "I think you shouldn't."

Those men were wrong, the way they passed over my grandfather's implied suggestion they reconsider, and his respect for his wife who was bothered by things pertaining to the military. I applauded my grandfather for stripping their living room of everything that said "Welcome" or exposed anything of her. And I imagined my grandmother's face when I told her how mistaken she'd been about this man all these years, and that those he'd expected were nothing and gone.

They stood. I heard three dull-colored but starched

uniforms rise to their feet and lead a tall, gaunt, elderly man limping to the door.

I cracked the bedroom door and listened to an exchange of dates and times instead of thank-yous or goodbyes in the living room. I stared at the worn little booklet that, gauging by its age, was probably written close to a time of war, maybe even the Second World War, the period they were interested in. I spun it toward me and glanced inside the front cover as the screen door creaked open. Grandma was right. I'd learned more from these few paragraphs about a man overseas than those men had in an hour from my grandfather. No author's name, no publishing date inside the cover or on the first page. If it was from the 1940s, or even the 1950s, I'd run it out to them before they drove away. Slap it in their hands and tell them what Grandma's favorite playwright, Henrik Ibsen, claimed—*Really good stories don't answer questions, but they ask them. Ask just the right ones so we can see our answers.*

Grandpa didn't say goodbye, just like they didn't to him. His guttural, "Yes, sir," was all I heard. I would beg him to go to Non Bookends with me and tell Grandma what he'd said to these men. I'd suggest it when they were gone, making him understand how much she needed to know that he cared. It would probably take a war-sized explosion to get him away from his favorite living room chair or from the front porch where he would amass piles of wood shavings at his feet. Whatever it took, I would do it. The two of them needed it. I needed it. And even Emerson would need it as he ran for the senate.

A car started in the drive. I opened the bedroom door farther and leaned around its edge. My grandfather's tall form listed to one side as he stared through the screen, relying more heavily than usual on his stronger leg. I snatched the booklet and flipped to the back. Maybe there was still time to give those three what they wanted so I could make sure they stayed away.

He said he'd return. His blond hair, almost white now it was dry, disappeared under a cap he tugged from a pocket. She shook her dress, damp and cool but no longer sticking to her skin. If he were anyone else, if this had been any other time, she would have asked, "When? When will you return?" But "when" didn't matter with him, because in her heart he'd never leave. He would always be with her, even as she watched the tall back of his jacket disappear.

~Amabile

The car drove away. I slapped the book closed and tossed it onto the bed next to its envelope and the other two, instead of into the trash like Grandma eventually would. Or maybe wouldn't, once she realized Grandpa truly loved her and stories like this had a place in her store. Maybe Non Bookends would have a new crusade. Maybe everything my mother had wanted and I had worked for was finally here.

"Grandpa," I said to his tilting frame, "we're going for a walk."

Chapter 3

Grandpa nodded at my suggestion to walk, took the front steps the way I took runs—fast and feverish, in spite of his limp—and veered left instead of right at the end of his front sidewalk, pivoting on the leg he relied on, ignoring my raised hand pointing the opposite direction toward Non Bookends.

"Grandpa, slow down." I hurried to catch up with him. "I asked you to walk, not race." I glanced his way as I came alongside him, at his lean form stretching and dipping a good full stride beyond my shorter one. His white hair fluttered with his pace, his limp and age the only things keeping him from an all-out run.

"Racing isn't in me. Neither is fast." Grandpa slowed and glanced down at me, the sort of half-smile on his plainly handsome face that never made it to his eyes.

"Well, take it easy and save some energy, then." I grinned at him. I wanted his energy for far, not fast, a square of blocks that would end us at Non Bookends.

"You still entering that marathon?" He gazed down the sidewalk as we went. The man who'd asked almost nothing of me asked again in his own way—stop running. Not just the sidewalk between their house and Grandma's store, but altogether.

"Entering, yes, but not to win. Unless you want to loan me your legs. Then I could win." I didn't run to win. He knew that. Everyone knew that, but if I reminded him now I'd sound more like Grandma than myself. I didn't have his legs, but I was fast. Fast enough I'd been forced to race to win in high school, where Jill—taller and older, now someone who thought of herself as a friend—had beat me. Even Jill's husband Frank, who bicycled alongside my runs, his worn-out knees turning him into everyone's except Jill's coach, carried a stopwatch and set imaginary finish lines I ignored.

"Running's not in the family. And speed takes more than just legs." Grandpa said it the way he'd said it hundreds of times before.

"Legs that stopped with my mother." Seeing Grandpa was like seeing my mother—light hair, fair complexion, long legs, and lithe build. My mother could have raced and won; she carried more energy in her than anyone I'd ever known. She was feverish like Grandpa was now, even with me lagging enough to slow his limping stride. "Dad always teased Mama about all the shoes she wore out, the way she raced around. He said she could have made a fortune as the cover girl for someone's vitamin ad campaign." But her energy hadn't been like that. She was feverish and frantic, always running, hammering out her dreams, her ponytailed blonde hair making her look like a cheerleader ready to throw herself into a flip.

I tossed my head, sending my own hair back, loose and brown, like my father's. I wasn't like Grandpa or my mother, I was my father's everything—shorter, smaller, and darker.

"Mom could win the marathon." If she could channel her nervous energy into a straight line.

We were straight-lining far enough from Grandpa's house that it was time to turn. His limp and my steady stride were taking us nowhere except away from where I wanted him to go. I glanced down the sidewalk, a block and a half ahead, where grandiose flower bushes spilled over someone's front fence, crowding the walkway. "Maple Street?" I asked. He nodded at the nearest intersection, and we veered left at the corner, his limp an advantage as he leaned into the turn, and then into the next, our off-rhythm footsteps carrying us back toward his house instead of to Grandma's store.

Grandpa's pace quickened the final block to his home, a comfortable Cape Cod style, just like every other house on the block. My grandparents began on this street with other World War II-era newlyweds, those families eventually moving on. I glanced up at my grandfather. Today their world would finally make it past 1940. "Grandpa, I need to walk more. How about we…"

"Whew." He slowed at the end of their sidewalk, stretched tall and lean, pinching his waist at one side. "Like I said, running's not for me."

I eyed him, seeing if he really looked tuckered on the outside or if it was just on the inside like he always looked. He stared up toward their porch, his towering height accordianing back down to his usual tired slump.

"Who's going to be on trial?" I blurted the same moment he asked, "How were the books?" He turned up his walk, and I followed, both of us heading toward their porch, side by side in a sudden silence.

He shoved his hands into deep trouser pockets, blousy beneath the belt he had cinched around pants far too large. Bony fingers and scars I hardly noticed anymore disappeared, only the cuffs of his long sleeves showing above the pockets' edges.

"No one you'd know, and possibly no one," he said the same moment I asked, "What books?"

He frowned down at me. "The books you had in the house, the one in particular I saw you looking at for your grandmother."

"Oh, that book. Not her type." I shook my head, knowing I was wrong. It might take time, but once Grandma heard what Grandpa had done for her, the ice would thaw. "And so if it's no one I know who's going to trial, that leaves you out. Right?"

He paused at the first step up to his front porch and stared toward the screen door above. "A man's always on trial, don't you know?" He managed a half grin, a wobbly streak of thin lips penciled across his face. "Even an investigation is a trial, and that's all this is. You'd best get on, now. Go take a picture for that photo display you've been hired to do. Or take one of that politician you've been dating…Emerson. Or go eat."

"Need help re-cluttering the living room first?" I asked as he headed up the steps. I did have pictures to take for the display, my hobby turned profitable—The Faces and Hands of New York—and Emerson took every chance he had to be in one of my photos. He was handsome, and the only part of me that ran to win as he raced toward the senate. "I have time." I didn't want my grandfather left on trial or a part of anyone's investigation, nor did I want him living as if he were. I wanted him living with Grandma, and loving her by avoiding military paraphernalia. I wanted him in my pictures, his face bent over long, wounded hands carving wood into something instead of nothing. And

Grandma's face soft for a change, half hidden behind one of her books, her hands clasping some author's gospel, no longer determined to make it her own. Both heads, both sets of hands, together. "You had it too neat. I could un-straighten the magazine stacks before I go, bring out a book or two, or leave a glass of iced tea beading on the coffee table."

He shook his head when he made it onto the porch and to their door.

"You sure?" I asked as bony fingers and a scarred hand reached for the screen door's handle. He pulled it his way, still shaking his head, the familiar creak masking any chuckle I hoped he had. "Have it your way, then. I left Grandma's books on the bed," I called as he stepped inside. I would go run now, to Non Bookends, to cover my lie and tell Grandma I left her three new arrivals at their house. Grandpa'd done his part; he'd silently loved. I looked at his shadowy form through the mesh, the lanky man with the limp, the non-runner with the scars. It was Grandma's turn to love back now. And if she refused to come here and hear it from him, I'd tell her everything she needed to know before I ran to take my pictures.

Grandpa raised a hand and waved from the doorway, not even turning as he did.

"I only read that one, by the way. Amabile. Just stuff hers back into its envelope, if you would. I left everything lying there together."

He caught the screen door behind him, the hand he'd raised dropping to his side.

"Grandpa?"

The other hand dropped, and the screen door closed, the heavy inner one shutting behind him.

Chapter 4

Dietrich showed the cards he'd brought to the US, his identifications as a journalist in Germany for *Der Spiegel—The Mirror*, oddly enough—and for *Süddeutsche Zeitung* that he sometimes contributed to. Then his International Driver's License, all to gain access to archived photos in the Library of Congress, for permission to search in ways and places the general public wasn't allowed.

The clerk at the desk checked Dietrich's information, then slid him a registration card, room enough for Dietrich's basic information followed by a statement promising to treat the archives with care. He filled it out and returned it, then waited for the nod of approval. Dietrich was media; guards and monitors of any sort were seldom friendly to people like him. Dietrich felt it now as the guard perused his information—that extra disregard, the almost distaste reporters received. *I'm a research journalist.* And he was, but to most he was still a gossip hack.

"Archived photographs are here…and then where is the microfilm?" Dietrich glanced at the clerk, already aware of where he needed to go. He'd studied the floor plans before coming, all international and military libraries falling into similar grids of organization, patterns complicated only by cultural and architectural flair. Dietrich smiled and made a show of his hands when the clerk glanced up. He rubbed them together, then brushed them down the front of his corduroy jacket. Cooperation. *No enormous camera, no recording devices, nothing so large it exceeded the limits Prints and Photographs allowed.* All he needed was time, time enough to prove there was no such man as Amabile had written about.

The clerk nodded toward the door Dietrich had come through, where elevators could be found just outside. Dietrich preferred stairs, most often nearly empty, quiet, with only a few hushed voices, others' footsteps, and his thoughts…about Oma and Monika today, and the fictional American runner who was wasting his time. "You're in the right place for photos, this section of the third floor. Microfilm can be found in Jefferson, on the first floor. That's all I need from you. Reference Desk is over there." The clerk nodded toward the other side of the lobby and dropped Dietrich's card into a file.

"Thank you." Dietrich turned and glanced around the room and rubbed his hands together again. He loved facts, thrived on details, and could spend days at this complex absorbing minutia, if he had the time. Truth made far better journalism than sensationalism or lies, which was why fiction writers and their stories could never be credited as reliable sources.

Dietrich ran his hands down the corduroy of his jacket again. He had to give credit to the Madison building, and the Jefferson Building he'd toured earlier, sauntering amongst art and architecture, gazing through glass windows and doors. The library's Research and Reading Rooms he'd peered into were gratifyingly enormous, immense ceremonies of book and periodical-laden shelves towering one after the other, fanned like pages along the sides. Long wooden tables filled open areas, creating kaleidoscopic symmetries of beautiful woodwork for people to hunch over while reading, their faces mirrored in the shiny surfaces. *Mirrored...*he turned. He was here to prove there never existed such a gift from a blond American runner. If the Prints and Photographs Reading Room didn't have evidence of such a man, he'd give the periodical room a chance after checking through microfilm. Then he'd go home.

Dietrich walked to the reference area, drinking in the sensation of data, information that would be difficult to argue. Truth. And here was irrefutable truth—a chamber with endless cabinets, shelf after shelf of bound photos to verify Monika's claim—or not. He inhaled the swarm of information. Uncovering hidden gems was his greatest thrill. Standing at the main desk, he rifled through notes he'd made and brought with him, along with others he'd created in the library's Main Reading Room.

One face and one name he didn't expect to find, amongst the three possible names he'd whittled Olympic participants down to while still in Germany. He rearranged his notes, slid the names into his pocket. He'd be limited how many photos he could study at one time. That's why he'd narrowed the dozens of potential "he's" down to three in particular who seemed to fit the physical description from what photos he found there. Today he would narrow those three down to none.

"I'm interested in the Olympics. Looking for information on US summer teams from the 1920s to the 1950s," Dietrich said to the young male clerk at the counter. Dietrich slid his notes from the Main Reading

Room across the counter's slick top, legwork that narrowed his search, reducing location suggestions. "That's still several volumes, I imagine…maybe too much for one request?"

The man was bright, too bright for this job. Dietrich caught it in the bored tap of his toes behind the counter, the "hurry" in his expression. Dietrich read this man's impatience the same way he read what was behind anyone's face. The man eyed Dietrich's notes. "Special requests can be managed. Even on short notice. Let me see if I can help." He grinned, and his fingers were quick as he punched keys and flipped through some files, his digital speed rivaled only by the pace of electronics. Dietrich admired efficiency that surpassed the machines and system as the young man determined more precise locations for the selections Dietrich wanted. "Got everything in storage decks. I'll fill out a call slip and have them brought in." And he did. Before Dietrich could choose a seat, a wooden cart was rolled in with books on top. "Follow me, please. I'll show you where you can view these photos." He stepped from behind the counter and led Dietrich to a table, parking the cart alongside it. "These have a large number of pictures for those years—many of the events, entrants, results… Were you looking for something more specific? I'll allow more than the standard fifteen, if it's a single subject. And I could help narrow your search to save you some time."

He probably could. Too narrow. Too close to the ludicrous mission of researching fiction Dietrich preferred the young man merely help with rather than understand. "No, but thank you. Just whatever you can give me of these will do, to start with." Dietrich watched the young man bend and stoop as he gathered a few volumes holding photos, catching the man's nametag as he straightened. "Carl. You've been a great help."

Carl grinned as he settled the books in front of the chair. "Here you go." Carl tilted his head and ran a finger down the horizontal spines. "Beginning with the 1921 games and all the way to 1956. Special sorts of heroes, don't you think?" He looked up, Dietrich's smile satisfying him. "I'll be at the counter, if you need anything else."

Dietrich nodded as Carl walked away. When he was alone, he sorted the volumes into three stacks, leaving 1936 by itself in the middle. If he didn't find anything there, he'd go to the games right before and after the Berlin games in case Amabile's heartthrob ran other years. Dietrich settled into the seat and opened 1936 and began maneuvering through its pictorial history. The photos of those particular games flashed by, evidence of the politics behind them clear, in hindsight. Fascinating material, but information he already knew better than most. And not what he was looking for. He flipped to the next section and the next, until he came upon the events—swimming, diving, hurdles, gymnastics...

Athletics. Track. Amabile's "he" ran in her stories—ran a race, ran to her, then ran away.

Picture after picture went by. Dietrich scanned each one, watching for the three he'd come to the US to find. He paused at each photo of a man with blond hair and studied the build, if he'd won, and searched for the name, English names as manageable to him as German names were.

None fit well until Graham. And then, eventually, Winston, two of the three he was considering. He checked their physical descriptions and then their names against the medalists in another section. All of the US medalists, not just the ones in track, on the off chance Amabile's fiction was just that. Both were medalists, both in track, and both rather tall with fairly light hair, but slightly wavy. US records agreed with what he'd found in Germany, but like he'd hoped, with more pictures and better, of the American teams in particular.

At the end of the book he found group photos. He'd pored through enough in Germany he practically had them memorized. He counted the heads of the group after they'd reached Berlin, the 344 athletes that rode over on the *SS Manhattan*. He counted the heads in the team for athletics alone, those who'd won and those who hadn't as the games came to a close. He compared the faces in athletics to the ones fresh off the ship in Berlin. He'd done it before in Germany, but he did it here again, especially in photos Germany hadn't had.

Counted and compared, everything the same…until one. One wasn't right. Dietrich knew Carlson had been in the first pictures, but he shouldn't be in the last. He had run the quarterfinals, then was hospitalized with food poisoning, the only athlete who had come down with it, creating a stir of alarm followed by hurried relief. Therefore, every picture of the team at the end should be one runner short from what they had at the beginning. And most pictures were, except for one.

One had the same number of competitors at the end as there were at the beginning. Dietrich went back through every face in the picture, comparing each one to the other photos until he found him. A very tall man with hair that looked almost white in the photo, thin build with a medal hanging around his neck. Dietrich sat back in his seat. The man fit Amabile's description. But ringers who hadn't been through the trials couldn't just drop into the games. He bent forward again, walked his fingers meticulously over every photo in the 1936 book, then set that one aside. He next looked at the years before and the years after. The mystery man wasn't in any of them. Only that one picture, and it looked like an amateur shot.

He matched the names below one of the professional photos to each face, spotting the three he'd originally considered, writing every one down as he went. Some of these men would still be alive. He checked the ones who stood nearest the mystery man and starred their names. Someone would know him. Too bad the photo he was in didn't list the names. It would take a lot less time to explain him away if he had a name. Dietrich stood and summoned the clerk to return the stack.

"That was fast." Carl smiled. "I admire fast. Find what you wanted, or do you need something else?" He tapped his fingers on the table next to Dietrich's books, four tiny race horses ready to take off.

"Those were helpful." Dietrich eyed Carl's fingers, hands Dietrich could put to use. The tapping slowed with Carl's disappointment. "You're quite adept at the filing system. Quicker than most."

"I like order." Carl nodded his head. "This system is good, and I've worked with it enough I've mastered it. But if they'd let me, I'd write a whole new system that works even better."

"Really? Better than this?"

"Much better." Carl leaned against the table's edge. "Try me. I can get you anything with my method, anywhere in the library, even faster than I did before."

"All right." Dietrich stroked his chin, the scrape of fingers against stubble priming Carl to dive into what Dietrich needed to know. "I won't make it too hard on you, but I'll give you two at once to see how well your system does."

"It will be a cinch." Carl straightened and rubbed his hands together. "Give them to me."

"Okay, find me the names of the US Olympic participants in 1936 who rode the *SS Manhattan* from here to Europe and then back again. That's not too tough. And for the second search, let's do something totally different. How about well-known wood workers in the US in 1950?"

"On my mark, get set, go!" Carl's face transformed from a grin to a machine.

Dietrich watched Carl scoop the books up, set them on the cart, and hurry them to the counter, his hands thrumming as he took his seat at the filing system. The race was on, Carl's fingers competing with the speed of his mind. If anyone could help narrow Dietrich's search to one American in Berlin, one unexpected Olympic medalist in those games, and one wood carver in Amabile's fiction, it was Carl.

A pad of paper slid across the counter and stopped in front of Dietrich, file numbers and locations scrawled on the top sheet. Carl swiped his forehead with his arm.

"Impressive." Dietrich tapped the pad. "Patent your idea. Soon."

"Yes, sir, I will." Carl's mouth kicked up on one side as he snatched the pad back and tore off the top sheet. He slapped his hand over a pencil. "Right now, in fact."

"Good." Dietrich turned away, then looked back. "Mind giving me that sheet you tore off? I want to check you."

"You bet." Carl handed the sheet to Dietrich.

"And who do I see about copies of a couple of these photos?" Dietrich folded the paper and slid it into his pocket.

"Let me guess—of the team on the *SS Manhattan*?" Carl's eyes sparkled.

"Very good. You're right." Dietrich smiled. "Leaving New York, and returning. And a few of the other smaller photos also. You had some I'm lacking in my collection."

"I can take care of all of those for you. Just show me which ones, and we should have them by tomorrow."

Dietrich made sure the one photo he wanted was almost invisibly chosen as he pointed it out to Carl along with ones he didn't particularly care about. Carl would be useful if Dietrich needed anything else. He would remember today as the day he set out to improve the Library of Congress's system, and Dietrich as his inspiration.

"I'll be back." Dietrich nodded. He smoothed his hands down the front of his jacket as he watched Carl and his pictures go. "Okay, Amabile," he whispered in German as Carl disappeared. "As far as I'm concerned, fiction has as much credence as romance. Let's keep it that way."

Chapter 5

Sweaty and unattractive, my reflection trotted across the glass of Non Bookends' front window as I trotted along the sidewalk to the door. *Reflections should lie.* I stared at soggy brown strands too heavy for their normal wave, tucked behind my ears, my soaked running clothes clinging to my body. It was my own fault. I couldn't help but take a jubilation run after leaving Grandpa's house before coming here.

The bells above Non Bookends' front door jangled as I opened it to faces I recognized and others that I didn't. Fingertips of all ages and sizes halted over yellowed pages and dusty spines as they eyed the wet me. Grandma's flock. I nodded at the faces that had been growing old as I'd been growing up, faithful patrons living Grandma's claim that Non Bookends was the place where life that had only been imagined could finally be realized. They could continue to believe her adage as long as they wanted. In a few moments Grandma no longer would.

I wended along the path I'd exited earlier, breathing in air normally congested with tiny print and author wisdom, it feeling clear, light, and refreshing for a change. I darted between shelves and around customers swallowed by cozy chairs and sofas with books poking up from their laps. Grandma's seemingly haphazard arrangement of shelves was an obstacle course that had entertained me for hours as a child, but I understood now they weren't arbitrarily situated at all. There was nothing sporadic about this layout. There was purpose in the placement of each group of shelving, meaning in the quotes she'd attached to their sides, and specific themes boxed within these clusters of small sofas, chairs, and tables with lamps. Grandpa's war was in this arrangement, according to Grandma. Truth in fiction. She was going to be shocked to learn there was no war for Grandpa and the truth was in him, not in her stories after all.

I grazed my leg as I rounded a sofa and apologized to the jarred woman looking up. I waved as I rushed on, hurrying past a tower of shelved books as I searched for Grandma. Grandpa inspired me, not the stretch of his legs and the way they could eat up twice the sidewalk in one step that mine could, but the pace of a man who claimed he was always on trial and who very soon wouldn't be.

"Grandma," I whispered around a block of shelves. She was here somewhere. This store was a map instead of a maze, islands of supposed truths all neatly hemmed by a border along the ceiling, every wall topped with a row of framed somethings—pictures, photos, or mirrors so high each one's glass was a reflection instead of a scene.

Grandma refused to lower them, even when I offered to replace whichever ones needed it with photos I'd taken—Grandpa's limp from behind, her hair as she bent over a book, and her customers' fingers charting courses along her books' spines. Her glinting border remained untouched and where it was…too far up to see, a rim of reflection capping her flock's reflections below it. And her…somewhere.

I reached the back, the smell of old prose catching up with me as I glanced from side to side. Faded oils, dried wood, and the waft of warm lamp bulbs overpowered the drench of my skin and wet clothes. I looked back at the labyrinth she was hiding in.

"Grandma!" I whisper-hissed. Not the "store voice" Grandma had taught me to use the first time I came to Non Bookends to "help" as a girl. I headed back toward the front. Slower, taking wider swaths, pausing at the center and listening near a singular tier of wooden shelves, the hub—the king—of Grandma's literary marvels: Henrik Ibsen, his plays, and his life. Grandma said he wrote strong women, even when they were weak. Strong women like Grandma, crusading through a war that was about to end. I glanced at the volume Grandma cited from most often, raised a finger, and tapped the binding that housed Nora, Henrik's most famous heroine, the one who dared to leave her husband, Torvald. Grandma said he deserved to be left, caring for Nora by building his castle around her, adding a moat of provision and protection to keep harm out. But it kept her in. Until she exploded through his walls, leaving him and his moat behind.

"Here." A towel appeared between me and Nora. "You're raising the humidity around my books." Grandma swiped my sweaty finger from the gold of Ibsen's name.

I took the hand towel and dabbed at my face, rubbed it around my neck and down my arms. "I have something to tell you. Something important."

"You went to the house like I knew you would."

I nodded to her gaze that passed from me to her

hero, to the rest of Non Bookends, to the volumes of carefully selected titles, and then to the row of framed somethings around the ceiling. I glanced up at what looked like a border of pictureless frames holding nothing but glass, the lights turning them into a ring of mirrors.

"Look at me, Grandma. Yes, I did, and that's another thing I need to tell you. Those three envelopes I took…"

The bells clanged as the front door opened. Emerson's voice rang with them, masculine and pleasant, greeting Grandma's customers in his way that brought eager hellos racing back. I paused. I loved Emerson's voice, along with his pace, his finish line, and his determination to win. I made it a point to slow my run to a trot when we jogged together. I did it for him, slackening enough that newspaper photographers could catch his smile and wave. Then after we were done I ran hard. I glanced at my watch. He had a political dinner tonight. We were to catch up afterwards and talk—about his night, his campaign, and about my day, the pictures I had yet to take. But not about my family…not yet anyway, but with a couple more minutes alone with Grandma we might be able to. "He wasn't supposed to come here." I tapped my watch. "Don't run off, Grandma."

"I've no reason to run off, but maybe you should." Grandma eyed my wet shorts and T-shirt. Emerson never looked like this, even after he ran.

"Catharine?" Emerson, black hair, dark eyes, a handsome smile above his even blacker tuxedo, stepped around a shelf to Grandma's center, to Ibsen whom she'd introduced Emerson to when we first dated. He hadn't hailed Nora and Ibsen the way Grandma thought he should, putting her into a perpetual pounce position, ready to spring on the man who'd disregarded her heroes. I stepped between them, touched his arm, and searched for a safe place he could wait until I talked to her. "I tried to find you at home, Catharine. But since I couldn't...well...I hoped I'd find you here."

I paused and looked at him. Emerson was handsome and impeccably dressed for his political gathering. We traded looks, he at my running clothes and me at his tuxedo, my frantic sweating beside his black and flawless.

"Either your grandmother's working you way too hard, or you slipped in a run."

"Neither. I mean, both. Grandma and I were about to..."

He lifted a sopping strand of hair from behind my ear and snaked it around a finger. I felt the warmth of his hand and then the cold of my curl as he let it go. "Here," he said. He dried his finger and then my cheek with a white handkerchief that was there and then gone as he folded and tucked it back inside his jacket. He glanced at his watch, then back at me. "Speaking of running, Catharine, you have just enough time to run and get ready for my dinner. I want you to go with me."

"Me? At your dinner?"

"Yes, you, especially you, at my dinner. But I'd like to talk to you first. Privately, if we could."

I glanced around us, Grandma's pounce amongst the faces looking our way and then his profile as I turned back. Emerson's was truly one of the faces I intended to photograph for my display, and his hand also as it gripped a potential voter's.

46

"Over there." I nodded toward a tier of shelves far from Grandma, leaving her with a look to stay where she was.

He laced his fingers through mine, and I led him to the shelf of books, stopping below one of Grandma's hand-printed quotes on its side: "An illusion which makes me happy is worth a verity which drags me to the ground." *Idris and Zenide.* I frowned and drew Emerson two steps farther.

"I preferred to do this at your apartment..." He glanced at the spectators who had streamed his way, then looked back to me. "But since time is short and you're...so..." He smiled at my sopping hair and soggy clothing. "So beautiful, I couldn't wait to ask you to be with me, to be beautiful and dazzling at the most crucial of my political dinners..." He lifted my hand, my left hand, and threaded a ring over my finger. "As my fiancée."

I stared at the hand he held, the shiny brilliance he'd placed on my finger.

"Catharine, would you do me the honor of becoming my wife?"

His wife...I'd worked so hard as his girlfriend, even harder as the photographer for this attorney running to be a senator, to protect him from the damage my family could cause...

Applause broke out behind us from Grandma's flock. I turned to see them flocking our way.

"Wait." Emerson raised a hand. "She hasn't said yes yet." Emerson did what he was so good at, managing the advance of the circle of happy onlookers with one of his winning smiles.

He took both of my hands in his then, faced me,

and held tight. Eager sounds rippled around us. I listened for Grandma amongst them, the one voice that would say I shouldn't…when really, I could. Just as she could, and she would as soon as I told her what Grandpa had said.

"I will," I said to Emerson. "Yes." I saw his relief, his dinner and the importance of it, his excitement, and the race he'd asked me to join him in forever.

Emerson's face, his handsome face, raised above the squeals and arms that wrapped around us. "I'm sorry this wasn't a more private moment." He winked. "Maybe at your apartment later. My car is out front. You have just enough time to clean up and be the beauty I know that you are."

I would. And I was. The same things my grandparents would do and be for each other now that we were all finally grabbing hold of love. Grandma had to know before I left, though. I scanned her congratulating flock for the one set of eyes that had marched away from marriage earlier today. I spotted her, the reluctant bride gazing back at me.

"Ready, Catharine?" Emerson, with his finesse, extracted me from the revelry, his fingers finding mine and drawing me his way.

I glanced back. Grandma had to hear about the three pieces of mail and the lie I'd told Grandpa, but more importantly…

"Catharine."

"I need just a moment." It was for him, for the race he'd asked me to join. The chaos of warm wishes separated our fingers as potential voters' hands clapped him on the back. Voices around us rang with plans we hadn't yet made when one voice, a store voice, spoke behind me.

"The books you took earlier, I assume you wanted to tell me how I am supposed to get them back."

"Yes, I did want to tell you how." I turned to Grandma. "I thought the one I read by Amabile wouldn't be something you'd like, until Grandpa told..."

"Amabile?" Grandma's store voice vanished and her real one exploded.

"Yes, Amabile. That's one of the books you ordered. It's over there. Just go to the house and ask for it and the other books," I said. "And ask Grandpa for some of his army mementos while you're there." *For my wife.* I heard the sentiment again, Grandpa's voice, while Emerson's called my name behind me. Grandpa had done this for his wife, and he had done it in love. I turned and looked across the room where Emerson waved, beckoning me his way. What Grandpa had done was for Emerson too. Grandpa had left behind what mattered because to someone else it mattered more.

Grandma sputtered behind me. "What were you thinking, Cate? What have you done?"

"Well, I lied to Grandpa, for one thing, so please go along with it. Tell him you wanted me to read those books there. And as for the books and his military souvenirs, just ask." I looked from Emerson to her, and back to Emerson again. He gripped the shoulder and hand of a vote he hoped to gain, but he pointed to me, made his excuses, and came my way. "See that, Grandma?" I nodded toward my fiancé, then looked at her. "Grandpa did something like that for you."

She watched Emerson, her arms planted across her chest. "You don't realize what you've done, Cate."

"No, you don't. Just go ask Grandpa. You'll be surprised."

Chapter 6

I ran my hands down the front of my dress, the same one I had worn the first time Emerson asked me out.

"Wow." He said it as I thought it. The dress was perfect. Emerson's reflection appeared behind mine in the full-length mirror I stood in front of, the black of his tuxedo becoming one with my dark dress. "This is just what I need when I announce our engagement. Beautiful dress for my beautiful fiancée. But we'll get you more. Can't have you wearing repeats on the campaign trail."

I glanced again at Emerson's reflection, his handsome face near mine in the otherwise black background. He belonged on the campaign trail, at dinners like tonight, on fliers, and on billboards. His parents' money would make sure he was there. It's what families did.

"I'm ready." I glanced at the shiny ring. I was a fiancée now, a part of his family and he a part of mine. Grandma would put a stomp into her march over to Grandpa's house for her books, likely make a show of tossing romantic Amabile into the trash. But when she asked him what I told her to, she would hear what I had heard. *For my wife.* It spoke of love, and she would be pulling Amabile back out. I smoothed my hands down the front of my dress. "I'm very ready."

****

"Mr. Marcus." I lifted my hand, my right hand, to Emerson's fellow attorney and campaign manager. He took it in his and brushed his lips across the back of my fingers.

"Let me reintroduce you, Miles." Emerson cut in and lifted my left hand. "She said, 'Yes,' so I want you to welcome Catharine Hunt, soon to be Catharine Cosnik."

Soon…I glanced at Emerson as Mr. Marcus pulled me into a light embrace. Smooth congratulations and chortles of, "I told him you had what it took to be the right woman," were whispered in my ear. "You have a way of making bad look good, ugly fetching. Even beyond the pictures you take."

I frowned my thanks into Miles' ear. Had what it took? Made bad look good? And ugly fetching? I pulled back and checked my dress, then looked in Miles' eyes for the only other possible bad and ugly—my grandparents. "Is that a campaign manager's observation, a man's, or a friend's?" I asked, as Emerson took my hand. He excused us and led me away. I checked my dress again, and patted my hair, then glanced back at Miles, who was greeting newcomers to Emerson's dinner, his compliment apparently best left behind. "Soon?" I turned to Emerson. "Did you really mean we'd be marrying soon?"

"It doesn't have to be an elaborate wedding," Emerson whispered as he led me toward our table, a smile going to a banker he greeted on the way. "That way we can work it in around the election."

I shook my head, then nodded. I held onto my ring.

I'd gone from girlfriend to fiancée to nearly a bride in too short a time. Emerson looked down at me as I wagged my head every direction.

"Catharine..." He stopped, took my hands, and squared himself in front of me. "I'm so sorry. You're overwhelmed. Here I am sweeping you along as if you're nothing more than a part of my evening, when you're to be a part of my whole life."

A warm wash of the anxious, new fiancé overtook Emerson's serious attorney look, his heightened senatorial one also, as we stood toe to toe like we had in Non Bookends. He held us there, and turned us into the only people in the room. "I don't want an elaborate wedding. It's just you I want. No distractions, just us."

My heart beat within a ring that formed around us, a more cultured circle than Grandma's flock had been at her store. Miles became a part of this one, watching and starting a round of polite applause. Emerson's hands tightened on mine. He bent and kissed the top of my head, burrowed his lips into my brown waves. Then he let go, one hand with me and the other extended to the onlookers around us. "My beautiful bride-to-be," he announced. The applause grew with the warmth in my cheeks as he eased me forward, led me past Miles, through the ring, and guided me to our table. "Let's sit," he whispered.

I didn't want to sit. I wanted to stand, to hold his hands, and feel his kiss on top my head again. But I took the chair Emerson held for me, faced the crowd that followed Emerson's lead, heard their congratulations transform into conversations as tuxedos and evening dresses found tables for themselves.

Emerson sat next to me. He looked composed, his

romantic notions appropriately contained, completely unruffled by this gathering and the announcement we would marry. Soon. I glanced at him, the man I was the right woman for, his hair flawless, his clothing without a crease, no bad, no ugly, nothing to make look different. "Thank you," Emerson leaned close and whispered. "You are the perfect touch to my evening."

"Thank…" I leaned even nearer, but he was gone, speaking to the man next to him. Emerson's arm stayed with me, draped across the back of my chair. He laughed, and the man joined him. So did the man's wife at his other side. My legs bounced beneath the table, I felt like running. I slowed them as Emerson said my name, leaned back in his chair to introduce me to the couple at his far side. Soon. I heard it in Emerson's praise of me and the couple's congratulations. Soon, faster than his usual trot. My legs picked up his new pace and began to bounce again.

Chapter 7

"Mr. Williams? Thank you for meeting me." Dietrich extended his hand, saying everything the same way he had two times previously except for the man's name. "I'm Dietrich Schmidt with *Der Spiegel*, and contributor to *Süddeutsche Zeitung*, doing research on our 1936 Summer Olympic games, as I told you on the phone. Your input is greatly appreciated, and I promise not to take up too much of your time."

For the third time a thin, weathered hand reached for and clasped his, cool to the touch, an equally weathered smile much stronger. These were star athletes he was meeting, men who were proof of what time could do to even the most fit.

"Come in, come in." Mr. Williams was eager, just like the others had been, his eyes sparkling with watery excitement, ready to talk about his day...their day. A day that lived on in all of them. Dietrich let go of Mr. Williams' hand. Someday he would write an actual article on these men. Good truths worth being told.

"Please come in and sit down." Mr. Williams' voice crackled with that airy sound that came with age.

Dietrich entered the man's modest home, not markedly different from the first two he'd visited for pretend interviews, men he hoped could help identify the nameless runner so Dietrich could eliminate him as a possibility and go home. The house felt comfortable, although the slightly worn, modern furniture scattered throughout was no longer modern.

"You can sit here. Can I get you anything?"

Dietrich sat where Mr. Williams indicated but refused the offered refreshments. "Like I said, I don't want to take up too much of your time. I'm happy to just sit and hear about your experience at our Olympics."

Mr. Williams smiled as he took his seat. He continued to smile as Dietrich led him through the same questions he had the first two US Olympic runners from Berlin's summer games...the trials, the ship, the residences for athletes, and the games themselves. The war that followed, and the fellow athletes who fought, died, or were captured in it. Everyone had heard of the two captured. Their stories were personal to these men, heroes innumerable times over as fellow athletes suffered as if with them. Dietrich waltzed Mr. Williams on to other heroes, the victories, and the disappointments. And finally to the man who'd taken Carlson's place, but hadn't. A face, a number, the name of Marvin Shanks, according to the other two men.

"Shanks," Mr. Williams said. "Unconventional the way they let him in." He leaned close, his crackling voice dropping to a whisper. "He was Aryan, that's what some of them thought. Rumor had it he fit the Aryan ideal. That's why the Germans...I mean, you...let him in."

Dietrich glanced up from the notes he'd been pretending to take. Notes he'd pretended to take two times before.

"I beg your pardon?"

"He was notably tall, very blond, fit, and good-looking. He was where Germany was headed. Even found himself a German girl right off. No wonder, since he was their type. Some thought the whole thing odd."

Dietrich nodded, relaxed the clench on his pencil. "Another runner? Was she one of the female competitors?" He kept his tone level; he knew how to be the disinterested third party. But the girl, an observation the other two Olympians hadn't noted, spiked his interest, setting off an explosion inside.

"No, she was one of the ones brought in to entertain us. Local folks, artist types who came to Hindenburghaus in the evenings, where we athletes stayed. I never actually saw them out together, but I noticed the way he watched her there, the way he singled her out when he first spotted her. He disappeared sometimes, probably to be with her, but sat whittling little flowers when he was around the rooms. I teased him about them being for the girl. He never said."

"He ran." Dietrich's professional mien began to slip, his comment too quick. He took a breath. "Yet there is no record that he did, other than what I've been told in interviews. And saw in one photo of the group."

"Yep, he ran. And medaled. But they took it away from him. Someone reported him as a money-making ringer. Paid when he won. So much for Aryan. He was a disgrace instead, and stripped of his prize. I saw it happen. Well, overheard it. But I did see Marvin walk out with someone. Some man. Stiff, like a cop."

Amabile's lover ran, he didn't walk. And he wasn't escorted away. "That must have happened near the end."

"It was. He was a good fellow, actually, even took

it well when some of the athletes teased him about his last name. Shanks. Perfect for a man built on stilts while most of us had more muscle. He was quiet and considerate, except for what he did. He looked bad even before he lost his medal. White. Shaken. Almost like Carlson looked when he took sick."

"He maybe knew what was coming?" Or what had happened in the explosion. Dietrich tapped his pencil. He was getting fact mixed up with fiction.

Mr. Williams shrugged. "Maybe. Losing a medal is quite a blow. But as bad as he looked after, he sure squared himself when he walked away with that man. Like soldiers, is what I thought as they passed. Made me think of a court martialing."

Soldiers. Court martial. Mr. Williams rambled on. Dietrich continued to scribble, pretending more notes. Marvin Shanks was probably a no one, but he had been in the US Armed Services, maybe? He wanted to interrupt Williams and ask about the girl—her name, her hair color. Did she write? He wouldn't interrupt and ask. He knew better. He let Williams ramble on, saving leading questions for when Williams was spent and distracted, when his reactions would be candid.

"Mr. Williams, can I see your medals? All of them? Not just from the '36 Olympics." Shanks, soldiers, Hindenburghaus, and the young woman were swept away from Williams, but not from Dietrich. The past Olympian stood, wobbled as he straightened, then led Dietrich to another room so Dietrich could lead him to the answers he really wanted. Or didn't.

When this interview was done, Dietrich would fly back to Washington and find Carl at the Library of Congress. Carl had his ways. And if his resources turned up nothing, there were other military history institutions in the Capital. If there hadn't been a girl, if Shanks hadn't whittled or carved... Dietrich stared at his pad as Williams rambled on. If Amabile had a lover, he could be Marvin Shanks.

Chapter 8

Non Bookends was dark after Emerson's dinner. I stretched an arm halfway across the car seat toward him as he slowed in front of Grandma's store. Our reflection idled in her window, the black interior of Non Bookends framing Emerson's car, my face a tiny light spot in its passenger window. If my reflection was closer, I'd see the smile on my face—Grandma wasn't in her store.

"It went well tonight." Emerson talked from behind me. He'd begun the moment we left his dinner, a rehashing of what everyone had said or done and what he'd said and done in return. I'd slipped in a request to drive here, rehashing Grandma's words during his third rendition of his dinner, whether she had truly said she'd go to Grandpa's house when we were gone. No lights in Non Bookends told me that she had.

"I was so proud of you tonight." I turned his way, stretched farther across the seat, and took the hand he offered.

"It was a success. I know it was. Even Miles was relieved how well it went. Thanks to you." He squeezed my hand while success effervesced in his eyes. "We should share my victory. I mean, our victory, with your grandparents. And we should call your parents."

I glanced back at the store's window, tried to see past our reflection for any tiny glow inside. She wasn't there. "Grandparents first." My mother, like Emerson's campaign, would be a breeze now that Grandma's storm was subdued.

"Grandma and Grandpa, here we come then." Emerson resumed his drive, and his monologue, tapping my hand with each happy mention that I was there.

I looked his way. I'd never taken these two blocks so slowly before. This was Emerson's candidate pace, not my old pace, and certainly not our new "soon" pace.

"That's quite a grip you have there, Catharine." Emerson tugged his hand from mine.

"Oh. Sorry. I guess I was excited…for you, I mean. You did so well. I could see how pleased they all were." I looked down the street at the pencil line glow framing the heavy drapes in my grandparents' front window.

"Looks like they're up. Or one of them still is." Emerson eased the car into the driveway. "I have another dinner on Saturday. We need to get you a new dress before then."

The draperies were too heavy to see through. I stared at the curtains; the two of them should be sitting together behind them, talking civilly for the first time. Emerson tugged at my finger.

"Yes. Of course, a new dress for me. I can get one before Saturday."

"I'll buy it, since it's for me, ultimately. How about tomorrow?"

I wrapped my fingers around the door's handle. "I have to get a run in tomorrow, and I have a camera shoot lined up. I can get my dress in between. You don't have to do that with me."

"For you, not just with you, and I insist. You'll either have to squeeze me in or give something up. I know what's best for you to wear, so let me choose it."

For me, like the *for my wife* Grandpa'd professed earlier today. The dark store, Emerson's offer, and the glow coming from my grandparents' living room proved it was finally happening—for all of us.

I let go of the door's handle and looked across the seat at Emerson. "Shopping together is perfect, and we can decide when after we leave here." Everything was changing. I glanced back at the house, imagining different photos I could include of my grandparents now.

"After we leave here it is, then." Emerson shut off the engine. "You know, you did well tonight, Catharine. Proving yourself with everyone, but especially with Miles. It was silly, but when I told him I was asking you to marry me and inviting you to the dinner, he wouldn't let me invite them too." Emerson nodded toward my grandparents' house. "He was adamant, but I promise you they'll be at the next one. In any case, it looks like they're still up. Let's go in and tell them about my dinner."

I looked at the draperies and the light behind them. The bad and the ugly finally gone.

Emerson slid out and came around the car, swinging my door open. "My lady. The beautiful soon-to-be Mrs. Cosnik." He stepped close and extended a hand.

I took his hand, took my place near the man I was to marry. Soon. Emerson was happy and relaxed, and he smelled heavenly, the cool night air keeping his fragrance close. I laid my fingertips on the chest of his black tuxedo, dark, like a hole in the night. "I'm so glad tonight went well for you. And…and I understand about Miles and my grandparents."

Emerson's fingers laced around mine, and he led me to the sidewalk and up the porch steps. He buzzed the doorbell with one hand while his other never let go of me. I listened to the irregular rhythm of footsteps coming to the door. Grandpa. The porch light came on, a cone of luminescence capturing us as the heavy inner door drew open.

"Cate?" Grandpa squinted through the screen. It was the same as earlier today, his face close to the mesh, his body hunched, the tiny squares of wire dulling the sparkle he should have had. "What are you doing here?"

"Hi, Grandpa." The room behind him was quiet, the way it always was. I held Emerson where we were. The whole house was too quiet.

Grandpa leaned into the screen door, one arm stretching and swinging it our way. "Come on in." He bent more and took a half-hobble backwards.

Emerson let go of my hand and took hold of the screen. "We don't want to disturb you."

The same light that turned Grandpa into a skeleton cast just the right shadows on Emerson. It would have made a harrowing photo, the good and the bad, the ugly and fetching, the contrast of Emerson's anticipation for the future and Grandpa's shackles to the past.

"You're not disturbing me. Come on in." The day showed on Grandpa. I glanced into the living room, past the man, to where nothing had changed since I'd left.

"We won't stay long." Emerson nodded me inside,

then stepped in behind me.

Grandpa hobbled out of our way. "Like I said, you're not disturbing me. Come on in. Happy to see the both of you."

Me. He said me. I made a hurried scan for *us*.

"Actually, I'm more tired than I thought, Grandpa. You must be too. We'll come back tomorrow."

"Come sit, Catharine. We'll just stay a minute." Emerson latched on, nearly dragging me to the sofa where the three military men had sat earlier. I glanced at Grandpa. He surely wouldn't talk about them in front of Emerson.

"Have a seat." Grandpa dropped into his chair, leaned back, and studied the ceiling. "Been a long day, that's for sure. You two been out somewhere?" He lifted his head and looked at me. "You didn't tell me you had plans, earlier."

"I didn't know at the time." I watched for a spark in Grandpa's eyes that said the army was gone and Grandma back, that he'd been told I was engaged. The emptiness of the chair next to him and in his gaze said she wasn't and he hadn't. She hadn't even been here yet. "We can't stay, but Emerson's political dinner went wonderfully. That's where we were," I said as I stood.

"Catharine, sit back down here. Anyway, that's not all the news, sir, but you've probably already heard the biggest." Emerson turned from me to Grandpa.

"News? No, I haven't heard any."

"You don't know?" Emerson's smile became a frown, one he passed from Grandpa to Grandma's empty chair.

"Well, then…" I shot my left hand into the air, waved it until I caught the low light with my ring.

"Right before Emerson whisked me off to his dinner, he gave me this."

Grandpa squinted from the ring to me. "You're engaged?" He hadn't expected this, not like he'd expected those three men earlier today.

I dropped my hand. "Yes." It was the store voice Grandma taught me to use. "I know it's sudden, but we…"

"But we intend to marry soon. You really didn't know?" Emerson frowned more.

"No…" Grandpa shook his head.

Emerson stood, he walked across the room to my grandfather's chair. "I'm sorry, sir," Emerson spoke softly. "I've behaved unconventionally. Disrespectful of her parents, as well as you and your wife. I should have asked them, and certainly you, first, but when I knew Catharine was the woman for me, I couldn't wait to sweep her into my world, starting tonight at my campaign dinner." He turned and smiled at me. "She's perfect, don't you think? A perfect senator's wife."

Grandpa stood then. He struggled to his feet, leaving his cane lying unused to the side. He glanced at me, an almost imperceptible flicker in his eyes. I studied the mouth that rarely spoke yet had spoken of love today, and eyes that had always lacked any sort of luster glinting with a phantom of that same love. "Hold on to her," he said, looking to Emerson.

Hold onto her…Grandpa's heart, his desire, the one thing Grandma had never let him do. And apparently hadn't come here tonight to let him do, either.

I stood, walked to two of the most significant men in my life, and laid a hand on each of them. "And I'll hold onto him, Grandpa." I clasped a shoulder far too thin, conveying the promise Grandma would be holding onto him soon.

"Mrs. Crawley didn't tell you? Is she here? I'd love to do a toast." Emerson glanced toward where their bedroom was.

"No. She came and went." Grandpa's posture waned as mine stiffened. He slumped from my grasp.

"I thought she was here. I assumed she was in another room." Emerson looked at me.

"Haven't seen her since early this evening." The handsomeness that must have been Grandpa's in his younger years still showed through. Grandma surely saw it when she came for her love story. Saw what I did when she was near the man she'd married—the handsome young soldier coming home—still dashing, even in his losses.

"She wasn't at the store." Emerson nodded toward the door. "It was dark when we drove by. Where would she be this late? Should we go look for her?"

"She must have been reading in the back," I said before Grandpa could say she might be sleeping back there.

"This late?" Emerson's frown deepened. "She shouldn't walk here alone after dark. Let's go get her and give her a ride."

I glanced toward the door and noticed Grandma's bags at its side, the two she'd brought this morning before she changed her mind. They lay slouched and toppling over like they'd been tossed.

"You can take those with you, if you go see her." Grandpa nodded at the two bags. "She won't be needing them here."

"No," I said. "A lot of books came in to look over.

We shouldn't bother her. We should be going."

"Catharine, you're being silly. Of course we should check on her, and we'll be happy to take those with us, and then bring her home." Emerson wagged his head at me. "Too much excitement for her tonight," he said to my grandfather. "We haven't had one minute alone to just sit down and breathe, catch up with ourselves. But we will." He walked to the bags, fished the cloth handles from inside the tops, and lifted them. He stared at the contents as he walked my way, his frown growing at nightgowns and slippers—things that didn't belong in a bookstore.

"Are her books for the store in there?" It came out too loud, no longer my store voice. "She might want them, but probably nothing else." I nodded at the bags. "Might just throw everything else out since she left those behind."

"This is just trash? Why are we bothering to take it to her?" Emerson lifted each arm, raising the bags in the air.

"Just the books were trash," Grandpa said. "I burned them. She knows. The rest of that stuff can go."

I turned to my grandfather. I stared at the man who got rid of everything pertaining to the military for his wife's sake. Then burned three books pertaining to her store. He'd turned Amabile, the love story I thought would be theirs, to ashes. "Grandpa?"

"Not the sort of book she would want." Grandpa leaned into his good leg and took the bags from Emerson. "Mavis doesn't need these things tonight. You two go on." He held the bags in the wrong hand, tipping him farther toward his weak side. "Make the most of your engagement," he said to me. "So you can make a good marriage. The right marriage."

"She will. I'll make sure of it. And we'll get your wife and bring her home. Then we'll…" Emerson reached for my hand, his fingers fumbling for mine.

"Mavis will be fine. We've been managing for years. You two go on." Grandpa nodded toward the door.

I followed Grandpa's nod, my fingers connecting to Emerson's, our arms stretching as I went and he stayed. "Just a minute, Catharine." Emerson looked at my grandfather. "So, sir, I will ask Catharine's parents also, but do I have your permission to marry your granddaughter?"

A glow flickered again behind Grandpa's years of no expression. He nodded from that place too far away. "Yes, son, you do. Just do it right."

"It's going to be a small wedding, but it will certainly be done right. Would you please do the honor of walking Catharine down the aisle along with her father? That much we want in an otherwise simple ceremony."

I saw "when" extinguish the glow in Grandpa's look. I saw "trial" and "investigation" in the way he let Grandma's bags settle to the floor. He reached for his cane. He steadied himself, pivoted slightly, and stared at his feet. "That might not be…"

"Don't let your injuries stop you." Emerson touched the shoulder of the man looking at the sofa where the officers had sat. "They are a tribute to you, as they'll be to me. And to our state when I become our next senator. You'll be our shining example. I promise."

Chapter 9

He burned them for you. Grandpa had burned Grandma's books for her, books she wouldn't want anyway. I hammered my argument with my feet as I ran. *He. Burned. Them. For. You. He. Burned. Them. For. You.*

He burned them because of me. Grandma's retort sent my feet hammering even harder. *Just like he burned his military things. Because of me, not for me. I was the reminder, not them. Especially those books. He burned them because of me.*

She'd known all along Grandpa's military items were gone. Burned also, according to her—*Because. Of. Me. Not. For. Me. Because. Of. Me. Not. For. Me.*

She was wrong. I'd heard Grandpa with the army officers, and I knew what he meant. *For my wife.* I'd suggested it as chivalry to Grandma, but she countered it was selfish. I'd claimed he did it for love, but she said it was from hate. I saw the sacrifice—she saw only the flames. *I don't know why the army came,* she'd closed our argument. *He expected them, I didn't…I expected someone else.* And she marched away from me.

"Cate, you're losing time. What's wrong with you?" Frank pedaled alongside me, Jill's husband, still coaching everyone except her, probably because she was already a winner. "You're putting too much force down instead of forward. Keep that up and you'll not only lose, you'll be riding tandem with me when your knees wear out."

"There's more to running than winning." I knew Jill would laugh at that, and Emerson would disagree.

"Uh-huh." Frank grunted the way he always did through my "I don't run to win" claims. I ran to run; I ran because I had to. Somehow, fast wasn't fast enough and far wasn't far enough when finish lines imposed unwanted goals.

I slapped my shoes harder against the pavement to drown out anything that followed Frank's grunt. My feet burned from the concrete and from crushing Grandma's argument into it. Frank's bicycle ground along beside me, too close, too sure he knew what was best.

"Lean into your run, Cate. Stretch, pump, stretch, pump." Frank stared at my feet and knees, his head bobbing as if they were his instead of the two tires he was on.

I slowed. "Okay, maybe you're right." I let up. I focused on my feet instead of on Grandma and the fires my grandfather had set, forward instead of down.

"That's better. Now lean even more into your run." Frank increased his speed and pulled ahead, dragging me with him.

Stretch. Pump. Stretch. Pump. For. You. Not. Because. Of. You. I grew into my stride, my regular stride, the one that wanted to outrun everything that was supposed to be behind me. *He. Burned. Them. For. You. Not. Because. Of. You.*

"That's the way to do it." Frank matched his bicycle to my speed, coming alongside me again. "By the way, Jill said to invite you over tonight. She's making Greek salad. She thought you might need to talk."

"Talk?" I glanced to the side at Frank.

He shrugged. "You know Jill, she's always trying to be nice."

Stretch. Pump. Stretch. Pump. Because. Of. Me. Not. For. Me. "Tell Jill thanks, but Emerson is taking me shopping tonight for a new dress for his next dinner. And I have this photo shoot to do first. That's why I called to tell you I was running extra early today if you wanted to join me."

"Campaign," Frank muttered over the sound of grit being crushed beneath his tires.

"What?"

"Campaign. A means to a goal. A strategy. A plan. A series of actions. Jill looked it up last night after you called about running this morning and told us you and Emerson were getting married."

"What does 'campaign' have to do with getting married? And why would she drag out a dictionary so late? What time did I call? Midnight?"

"It was pretty late, but you know Jill. Nothing slows her down. She's always off on some tangent that sticks in my head more than hers. Especially when that tangent is in our bed with the lights on and her bent over a book reading definitions out loud. She said campaigns aren't organic. Not entities in and of themselves. They are nothing more than methods to gain something real at the end. Means to ends, not ends."

Like burning books and military mementos, reading too many authors, carving sticks until nothing was left. "Isn't 'campaign' a noun, an actual thing?"

"It's a verb too. Even an adjective. If your dress fits Jill's definition of 'campaign,' it will make Emerson look better than you."

Hold on. Hold on to her. And I will hold on to him, Grandpa. And I would.

"Pick it up, Cate. You're lagging behind again."

Stretch. Pump. Stretch. Pump. For. Me. Not. Because. Of. Me. For. Me.

"That's a little better." Frank nodded at my feet.

It wasn't better. I dug my toes into the pavement and threw my weight backward, bringing my stretch and pump to a halt. Bringing everything to a halt—my running, Emerson's race, and Jill's campaign. Frank's tires caught on the pavement, dry skids rising from his wheels as he clamped down on the brakes. He leaned his bicycle into a circle that wrapped around and around where I stood, unhappy loops, frowning from every angle.

"Why in the world did you stop?" he asked. "Jill said getting engaged to someone so public might cause you to have some…"

I raised a hand. Frank's loops tightened around me, his final one bringing him to a stop right in front of me.

"Have some what?"

Frank fiddled with his brake lever.

"Look, Frank, that dress will be for Emerson and me both. It will fit his functions because it will fit me. I'm a part of his campaign now because I'm a part of him, not some tool used by him." My voice sounded rangy, not a good store voice. "That dress will be for me, for both of us, not because of anything else."

"Jill's just saying…"

"Never mind, Frank. I gotta go. I have some

72

pictures to take." Jill was a sprinter. That's why these immediate finish lines worked for her—campaigns, friendly dinners, opinions about my life. I was a runner, I was fast, and I kept going.

"Some questions," he shouted at my back as I turned and trotted away. "You might have some questions, that's what Jill said…"

That Jill would know the answers to better than I would? I ran hard. I wanted to keep going and never stop.

Chapter 10

"Marvin Shanks…Marvin Shanks…" Carl's hands slowed as his mind searched to pinpoint a detail in a broad subject.

Counters were obstacles, and Dietrich wished he could step to the other side of this one and peer over Carl's shoulder as he struggled through the Library of Congress's system while meshing it with his own.

"Army. Nineteen thirty-five. Also a Marvin Shanks earlier than 1930, but no tie to the Armed Services." Carl glanced up. "There are others. You want me to go on? They're slightly outside of the time period you asked about."

Dietrich shook his head. "I think you've done well. Again. Where can I find information on the Shanks in the army?"

Carl was quicker this time, his eyes and his hands scouring through information. "Here," he said, pushing toward Dietrich a notepad he'd written on. "Look in those spots."

Dietrich stared at the numbers and letters. Codes to the man he'd been searching for so he could dismiss him. "Thank you. He sure was the Olympics' best-kept secret, it seems. Maybe I won't even need him for my article, but good journalism leaves no details to chance."

"Yes, sir. If you need anything else, you know

where to find me."

"Unless you patent your system and become a wealthy man."

"Working on it." Carl grinned. However far along he was at turning his nervous energy into profit, the challenge had changed him into a peaceful man. Contented, leading his life instead of dragging behind it, like Dietrich felt himself doing now.

"Keep at it." Dietrich returned a smile as he lifted the top page from the pad of paper. He stared at the numbers, nodded goodbye to Carl, and set off. To find Marvin. Hopefully pure fiction.

****

The Library of Congress was like a giant encyclopedia—pages and pages, floors and floors, of carefully segregated categories of information. Pulling the pieces...the few pieces...of information about Marvin together wasn't simple or quick. Other clerks, other books and files, finally turned up a single photo of the man in military records. Short. Dark-haired. Stocky.

Dietrich dropped back against the seat he was sitting in. Wrong Shanks? Not a soldier? Or worse, a fictitious name? Dietrich rubbed his temples. He needed coffee. He needed fresh air. He needed to relax so his inner intuition could sort out the jumble of details in his mind.

Dietrich let his head fall back, and his eyes traced the patterns of the ceiling. It hadn't been a strong clue Williams had given him that Shanks may have been military, only a hunch. Dietrich's own hunches were most often right. Evidently Williams' weren't.

Dietrich stretched his arms upward, locked his fingers over his head, and stretched farther. Research was invigorating and frustrating. Miles and miles of data to run through, and sometimes there was no finish line. He loved it just the same, when it wasn't so personal. He couldn't stop. He had to reach the finish line, even if he couldn't see it yet.

He dropped his arms at his sides and straightened in his seat. He reached for the volume Marvin's troop photo was in. He was done with this book. He had to find a new thread to follow. As the front cover closed, a tiny face, just like all the others but taller, caught his eye. Dietrich grabbed the pages and laid the book open again. There he was. Marvin—another year, another unit. The man was certainly tall. He was in the background, and even though he truly did blend into the black-and-white picture, Dietrich would know that face anywhere. He was the runner, the singular runner who took Carlson's place. But his name wasn't Marvin Shanks.

Chapter 11

I stared at the dress Emerson had bought, the one he'd insisted was right for me...for him, according to Jill's definition of campaign. I ran the bright red fabric through my fingers. *That color is perfect,* Emerson had said when I held it up, then returned it to the rack and reached for another. *You must be colorblind.* I'd laughed, but he didn't laugh when I tried it on. *Perfect,* was all he'd said, and his dancing eyes agreed.

My mother would agree also. She would squeal at red the way she'd squealed when Emerson and I called to tell her we were engaged. It was an explosive conversation, her excitement drowning out my father's gentler congratulations, her insistence that the wedding be near her and far from my grandparents cut short as I promised to call another time and hung up. Call another time when Emerson wasn't around to hear our family war.

I let the fabric fall from my fingertips. Grandma was waiting. She had something to tell me. It wouldn't be an apology. Mavis Crawley never budged for anyone, but maybe she'd seen the light in Grandpa's fires. Something she'd never seen before, something she needed to see before I donned this dress or determined where my wedding would be. I grabbed my keys, my camera case with yesterday's rolls of film, and my purse. I cast one last glance at Emerson's fiery red, then ran out the door.

****

Grandma turned at the tinkle of Non Bookends' bells. Her face in crusade mode, she raised a finger the moment she spotted me—her sign to stay long enough to be her next audience. I raised my finger along with my camera case—*hurry and tell me some good news, I have things to do.* She ignored both and resumed talking to her customer. I strode to her little home-away-from-home in the back, dropped my purse on her cot, set the case next to it, and took my camera out. Photographing Grandma's customers would hurry her up.

I stepped from her room into the jungle of fiction Grandma called truth, truth without standard bookstore arrangement and without a section for romance—even burned romance. I focused my camera on a nearby tier of books—a woman in front of them holding *The Scarlet Pimpernel*. Average-sized book, hardbound, a faded maroon cover, her face barely visible over its top as I clicked, capturing her rapt attention to what Grandma said battles brought out in a man—patriotism paraded as chivalry when, in the end, true chivalry really began and ended at home. I caught the hunger in the woman's eyes. I clicked again.

Soft sounds hummed throughout the store as I adjusted the settings on my camera. Grandma's voice was one of those hums, still preaching her crusade, as I searched for my next victim. A book groaned, the soft sounds of a brittle spine being pried open to release a deluge of sleeping words. *Le Morte d'Arthur*. I focused on the title below another woman's hopeful face.

"Can I help you disturb another customer, young

78

lady?" Grandma appeared next to me, glassiness captured in her eyes with the camera click she wasn't ready for, a glassy sheen like the rain in Amabile's story.

"Trying to capture proof about your theory of fact in fiction."

Grandma shook her head. "You want proof of fact in fiction? Go find yourself a modern book on how to be married, and after you've been married a while, come to me for a novel. Then you tell me which is more accurate."

I shook my head then and glanced at *Le Morte d'Arthur*, now back on the shelf. It was about war, most likely. Love in war, maybe. It was in Grandma's W section.

"What's W stand for?"

"Write what you know."

I held back a snort. "According to you, this whole store should be under W, then."

"Don't get smart. The whole store is under Non Bookends. Limitless truth in fiction. Writing truth in a story doesn't create or change an outcome, it just helps you see why things turned out the way they did." Grandma glanced to other shelves with other letters. "Unfortunately, knowing why can hurt more than just understanding you lost."

I stared at the glassiness, at the why she thought she saw behind it.

"I contacted an attorney." She looked back at me. "I'm leaving him."

"You what? You can't do that. You can't do it to Grandpa, especially now, and you can't do it to Emerson and me. You need a reason...a solid reason.

Otherwise…" Otherwise Grandpa's well-set flames would go out. So would Emerson's campaign, with my fiery red dress.

"There are reasons, Cate."

"What reasons?"

Grandma raised her arms and spread them in the midst of her books. "It's all here, Cate. Ibsen was right. We learn our own 'what to do' as we find the truth. And it doesn't always make other people happy—like calling a lawyer."

I took a step back, spotting her hand-printed sign at the end of the shelf—"In this war, we know, books are weapons. Roosevelt." I looked from the sign to her. How could Grandpa's efforts to love survive this much opposition? How could any survive? "You're wrong, Grandma. You need to step out from behind your fictional characters and deceased authors and face the real truth."

"There's more truth here than there has been in the rest of our lives." Grandma glanced around Non Bookends, a gaze that ended at me. "It's time for me to leave, Cate. What he expected wasn't what I expected, but one thing I'm sure of—I'm a part of neither."

Chapter 12

Grandpa's car wasn't in his drive, so I rammed mine into his spot. Grandma couldn't leave him. Maybe he knew; maybe that's why he was gone. I shut off the engine and stared at his porch and his empty chair, and the pile of wood shavings where his feet should have been.

Grandpa never went anywhere, except to the store. And rarely that.

I hurried to the porch and up to the screen door, raised a hand, and knocked. My knock disappeared in the silence. I slid my hand inside the screen and hammered on the heavy inner door, but he didn't respond.

Wood shavings scuttled across the porch floor, swept by a light breeze. Grandma had started complaining about his whittled remains right before she converted the back of Non Bookends into a home-away-from-home. If Grandpa had actually carved something, especially for her, maybe they wouldn't have bothered her so.

I walked down the steps and to the garage at the end of their drive. Grandpa rarely parked inside it, and going through the side door, I found it empty. The vacant space was close and dark. It smelled of Grandpa—the aroma of wood and woodworking tools, oils, and cleaners. I felt for the light switch, flipped it on, and stared at the only thing I really knew about my grandfather—wood.

I walked along the workbench he'd built at the end of the garage, a long, high, wooden structure with everything he needed if he ever decided to build anything. Grandpa's work area was organized and ready, boards I used to play with, arranged by size, stacked at one end, jars full of small nails and screws across the back. Large equipment he'd told me the names of every time I asked stood along the adjacent wall, things that gave him the ability to do more than straight lines and sharp corners if he chose to. But he'd never made anything. He never even said whether he knew how, smiling quietly at my girlhood suggestions.

I tugged open drawers he'd hung beneath his long table, too high for me to reach as a child. Screwdrivers lined one, smallest to largest, Phillips in one row, flatheads in another. Pliers of all sorts filled the next, clean and shiny as if they, too, had never been used. Maybe Grandpa could make me a cedar chest for my wedding. Something fancy, something that would quiet Grandma's talk of divorce, something he could do to impress Emerson instead of walking me down the aisle.

I peered into each of the following drawers, everything inside shiny, neat, and clean, making his garage more like a store than someone's shop. At the last one I caught a tinge of grime around its handle. I ran a fingertip over the gritty blackness. This was his favorite drawer. This had to be where he kept his whittling tools. I looped my fingers over the handle and tugged. An assortment of knives and carving tools rattled in their rows, all looking well used and well loved. I smiled at the one thing I truly did know about my grandfather. He carved. He never made anything, but he whittled and carved.

The hum of a car came from the drive, a vehicle behind mine. Grandpa was home. I should have parked in the street instead of blocking him. I shoved against the drawer with my hip. It caught and jammed at an angle. Grabbing it by both sides, I jiggled it loose, set both hips against its front, and shoved once more. The drawer wedged again, jarring Grandpa's tools from their neat rows. The motor died as Grandpa cut his engine. I gave the jammed side a tug. I would tell him I was in here getting the broom to sweep off his porch. The drawer popped loose, and I clawed all of his tools from the back to the front to line them up again, three chunks of old and dried wood coming with them. I grabbed them, dragged them out, and carried them to the trash, pausing beneath the light as his car door closed. The chunks weren't trash, they were carvings. Flowers. Two round like roses, the other long. Like an iris, maybe. Or a tiger lily. They were beautiful beneath their ruin, finely carved, the work of a true artist.

I wanted to keep them, but I returned them to the drawer, guiding it shut this time. If Grandpa made those...if he could whittle flowers for Grandma... These were how his love efforts could undo the destruction about to come from her—carved in wood. Even old and splintering, those flowers spoke of love. I felt it. I flipped off the light and hurried out the door.

"Grandpa, I'm sorry about parking in your way." I shut the door behind me, the broom in one hand for my lie. Two more car doors closed, and I looked toward the car that wasn't his and faces that weren't his either. "What are you doing here? No one expected you."

Three staunch men in military uniforms stared back at me, their answer in a uniform look—what are *you* doing here?

Chapter 13

Dietrich spotted a small New York bookstore and a parking space a half block past it. A neighborhood store, from the look of it, one likely brimming with the sort of local information he needed. George Crawley's home was another block and a half ahead. A bookstore was the perfect place to pretend to be a tourist searching for books and an old friend, asking about the area, and learning what he could about the runner who had hidden behind a fictitious name.

Dietrich stepped from the rental car and strode around it to the sidewalk. He stared toward the bookstore. The perfect setting to prove fiction was just that—that fabled love stories and running under an assumed name for valid reasons had nothing in common. Pounding footsteps came from behind, the direction of the man he intended to quietly but speedily clear. He turned, kept close to his car as a young woman raced past, small but fast, her wavy brown hair nearly straight behind her. He glanced the direction she'd come from. A pursuer, maybe? This was an outer perimeter of New York City. No one was there, but still she was quick, impressive for as small as she was.

Dark haired and short—he was searching for tall, fair-haired, and thin. He gazed the direction the girl had run from, looking to the opposite side of the street, where the Crawley house would sit. He'd driven by it before coming here. Two cars had been in Crawley's drive, but the house had looked quiet, no sign of the man who'd run when he shouldn't have. He turned back toward the bookstore. This shouldn't take long.

Chapter 14

They were back, three stolid expressions I hadn't expected, watching Grandpa's pale one as he struggled from his car on the street.

You need to go. I saw it in Grandpa's eyes the moment his head appeared above his car, an invisible shake as he singled me out from the faceoff between his granddaughter and the three military men in his drive.

"My car..." I said it in a gesture, pointing to mine pinned in the drive by the heavy gray vehicle the men drove. *Make them go. You've burned everything pertaining to them.*

"Go on," Grandpa said to me, their three backs saying the same. I ran then, their faces photographs in my mind—photos I didn't want. I ran harder and faster than I'd ever run, their three faces chasing me the two blocks from the crippled man with his military intruders to Non Bookends. From a place with carved flowers, where I wasn't wanted, to one I didn't want to be, with divorce.

I flew through Non Bookends' door, the bells shrieking their violation.

"Grandma?" My voice further violated her atmosphere, too loud for her crusade. "Grandma?" I slowed, spotted her dusting Ibsen in the center of her store. "They're back, Grandma," I whispered, stopping at her side. "The army, and I don't think Grandpa was expecting them this time."

Her duster fluffed across Nora and Ibsen's other volumes until I snatched it from her hand.

"I said they're back, Grandma, and I want to know why. Why you can't be there, why you didn't expect them, and why you'd want to leave him at a time like this."

"I told you before, Cate, he was the one expecting them, not me. He never said a thing about it until now, and all he told me was maybe I shouldn't be around. So I'm not. I'm giving him the added space I should have years ago."

"You know that's not what he meant. And they shouldn't have come back."

"Was one a woman?"

"A woman? No. And what does that matter?" I grabbed her elbow and steered her away from the center of the store, to the front and off to one side, where there were no sofas or chairs filled with listening ears, only shelves and another of her hand-printed signs— "Medicine is my lawful wife and literature my mistress. When I am bored with one I spend the night with the other. Chekhov."

"They were all men, Grandma." I dropped her elbow. "Three army men, and what they said the first time wasn't even about Grandpa but about some other officer."

She ran a hand over her mouth as she stared at the feather duster I held onto. "I have no idea, Cate, but things could be worse."

I leaned close but spoke louder. "This is the man who stuck up for you when they asked to see his military memorabilia. No matter what you say, Grandpa did something for you."

"He got rid of it because of me. Not for me."

I straightened. I stared at her as I took a step back. "I can't do this anymore, Grandma. I'm tired. Do whatever you want. But the good things about Grandpa will still stand, things Emerson will honor when he's a senator. Grandpa's a hero for efforts you should never forget—he suffered, he was wounded, and he got rid of everything pertaining to his military past—for you, because they bothered you. He did it for his wife."

"He didn't want to get rid of those things, Cate, but he did. Because of me. Let him explain that to the army."

"He will, then, and I'll be there with him, if you won't. And so will Emerson." My voice cut through the silence that had settled over Non Bookends...a heavy hush except for the jingle of the front bells as the door opened and then closed.

" 'You shall judge a man by his foes as well as by his friends.' " Grandma's voice rose over her newest customer's steps. "Joseph Conrad."

"I don't care who said it, Grandma, or what they said. It doesn't matter. I wish you would be a part of what's ahead for Grandpa and for Emerson and me. But since you won't, I'm done."

"Pardon me."

The accented voice interrupted the "It's about time" I expected Grandma to store-shout at me. I watched her face, waiting for a blaze of triumph over my surrender. She could carry on without Grandpa and without my interference from now on. The intruder towered nearby as I waited, a man foolishly expecting one of us to pardon him when we could barely pardon each other.

Grandma didn't acknowledge him, so I did, looking up into a face I'd never seen in her store before. He stood above me, a man almost as tall as my grandfather, with hair nearly the same color as what his had been. This man's was coarser, wiry and wavy instead of straight. He held one of my grandmother's books, lifted it for me to see—a small book nearly covered by long fingers jutting from the sleeve of a soft corduroy jacket.

"I have a question. Could you tell me who manages this store? Then you can continue with your literary discussion." He nodded at the feather duster in my hand. "And cleaning." His accent had a comfortable lilt, a rolling German inflection. One that brought Grandma's brows to sharp peaks.

I pointed the duster at her. A German convert to her crusade would be the perfect icing on the cake of the war she'd just won. "She owns the store. She can help you."

Grandma yanked the feather duster from my hand and walked away, her march stilted as she disappeared around the shelves that aired Chekov's admission. "My grandma is apparently busy." Busy, rude, and selfish. "But I can help you."

"Your grandmother." He rolled it off his tongue, an accented sentiment that was neither a statement nor a question as he stared where Grandma had gone.

"So you needed help with something?"

He waved the book in the air, but it was his eyes I noticed. Irises the color of donuts, deep rings of hazel sectioned by thin rays of gray fanning out around bottomless pupils. "Shakespeare," he said. I looked from the steel-colored gray toward the book. "Do you only carry fiction in here? I'm interested in nonfiction. Books of local interest, in particular."

"Yes, only fiction. No nonfiction." Unless you're crazy enough to believe fiction is truth, like Grandma does. I shot a glance the direction she'd gone, then looked back at a customer who would go away and a crusade she'd for some reason let slide.

The man's gaze traveled down my clothes to my shoes, then back up to my sweat-tinged hair. "You were running to the store a moment ago. I saw you. Were you late for cleaning? Or do you think of yourself as a runner, though you are rather *wenig*? I mean little. German for small." His accent was melodic, his inflection sincere, his jacket comfortable and loose, but calling me *wenig* sounded like an insult.

"Running is more than just legs, and like I said, we have no nonfiction."

He raised the book higher, pinched it between two long fingers, and pointed it toward the front of the store. "I found this near the entrance." He opened it, then searched through a few pages until he stopped. " 'Wisely and slow; they stumble that run fast.' " He closed the book and looked at me. "It's underlined. It was important to someone. Did you do that?"

"Of course I didn't mark in a book. Didn't you say you were looking for nonfiction?"

"Yes, I prefer nonfiction, and for obvious reasons. I would underline facts, but this? No one would consider a line of fiction an adage. Would they? Would you? Is that how New Yorkers think?"

"I can't speak for all of New York, but I can give you some suggestions of other stores you might try." I reached for Shakespeare.

"So I would assume this store suits the local neighborhood…maybe mostly romantic sorts of customers and stories?" He held Shakespeare out of my reach.

"I'm not sure who all comes into this store, and since it's not my store, it's her decision what's stocked here." I jerked my head the direction Grandma had gone. Where I should have gone while she dealt with this man. I was done with her wars and her crusade. I was finished patching up the men she left behind. "But I can tell you she keeps no romance section here." Not in Non Bookends, not in my grandparents' lives. "And no nonfiction. I'm sorry we can't help you." I reached for Shakespeare again.

"No romantic section?" The book moved higher.

I listened for Grandma's voice. I needed to turn this customer over to her before I switched to my non-store voice. "I told you, no romantic section. And no nonfiction. Was there anything else?"

He lowered Shakespeare against the soft beige of his jacket. "This is an unusual store, especially for a woman and her small but fast granddaughter."

"Grandma has her reasons for what she does in here."

"Interesting woman. And her name would be?"

"I call her Grandma." I extended a hand, palm up, for the book. "If there is nothing else…"

"Your patience is appreciated." He waved Shakespeare. "I can return this to its proper place. But maybe you can help me anyway. I'm here from *Deutschland*…I mean, Germany…travelling and searching for an old friend that…"

Grandma appeared, drawing the accent and the hazel eyes from me to her. "So you are the owner of this store."

I braced for her usual proud expository, followed by an excuse for my behavior instead of hers. The stony profile I'd been watching for years softened as I stood there, her face like a child's, staring with thrill and terror at her first carnival ride. "Grandma?"

"We're getting ready to close."

I glanced at my watch. Grandma never closed early. "Grandma, you have customers still."

"It's time to close. Please lock up the back." Grandma turned away from me and the German again. She made her way toward other customers. "We're closing," she explained as she went, her march broken like Grandpa's limp. Grandpa. That had to be what was bothering her. Winning their war wasn't as gratifying as she'd thought.

"Excuse me," I said to the German. "Good luck finding a book somewhere. And your friend. Or whoever."

He nodded as I left him behind.

"Grandma." I caught up with her near Ibsen. "Have you locked the back yet?"

"No, not yet, but I will. I want to talk to you first."

She glanced over my shoulder where we'd been. "Lock up the back, and go on out that door when you do. I'll get the front."

Customers padded past, saying goodbye as they did. No one questioned Grandma. Non Bookends was always open, but Grandma was also always unique, distinctive enough no one wondered at anything she said or did, never thinking it odd. At least for her. But this was. The end of a battle had finally fractured the stone in her face.

The bells over the front door jangled a nearly continuous peal as people left. I stared toward the door, listened to it open and close, the glass of Grandma's front window like a mirror of her emptying store.

"You never close early." I looked back. "What we talked about back there...it must be hard for you... I mean, it's the end of a very long..." I shrugged toward the books around us. "War."

She looked at the books. "It's surprising how many battles make up a war. It's even more surprising when those battles are about to run out. The way you expected...yet didn't."

"Maybe what you expected isn't what you really want. Maybe there's a better way to end this war."

Grandma turned at a noise behind me.

The corduroy jacket was there, working his way around fiction he wasn't interested in, tilting his head as he studied the spines of Grandma's books instead of leaving like he knew he should. He sidled to the end of a shelf and looked up to the border of framed somethings reflecting all around the tops of the walls. He was tall enough maybe he could see what was behind each one's glass as he rotated a tight circle, studying each one, stopping at the ones above Grandma's main table.

"I thought he understood we were closing." I looked toward Grandma, but her gaze joined his to the frames above him. "Do you want me to tell him to go? It won't be in German, but I can make it clear."

He stood with his neck craned, one hand slipping into his trousers pocket, fidgeting as he stared above him.

"Can I, Grandma?" I waited for Grandma to tell me to go ahead. Books were closing, I could hear them being slid back into their spaces, as the last few people were leaving. The bells on the front door tingled for everyone except him. "Grandma?" I watched her. She and the German stared toward the ceiling, both looking at the darkest of the frames, the darkest and the ugliest.

The German man glanced over his shoulder at the two of us, drew his hand out of his pocket, and rolled something black in his fingers.

"Sometimes we get dragged into a war we wanted no part of," Grandma whispered.

The German couldn't have heard, but a war was there. And the dislike of it, too, just like she had whispered. It was time for him and his battles to go elsewhere. We had enough of our own.

"You'd best be going," I called to the German. "We're closing. There are larger bookstores closer to downtown. You'll find what you're looking for there."

With a last glance upward, he returned the black lump to his pocket and walked to the front of the store.

"He's already found what he's looking for," Grandma whispered.

"He was looking for nonfiction."

Grandma shook her head. "That only means he was looking for truth."

I gazed toward the front, where the man in the corduroy jacket had disappeared. I listened for the bells. "And you're thinking he could find it here in your fiction."

"I hope not," she continued in a whisper. "Or maybe I hope so."

"Oh, my gosh, here he comes again." I watched the German man approach. Legs as long as Grandpa's, walking our way—smooth, no limp, determined in his stride.

"I've decided to buy this after all." He held Shakespeare up, toward Grandma instead of me. "Someone has underlined a phrase about running." He watched my grandmother. "I'm not complaining, though. As I told your granddaughter, I'm looking for an old friend. A runner, it happens. Such a coincidence. The underlining will always make me think of your store." He tipped his head at me. "And you, little runner."

Chapter 15

Little runner? I heard the *wenig* in the way he said it. Grandma must have also felt the sting; it was in her hands and how they shook. I waited for a nasty retort as she took the book, pressed it against her stomach, and led the tall German to her table.

I continued to wait as Grandma wrote his ticket and made the wrong change. The man stood over her table saying nothing, his hazel rings watching each coin as she recounted. She handed him the bag with his book, minus the usual bookmark touting Non Bookends inside.

"*Danke.*" He nodded at her, then swiveled my way. He studied me from head to toe, then left, the front bells at long last tinkling his exit.

"I don't know how you stood it, Grandma. Thank God he is gone."

She stared forward as if the man were still in front of her, focused on the empty space across her table.

"He's gone, Grandma. He was horrible, but he's gone." I stepped behind the table and touched her shoulder with my fingertips. My mother would envy this sort of rare contact; probably Grandpa would too.

Grandma didn't move, didn't shrug off my hand. "Maybe wars never really end just because there's a winner and a loser. What about the wounded? Will the pain eventually stop?"

"I have to admit he had some sort of chip on his shoulder, but he's in no war with us. He's someone else's problem. I hope he finds his friend or whoever he's looking for and goes back to Germany. Soon." I gave the front of the store one last look and listened to the silence. "Your war is done, Grandma. And it can be in a peaceful way." I turned to her. "That's what's really bothering you. You can lay it aside and start again, with Grandpa or without him, but trust me, you should begin again with him."

" 'Love and war are the same.' Cervantes was right. He's brought them both to our door."

"Cervantes did?"

"No. Your grandfather. Please lock up. I must lie down."

I watched the back of her, the near stagger that took her to her little home-away-from-home. When the slight click from her door came and went, I locked up, front and back, and then I ran—ran from what she said about my grandfather, about love and war being the same and at our door because of him. Grandma was wrong…still. There was plenty of war, but it had all been hers. It also belonged to the three military men I'd left Grandpa alone with too long. What they brought wasn't ours.

I ran hard. The military men were in the drive as I neared my grandparents' house. I slowed to a trot and watched my grandfather hobbling behind them toward their car, his cane like the only leg he trusted.

"We can send someone for you." One of the men turned my grandfather's way as I walked into the drive. None of them looked at me as I stopped behind their car.

"That won't be necessary," my grandfather answered. He stood still and straightened as he addressed the man speaking to him. "I'll be there."

"Very good." All three climbed into their car. I was invisible to them. Their car started up. I looked through the wide back window, then stepped to the side, moving into the grass opposite my grandfather. Grandpa deflated to his regular posture as the car inched backward between us. His fine white hair, visible over the car's top, fell over his forehead as the car eased out of his drive. Then it was just the two of us as the car shifted gears and disappeared down the street.

Grandpa stared at the ground, propped up by one hand on the cane, his free hand threading long fingers through the white strands that fell back where they'd been. I watched the streaks of off-colored skin appear then disappear near his cuff. What more could the army want from him? Hadn't the service cost him enough?

Your grandfather brought both to our door. This was McCoy's war at our door, not Grandpa's. And love? It was in the carved flowers he'd surely made, or at least admired enough to keep. In the way he told Emerson to hold on to me. In the scars that hinted of a man with heart enough to suffer. In destroying what mattered to Grandma. Grandpa was wounded love.

Chapter 16

Dietrich didn't wait for stories, he went after them. He didn't invent situations or fabricate truths, he met facts and his subjects face to face, like he surely had today. He hadn't expected to encounter a Crawley, yet all evidence said he just had.

He turned left out of Non Bookends, headed the opposite direction from the Crawley house and the rental car. Opposite from the direction the girl had run from. And would likely run to. He stayed along the sidewalk, peering in shop windows, guessing what would happen, and it did. She darted out and she ran. She was too small to be a real runner, but she was good. Not as good as Mr. Crawley must have been, the man Dietrich guessed to be her grandfather.

Dietrich watched the young woman. Amabile's heartbreak, just like her heartthrob, was taking an odd form—tall, blond, and fast over forty years ago, but small, dark-haired, and fast today. Mentioning a runner hadn't shaken the grandma as much as it should have. Maybe she didn't know. Maybe it wasn't her husband who had run as Marvin Shanks. But Dietrich's being there had seemed to trigger something, possibly something she'd only wondered until now. That woman had scars, though; so did Oma and so did Amabile, some inside and some out. She also had something odd hanging on her wall. He touched the rounded chunk in his pocket. But none of that proved anything…yet. He needed time, maybe more time than he'd thought. Two weeks might not be enough, even though split-second glimpses of truth on the grandmother's face today said a lot—the unexpected realization of the opportunity for revenge.

She needed time he really couldn't afford. Women's hearts could be fickle and faithful all in the same beat, love who they hated and hate who they loved. She had to simmer. In the meantime, he would gather more information on the man down the street before he met the grandmother again…or her granddaughter. Old newspaper stories would have details about Mr. Crawley's coming and going overseas. Wedding pictures maybe. Facts to substantiate what had frightened him, and the grandmother too.

Chapter 17

Red wasn't my color, in fact I'd argued against wearing it, but as Emerson led me into the large ballroom I understood why he'd chosen it. Frank was right...or maybe Jill was. Red was for Emerson.

Beautiful evening gowns and dark tuxedos filled the room. The gowns created a sea of understated pastels...soft hues that made the red of my dress stand out. The perfect complement to black—Emerson's black I glued myself to. He did well.

"Perfect." Emerson leaned my way as we walked, speaking from the side of his mouth, his eyes surveying the crowd ahead. "Exactly what I intended."

"You mean, beautiful? Dazzling?" I pressed against his arm.

He looked at me, an approving tour with eyes as black as his hair and his tux.

"Yes, beautiful. Always. And I want you to spread some of that dazzle around for me tonight."

"You mean talk more as we mingle?"

"No, I want you to mingle on your own. Your face is well associated with mine now, and that dress further distinguishes you enough we can be apart and cover twice the ground—as one. A senator's wife has much to do with his success."

Or his failure. I stopped. Red alone would look garish instead of distinguished. It could be a beacon of my grandparents' dysfunction and my mother's move across the city. Emerson needed his black to truly make us one, and not leave himself with me out there strobing like a solitary, beckoning light. "How about we split up at your next event?" I pressed closer. "I'm not ready to solo tonight. I don't feel all that dazzling. A lot has been going on."

Emerson slowed. He glanced at me, his black brows level above his eyes. "What has been going on? Anything you need to tell me before I begin talking to people?"

I searched for my grandparents in his eyes, the way I'd hunted for them in Miles'. Whatever had been brought to Grandpa's and Grandma's door—their love and their war—Emerson couldn't have it brought to his.

People swept around us. Miles stood across the room watching, his wife at his side, perfect and at ease. No expected army officers daunting her life or dimming her expression, her gown the softest mint green I'd ever seen. "A senator's wife has to be dazzling." I turned to Emerson. "Even when she's tired. Everything's fine. I can be dazzling on my own."

"That's what I like to hear." Emerson leaned down and brushed my cheek with a kiss. "You will be an excellent senator's wife. Won't you?" He squeezed my hand at my nod; then he ran off. Straight to Miles, who would help him run his senatorial race while I mentally ran from here to Non Bookends to erase the love and war that would trip Emerson up.

Chapter 18

"More books!" Grandma's mailwoman breezed into Non Bookends, in shorts because of the mild fall temperatures, showing off legs even more muscular than mine. Her eyes lit up as the stack hit Grandma's table, startling me off my seat. "Too much coffee?" There was a laugh in her smile as she headed back toward the door. "Tell your grandma I'll be in tomorrow evening for some of that new reading material." The bells clanged and she was gone, already speeding past Non Bookends' front window.

"Oooh, what did Mavis get?" Two of Grandma's flock crowded the table where I sat pretending to work, wondering where Grandma was, the word *lawyer* vexing my mind. She wasn't at the store, but she knew I was coming and would open it for her. She wasn't at the house, either. I'd just left there, only Grandpa at home as usual…saying nothing about the army officers and nothing I wanted to hear when I said, *I want to talk to you about the wedding.* Grandpa had turned in a clumsy spin to the right and hobbled away.

"Can you open the packages so we can see what books she got?" The two women rifled through the stack, squeezing the books through their envelopes and rattling the boxes.

"Grandma's pretty particular about what goes on her shelves…" I watched four crusader hands pass

Grandma's mail back and forth. "What's so special about her books?" It was meant to be a thought, but it came out of my mouth and showed on the women's faces.

The back-and-forth stopped. "You don't know?" Wide eyes stared at me over packaged books.

"Well…" How could they tell me what Grandma wouldn't? "I guess I know enough to figure out what she wants in here and what she doesn't." I just didn't know why.

I can't walk with you down the aisle. My eyes had been as wide as these women's when Grandpa said that, the why of his reasons as lost as Grandma's to me. He would be worried about being available, trapped at whatever and whenever the army officers had offered him a ride to. How Emerson would be affected set off an explosion inside me, maybe inside of Grandpa as well, one that wouldn't stop, that continued to roll and fire, even as I begged Grandpa to be there, then begged him to at least make me a wedding gift, instead. A cedar chest, I'd suggested over the rumbling that still shook an hour later when the mailwoman dropped Grandma's books where I sat.

"Well, your grandma's books tell the truth." One woman slapped her hand on a pile on the table, and I jumped again. "People will say in fiction what they wouldn't dare admit out loud."

"Even to their spouses," the other woman added.

I glanced around the store at Grandma's crusade, at honesty that had to be dug for. Like from Grandpa this morning, insisting he be there for me and walk me down the aisle or make the cedar chest at least. *Ill timing, Cate. It undoes even the best of intentions. Not to mention the worst,* Grandpa had said without looking at me. *I'm sorry. I won't be there. And I won't have time to make you anything, either.*

"Truth is much easier to face when it's couched in someone else's story." The nodding woman nodded more. "It helps me see what I was afraid to admit. It sneaks it up on me instead of being shouted at me."

"Misery loves company, that's for sure." The other woman put a hand on the nodder's arm. "If someone wrote it, someone knew it before you. Someone had to suffer for that story to be born."

"So, so true. Let's open the books and see what she got." The nodder clapped her hands together, and I jumped for the third time. "We won't read them, but I just can't wait to see."

"I hate to when Grandma's not here…" *I won't be there*, rang in my head from earlier, Grandpa's voice followed by mine. *Another officer's investigation shouldn't have any effect on you or my wedding,* I'd argued. *When are you going to see those three army men?* I'd move my wedding date so he could be there. So he could shine for Grandma as he walked down the aisle. Changing the date would be better than explaining to Emerson why Grandpa wasn't there. Grandpa had stared at me, the impending date like a story across his face. *Middle of October,* he finally said. I'd sputtered. October was before our wedding date. The more I sputtered, the clearer the story became. I finally said out loud the thing he wasn't. *It's bigger than October, isn't it?*

It's a lifetime. Then the man who was always on trial turned, and I had left his house.

"You can blame us. Your grandmother won't yell

at us." The two women giggled.

"The last book I opened without Grandma's knowledge ended up... Well, let's just say something happened to it and she never got the chance to read it."

Their eyes widened again, and glee spread across their faces. "Tell us what happened." In tandem they leaned close, another person's personal disaster a story for them to read.

"All I can tell you is she wasn't happy. It wasn't the sort of book she would have used here, anyway, but that didn't pacify her."

"Too technical?" One scrunched her face.

"Too romantic."

Both women frowned. "Your grandmother isn't against romantic stories," the nodder corrected me.

Now I frowned. My brows dropped like laden eaves over my eyes. "I beg to differ."

"It depends on who wrote it and why," the other jumped in. "If there is a reason why the author wrote it, that book would be in this store."

"Amabile," I whispered. I'd never heard the name before I'd read the story at Grandpa's house. Hadn't bothered to research it after he destroyed her book. And two others.

"That was the author's name?" one of the women asked. "Or the title?" The bells tinkled at the front door. If that was Grandma, it would be a death sentence to be caught talking about the book Grandpa burned.

"Amabile was the author," I whispered.

"What?" The women leaned close.

"Amabile." Beige corduroy came around the corner. Her name was said again but this time louder, and with the roll of a German accent.

Chapter 19

Dietrich spoke Amabile's name without the surprise and guttural shout he felt from the shock at hearing the name in this little store. "You are speaking of a German author from the era of the Second World War?"

The little runner stared at him from between two women, her brown curls dry today. Healthy, a nice wave around a face more attractive than he'd noticed before. But a Crawley face.

"I've read some of her work. Not what I usually read, but it's healthy to read a variety, don't you think?" He came close to the three, two of them smiling, the little runner not. He wasn't either.

"Why are you back? I told you we don't have any nonfiction here."

She had gumption. She should learn to channel it, the way he had.

"Pondering the name of your grandmother's store. Non Bookends. Makes me think there's more here than oddly arranged fiction. Possibly whatever a person could want to find."

The taller of the two women did what his journalistic side loved—she began to babble. She was slightly older, with an almost olive tinge to her complexion, details Dietrich noted without even having to look. He turned to her and managed a smile as she spilled the sort of uncontrolled effervescence journalists waited for. "Cate's grandma would agree with you about that. So even if it's nonfiction you're looking for, you'll find the truth in here. You just have to know where to look. Cate can help you. She's been helping here since she was a child."

He knew that. Cate had grown up near her grandparents, the Crawleys an unhappy man and wife. He'd gleaned that from microfilm of newspapers at the local library. This area might be part of New York City, but it had all the naïveté of a small town. It had been simple to read the whole story between the lines—a broken soldier returning, his fiancée not even at his side during the celebration welcoming him home. A wedding sometime after, two glum faces as far apart as they could be behind their wedding cake. But nothing about the Olympics, nothing about Crawley being a runner. Dietrich had wired Carl at the Library of Congress, asking what exactly were Crawley's injuries, thankful that injuries didn't fit Amabile's lover. Only her…and Oma…and now this man. How had they happened? Why had he come home when he did? He'd claimed to be asking for a friend, a brief but necessary diversion from his own research.

Cate gathered strewn packages from the table's top, her short arms quick, scooping everything her way. "He doesn't need help. There are plenty of other bookstores in New York. Ones that group mysteries with mysteries and romance with romance and have whole areas for nonfiction."

She was young, close to his age, but still Dietrich caught in her tone what he read in Amabile, saw in Cate's grandmother, and heard in Monika—unresolved angst—not something that would benefit a woman intending to become a senator's wife, an engagement he'd learned of from the microfilm also.

"Let me help you, instead, with the author you were speaking of when I came in—Amabile. In case you didn't know, she wrote around the time of World War II. I've heard conjecture she wrote love stories long before the war under a different name, then shortly before, she switched to writing under the name of Amabile, writing painful tales that people suspected might be true. In them she gave her heart to a foreign man, someone who was in Germany briefly around that time. A soldier? An athlete in Berlin's games? Both? Whatever his reason, he wooed her while there, and did it so well he won. Won a medal and won her heart. Then he left her behind, after an explosion, like a discarded prize. A medal he really didn't want. It broke her, shattered her, inside and out, her scars worn in both places." He watched for an explosion in Cate, holding back his own at quoting Monika and giving air to her presumptions he was here to refute, but the burst came from another.

The second woman, not as tall, heavier, hair too curly, gasped and clapped a hand over her heart. "Cate…" The woman looked at the little runner. "Your grandmother would want those stories here, especially if they were based on truth. Maybe that's why she ordered one."

So Mrs. Crawley had ordered one. Maybe more than one? The color had gone from Cate's face. "What I read was nothing like what Grandma would want." Cate pressed the stack of packages to her chest.

"You've read Amabile?" Dietrich asked. "Did you

think the writing was more real than not?" He wanted to hear the answer from her if she would, what she had to say instead of him so he could scratch Crawley off his list and go home. But Cate said nothing. She was running instead. Dietrich could see it in her waning color, the way she bound the books between her and what she didn't understand. "Did you think the man who wooed her was from this country? Could you tell anything about her lover in what you read?" He waited for her to say no, or dismiss fiction for exactly what it was. He could just go ask Crawley, skip his usual journalistic precautions, free his family from Monika's claims, and be done. But Crawley still had Marvin Shanks to explain. If Dietrich charged past the fictional world to get at the facts, the impact would be felt here, in this store, with this family. He would be the bomb Monika had been to him.

Amabile's lover was taking form again, the blond in her darker hair, the tall in her shorter form, the similarities in their differences on Cate's face. "I didn't read much of it."

Whereas he'd read all he had, and he was reading it again on Cate. The similarities Monika had inferred between Amabile and Oma were frightening, but what he saw on Cate's face was terrifying. "He may have been in the service, but I suppose solving who he was wouldn't matter as much in a fiction bookstore as why he did what he did. That may be something to ask your grandmother." That may be too much, but it had to be said. He had to separate his family from George Crawley's, distinguish his family's who or what from the Crawleys' why. To know why was personal, the chance that you weren't the reason why, but some other

111

person or object was more important than you. Dietrich's family hadn't lived that way. There had never been a why in their family, only the whisper of what…what was it beside Oma, that invisible presence that really was never there. But whatever sins lay in the Crawley family, the grandma had felt the sting of why and was choking on it. They had truths to face that likely weren't fiction, whereas in contrast, his family's still were.

"I won't do that." Cate shook her head, throwing off his suggestion, sending her brown waves slapping across her face.

"Why not ask Mavis?" The taller woman stared down at Cate. "This is exactly what she would be interested in. She probably knows, since she ordered one of that author's books. I'm going to ask her. You have too much going on with a marathon, the election, and a wedding coming up. Leave this to me."

"A marathon? So you really do run." The man in the story ran also. He didn't need to repeat that for either of them. "And you're getting married? Fiction says to watch your heart." He turned from the color streaking Cate's face to the other woman. "I'd be interested in what Cate's grandmother says. And if she is interested in my opinion, as a German, I'd be happy to…"

"She won't be interested in your opinion or why. Weren't you looking for an old friend? Shouldn't you be spending time with him instead of here?" Cate jerked her head toward the door.

"Did I say friend? Distant acquaintance might be more accurate. Old is correct, though. I found him. He lives not far from here. I just haven't been to his house yet." He couldn't look at Cate. Her "why" was mixing into his "what" in the same way her defensiveness lapped at his determination to prove Monika wrong. He glanced up at the frames surrounding the ceiling, the lights whiting out the glass, turning every one of them into a mirror. He wrapped his fingers over the dark lump of wood in his pocket as he stopped at the blackest of the frames, a lone chunk hanging on one side. Erika Müller wrote romance; the things in her attic that reminded him of Amabile were there because of her love of it. And the absence of writing had created the vacancy at Oma's side, not some untrustworthy fictional lover. Those were Dietrich's facts. Crawley's were much worse.

Chapter 20

"Why Amabile?" one of the women asked as Non Bookends' bells clanged the German man's exit. "Why choose that name to write under? I bet he's right, whoever he was. She fell in love, lost her lover, and everything she wrote after that was sad and true. Does your grandma have any other books under that name?"

Besides what my grandfather burned? My chest hurt. I couldn't breathe. Grandpa's back appeared in my mind, the way he paused in his doorway when I'd said Amabile's name after our walk. Why was this happening, and why now? *Ask your grandmother…* I couldn't, I didn't want to know any of the whys about Amabile, some silly fictional person just like all of Grandma's others. Amabile and this German needed to go, out of our lives, but especially out of Emerson's. "I hope not…"

"You hope not? I would think you'd hope she does."

I pressed the books tighter to my chest. No wonder I couldn't breathe.

"Why, Mavis might have one of Amabile's books right there, in your arms." Both women eyed what I clasped. I shook my head and nodded toward the back. I was taking Amabile away. *God, please don't let there be any books by that woman here.*

I left Grandma's two customers at her table,

chattering away, bringing life to something that needed to be dead. Grandma's crusade exploded in their zeal— a woman's plight, a woman's war, a woman who may or may not have survived her crisis. I didn't want to know what that German had made me feel, though I already did. He was giving form to something invisible and ephemeral I'd always ignored.

The women's voices carried like the buzzing of bees, a hive of excitement chasing me to Grandma's room. A little home that suddenly felt like a refuge. I hurried the packages to her cot and dropped them on her quilt. The stack hit and teetered, and I bent and fanned it to the side, exposing return addresses I really didn't want to see. Had Amabile's envelope had a German address? But the book had been in English, so it was a translation. Addresses beyond New York slid to the side, towns and cities all within this country. I straightened. I wanted to open every one, more than those two women had. More than I'd ever wanted anything in my life.

I glanced around Grandma's home-away-from-home. The miniature of what should have been her real world, minus a husband. Fictional people and authors who'd suffered were shelved in rows outside her walls, her companions instead of him. I stared at her quilt, her floral tablecloth too large on the tiny table, at tea towels and salt and pepper shakers from the fifties. I shook my head. This wasn't right, but it was her refuge, just like it was Grandpa's to carve sticks to nothing. Yes, they had a bad marriage; at least Grandpa had tried. That German was planting fictional thoughts I didn't want. He had no business in my head or in Grandma's store. I'd tell Grandma he was never to be allowed back. God help his friend he'd come to see...and the friend's family.

"It will be okay," I whispered to myself, the envelopes, and her room. "He's just some foreign man who will go away. He's stirring up trouble before he does because he's evil. Eventually he will go, and everything will be all right." I scraped the sweat from my palms onto my jeans, straightened the envelopes on Grandma's cot, and marched back out into the store.

The buzzing was still there, but quieter. I passed customers settled comfortably in Grandma's chairs. I was okay. Everything would be fine. An old acquaintance down the street meant nothing, especially if he was a runner. Fast wasn't in us, according to Grandpa. Neither was racing. That's why I didn't race and only ran. The buzzing stopped as I rounded Ibsen and headed to Grandma's table. The two queen bees were still there, their heads bent together over a large book.

"What are you two up to?" I swiped my hands down the front of my pants again.

"Look at this," one said. She swiveled the book my direction. "We can't figure it out." She placed a finger on a word in the first column. "There. Why do you suppose she chose that?"

"Who? And chose what?" I frowned at her, then at the dictionary and where she pointed.

Amabile—Am·a·bile—noun. Lilium amabile. The friendly or loveable lily.

Lily. Grandpa's garage.

Chapter 21

I watched my grandmother, followed her march, looking for *lawyer* in every step. She brushed past her table where I sat, her purse locked inside one elbow. "Anything happen while I was out?" she asked without slowing.

"New arrivals are on your cot." I stared at the back I wanted to run to, the hem of her skirt I wanted to cling to the way I had my mother's when I was little and things were going wrong.

She disappeared around the shelves and eventually through her door. I made myself breathe, listened above the pages flipping around me, the soft whispers and gentle footsteps throughout the store. She'd lock her purse in a cabinet and probably study the stack of new books that had come in. I stared at the pile of unmarked price tags and strands of ribbon I'd arranged into the shape of a lily, and at the closed dictionary on the table's corner.

Grandma marched back, the packages in her arms, books she might ask me to look at. I stared at the volumes peering from ends she'd slit open as she dropped her new arrivals on the table's top. She scooted a chair to one side, sat without a word, and began removing books from their mailers, sorting them into categories that meant something to her, and probably to the two women who'd finally gone.

117

"Any good books today?" I stared at each one, straining to see each author's name.

"I chose them, so they're probably good." Her smile came and went as she laid packaging aside and arranged her books into four piles.

"I'm sorry three you chose got burned." I hoped she wouldn't look up, and she didn't. She squared each stack, then squared each one again.

"That German man came back this morning."

The squaring stopped.

"I think we need to tell him he can't…"

She looked away from the books in her hands and glanced above where we sat toward the ceiling.

"Grandma, I don't like him." I sounded twelve. Not surprisingly, she didn't respond. "I mean…he's trouble. He might upset your customers."

"Did he say his name?" Grandma looked at me.

"No." I shook my head. But neither had I asked. Or even thought to. Or wanted to. "It doesn't matter. He's visiting someone, so he'll be gone soon, anyway."

"That's not true, I'm afraid." Grandma shook her head. "He's always been here. Even longer than you. And I hate to say it, but he'll never leave."

Chapter 22

"I brought you something." Dietrich held the small book Cate's way. It was meant to be a brace of sorts, a small sting so the bigger sting that may come later would hurt less. He kept his hand over the title and author between them, a half dozen other books balanced on her hip, old books like this one.

"Grandma approves the books for her store."

"How much longer, Catharine?" A man with black hair came around a shelf, good looking, a smart clip in his step. This was the fiancé Dietrich had seen pictures of in the newspaper. Emerson Cosnik, intending to smart clip his way to the senate—with Cate… Catharine.

"Just two more stacks to put up first." Cate glanced at her fiancé, leaning from her load. Emerson peeled back his sleeve and studied his watch.

Cate needed time as much as Dietrich did, for important things that could trip up the smart clip. "Let me help." Dietrich slid his book into his inner jacket pocket. He laid a hand above and one below Cate's— Catharine's—stack, and took it from her.

"What are you doing?" Cate grabbed at the books he lifted out of her reach. "I have to put those on the shelves…" She nodded her fiancé's way. "Fast. We have to be somewhere."

"Fast it will be. You lead, I'll follow."

"I don't have time to work with someone in the way."

"You'll be much faster if you're not carrying a load. Anyone's load. Trust me." Amabile was a story likely having been lived out in thousands of people's lives. Not in his and Oma's, though. A night of pacing and analyzing Erika Müller's writings had convinced him of that. But there was an Amabile of some sort in the little runner's life. He could help Cate face hers as he disproved his family's fictional one. Cate could go on then, marry her senator while Dietrich returned to Germany to tell Monika she was wrong.

"Excuse me." Emerson shook the sleeve back over his watch. "We appreciate your help, but we're in a hurry."

"Maybe you could collect the other pile," Dietrich said without looking at Emerson. "That would hurry things up. For you."

Cate eyed Dietrich. "Who are you? I don't know where you came from or why you keep coming back, but I'm telling you now to get out of my grandmother's store and stay out. Stay away from her and away from me. And him." She tossed her head where her fiancé had been, his smart clip taking his hurry away.

Dietrich slid a hand inside his jacket and drew the book out. "This isn't for your grandmother." He held it toward her. "This is for you."

"Let's go, Catharine." Black hair and impatience was back. "I asked your grandmother, and she said the books can wait until morning. All of them." Her fiancé clipped near and Dietrich let him take the stack of books from beneath his arm.

Cate stared at the dark green cover Dietrich held in

his hand. He let her see the binding that had faded to a dustiness, a single flower embossed on the front.

"Go on without me." She stared at the lily and Amabile's name below it.

"You need to be there, Catharine. You're expected."

"This is for his campaign?" Dietrich asked.

"That's right. My name is Emerson Cosnik, and I'm running for Senate." Emerson stepped closer to Cate's side, then slid his shoulder in front of her, between his fiancée and the book that had her attention.

This was Cate's hurry, not his. Dietrich turned the book and opened its cover, swept several pages to the side, then read:

"This is you. It's the way you really are. It's the way I see you." He turned his mirror her way, the bottom of its frame resting on his knees as she sat across from him. Her tiny apartment seemed so much fuller when he was there, so much more alive and warm. He steadied his hands at the upper rounded corners, careful where he placed his fingers near the carved lilies he'd added. "See yourself? See the water? See who's across it from you?"

She did see herself. She was much younger. She inched closer to the edge of her seat. How was it she could see herself in the mirror so long ago? It must be a trick. She looked over the mirror's top at him. Maybe it was the language difference. She wasn't proficient at his English, and he knew nothing of her German, only the niceties. Only words that told him to find his mark and ready himself to go.

They could hear the roar of the crowd far away, others learning those same words in her language. He didn't care. He was there. With her. She could see it.

Cate's face blanched. She saw what she had to in the mirror, something her fiancé didn't. And shouldn't. "Go without me, Emerson. They're waiting for you."

Chapter 23

Amabile. I think I said her name. I must have, for the German man nodded.

"Who are you?" I asked again, once Emerson had gone. Not happily, but rightly. Away from this man and the insinuations he tried to make. Away from the mess this German would make of Emerson's campaign. "I mean it this time. What is your name, and why are you here?"

"My name is Dietrich. And I told you, I am here because of an old acquaintance. Well, not exactly an acquaintance, personally. A family acquaintance is more accurate, but it turns out the presumed connection was wrong. A literary liberty misconstrued."

Grandma said he'd always been here and that he'd never go. One of them was lying. It had better be her.

"Dietrich what?"

"Cate what?" he asked. I studied the lines in his eyes. Handsome eyes, except for the lies they inferred. "Shall I read more?"

No. The word was a store shout neither of us heard. "Outside." We stepped through Grandma's store, her bells, and out onto the sidewalk, where I wheeled and faced Dietrich. "What do you do, if I can actually believe anything you tell me? You say you don't care for fiction, yet here you are, reading some to me while speaking of literary liberties. And romance, too? It might be okay to lie in Germany, but we frown on it here."

The lines in his eyes sharpened. "A common fallacy regarding my country in light of its history, but foreign liars are equally guilty of carrying out schemes."

I thought of their history and our army. I thought of McCoy, who was being investigated. I thought of the lily in Grandpa's workbench drawer...and the one on Amabile's cover. "Is that why you're here? To carry out a scheme?"

He came close, even nearer in the way he looked at me than in the way he stood. "I'm here because of others' schemes. But I'm staying to help. Not help them...but to help the victims."

"You call what you do help? From what I can see, you travel around and create problems."

"I'm not some bored troublemaker. I'm a researcher. I actually look for truth, and then I write it. I fix the lies everyone else tells."

"Truth? You write truth? And your research is in fictional stories like Amabile and stores like Non Bookends? I don't for one second believe you write truth or read fiction to find it. You sound like Grandma, except the two of you have nothing in common."

"I believe I understand your grandmother, possibly even better than you do. I can guess how she would feel about something like this." Dietrich opened Amabile again.

As he left, it was his face she saw. His back headed toward her door, but in the mirror—in the gift he'd given her...given the two of them—she saw him coming toward the water while looking her way. Walking across the gleaming expanse to her, a smile on his face, blue beckoning in his eyes, gentle waving in the loose strands of blond hair. Long legs destroying the distance between them. Legs that brought him there. Legs made to win.

She wanted to beg him to never go. To stay. But when she glanced from his retreating form to the mirror, she knew he'd always stay. He was running now, toward her, in the glass. She was his prize. One he would cherish forever. That's the way this love was supposed to be. She saw it, in his mirror.

"You know nothing about my grandmother. Leave her and her bookstore alone. Most people use the library for research. New York has an amazing one. You should try there instead of storybooks or used bookstores." I turned, my reflection catching my eye, the me I saw in Non Bookends' window doing the same. I gazed at myself, large gold letters splayed over my head and across Dietrich's much taller one as he stared with me. Our reflections looked back at us, the sheen of the pavement beneath our feet like water.

"I've been to the library. Several of them, in fact," he said to my reflection.

I looked up at him, at the profile of his real face as he continued to stare at Grandma's window.

He looked from the window to me, a fragile rigidity I hadn't seen in his reflection. "I told you. I was looking for a runner. You should be looking too."

The words exploded. I turned back to the window, to the two of us, the short and the tall, the brunette and the blond, the runner and the writer.

Chapter 24

Dietrich looked like a runner. I didn't. I worked in a bookstore and should have been a writer. But I wasn't.

"Leave me, leave all of us alone." I said to his reflection and then to his face. "I'm going to stand here until you go. I don't want you bothering my grandmother, so leave. Now."

"You needed to know. And you can rest assured, you're not the runner I was looking for."

"You couldn't catch me if I was."

Dietrich stepped around me, not even glancing down as he passed. Street lamps and car lights lit the sidewalk now, turning Non Bookends' front window into even more of a mirror. One that should have shown Dietrich walking away. Leaving the runner without the writer. His footsteps faded, but his reflection stayed. I could still see it. Right there next to mine.

Chapter 25

He would come. She knew he would. He'd been so near...

The outer wounds screamed until there was nothing to scream about—shards of glass extracted, splinters of wood withdrawn, ashes discoloring cuts and burns, bones fragmented into slivers now bound into place. But on the inside of her...the heart that hurt, and waited, screamed on. There was no balm, no relief, no way to remove the ache that lay there watching her doorway every day.

Dietrich slapped Amabile closed, a copy he'd found here in New York. He was right, he knew he was. Amabile was fiction Oma had admired and intended to use as inspiration so she could write again. Some truths were amongst its passion, truths he sensed in Cate's family, no matter how much the little runner fought them. He didn't have enough time for her battles, though. *Der Spiegel* had contacted him: they had an assignment waiting and wanted him back in Germany. Oma would be anxious, also, not to mention Monika. He looked from the window of his hotel room, from the highest floor of the building, onto New York City's life below. He'd come here for Oma, for his career. Crawley likely wasn't Amabile's "he"—not with his injuries—but he was someone's. Dietrich could only prove what mattered to Oma, then he had to go home.

Dietrich stared down into the darkness dotted with flickers of light. Was one of those lights the little runner as she hurried to her fiancé at his event, carrying herself fast, away from the pain she tried to avoid?

He tapped Amabile's book on his leg. Enough. Cate was going to run wherever and however she pleased…with an emotional limp, though, that she didn't deserve.

The phone jangled, and a small red button lit up. He walked to the nightstand and lifted the receiver… "A wire? Thank you. I'll be right down." That would be from Carl, a very resourceful and eager young man. Dietrich managed a fragment of a smile. Then he left his room.

The United States had no concept of old, but the hotel and its lobby made the most of what was aged to this young country. Lights like tiny stars glittered high in the ceiling, while sconces sent soft fans of illumination up the walls. The bustle of the lobby had a hushed pleasantness to it, pleasant enough he took his wire to the hotel bar and chose a seat in a far corner.

"Doppel Bock, please," Dietrich said to the young waiter bent in a slight bow at his table. It was a German beer this New York hotel probably wouldn't have, but the young man suggested a suitable Belgian replacement, a good suggestion, and very dark. Dietrich smiled as the Carl of brews walked away. He'd keep this young man in mind in case he ever needed to woo something from someone in a dark, discreet New York environment on another trip.

"*Danke*." Dietrich thanked the young waiter once the drink was delivered to his table. Dietrich leaned close to the wall and studied faces glowing over candles at nearby tables, close together, whispering love, promising it in their expressions. Which ones were genuine and which were fiction? Dietrich took a sip of the beer. Its heady darkness bit at him. It was genuine.

He leaned into his own candle, the fire's glow lighting the envelope containing Carl's nonfictional wire. "I trust you've done well again," Dietrich whispered. He broke the seal, and Carl began to whisper his facts back.

"Most of Private Crawley's unit stayed in France, where they were stationed, while he and several others were temporarily deployed to other locations in Europe, strategic locations, to ward off the possibility of an eventual war. Many were sent to Belgium for the elections, while Crawley was stationed in Poland with five others. He was sent there as a US presence in a country fretting over tensions to the east and the west. Lieutenant McCoy thought Crawley quite capable of tending to what little was needed in Wroclaw, sending Crawley there on his own. Crawley's eventual injuries brought McCoy there, and his involvement in Poland ended shortly after.

"Private Crawley sustained injuries to his hands, chest, and arms in an explosion, burns severe enough on the extremities to undergo treatment in Poland, where they were acquired. It was a severe break of his leg that finally sent him home. Crawley finished out what little was left of his enlisted time in convalescence at home. Not the usual way the army did things, but an exception was made for him.

"His burns were sustained from a gasoline fire he attempted to help with. Still too medicated from the burns to be back on duty, his leg was accidently crushed above the knee when he misjudged the nearness of a backing truck and was caught between it and a loading platform.

"It was McCoy who had Crawley sent home. Crawley insisted he stay active, even though hospitalized, but McCoy had him shipped out. No reason was given, other than McCoy noting Crawley had served well, was near the end of overseas duty, and was of no use in his condition for his final days of enlistment.

"Not all of this information was from the Library of Congress. I found some at the National Archives and the rest with army records. If there is anything else you or your friend need to know, please send me your request. Working diligently on my cataloguing system, by the way. Hope to have it ready to present in another month.—Carl Logan, Photographic Archives Specialist"

Dietrich stared at the page. He could hear Carl's voice as he'd read it, professionalism giving way to the youthful lilt of excitement at the end. Dietrich had also requested information about two other enlisted men he had no interest in, to throw Carl off. Those two pages lay behind Crawley's.

Crawley didn't fit with the Shanks story—no mention of running, nothing about Berlin. But photos didn't lie.

"McCoy." Dietrich spit the name as he refolded Carl's notes, slid them back into the envelope, and tucked it into his inner pocket. He glanced at his watch. The little runner had suggested he take advantage of New York's libraries. There he could find something about an officer who let one of his men just go home, bringing something with him that soured his wife. Dietrich would solve this for Oma's sake, and then he would go home.

Chapter 26

The main course was done and dessert was being handed out when I entered Le Bourgelais, the restaurant I should have been at two hours ago…instead of running from Dietrich's and my reflections, and Amabile's book. The dining area was dimly lit, candlelight and soft chandelier luminescence making everyone appear young and amorous. I glanced beyond their expressions, searching for Emerson, and spotted two empty chairs at the main table. One was surely mine.

I scanned the black tuxedos, looking for one worn by a man with black hair and dark eyes. I should have run faster. Dietrich was an awful man. Nothing like the one I was searching for now.

Emerson's voice came from across the dining area. His laugh, the way it pealed in genuine mirth. I glanced the direction it had come from, to the table where one of the attorneys who worked with Emerson sat, and alongside him, the man's wife. Their secretary and her husband were also there, she looking as beautiful as she was valuable to the office. The others were faces I didn't recognize, but I would soon know who they were. I left Dietrich behind and glided to the table.

"Catharine." Emerson's secretary saw me first. "Emerson said you might not make it. So glad you did."

Emerson looked up from leaning on the back of his

partner's chair, his laughing expression changing to a smile. "You made it."

"Yes, thankfully." I came to his side, threaded my fingers through his. He squeezed my hand, and I burrowed in his grip. *Blond. Runner. Blue eyes.* "I'm sorry about…"

Emerson squeezed tighter, a squeeze that said, *Not now.*

He was right. Grandma and Grandpa had no place in Emerson's world. Neither did Dietrich. I held on, knowing Emerson would soon shoo me off, send me around the room "running" for him, selling his agendas, helping him win. I leaned into his arm, holding tight as long as I could.

Emerson squeezed again, a promise he would never let go. He kept me close in his grip, included me in answers to questions, shared his dessert at my side, and whispered as we danced close. Amabile, Dietrich, runners, and my grandparents drifted farther away. This was my world, my real world.

"You have them eating out of your hand." The crowd thinned after Emerson's talk, and Miles spoke in a hushed tone alongside us, watching supporters leave who had promised their allegiances. Only the servers remained as the last guest exited, they and the four of us—Miles, his wife, Emerson, and me.

Emerson held onto me as he laughed, happy with Miles' compliment. "It's a large hand. I've promised them much, and I will deliver."

"He will…" I began.

Emerson let go of my hand, wrapped his arm around my shoulder, and drew me close. "Family. Can't do anything without loyal and solid family," Emerson said, too loud as he looked at Miles. "Can't if I'm exhausted, either. We must be going." Emerson nodded at Miles, thanked him and his wife, then steered me away, thanking each server and the caterer as we went. I saw Miles and his wife slip out the door as Emerson said his last goodnight to a custodian. Family. Emerson would make loyal and solid family.

He led me to the coat rack and helped me into my coat.

"Thank you." I glanced over my shoulder and up at him. "You don't know how good you've made me feel this evening. Like family." I reached for his hand.

"Family," he said almost too low to hear. "When we get outside, I need to talk to you about that."

"What?"

The fingers I reached for wrapped around my elbow and steered me from the building.

Chapter 27

Mc-Coy Mc-Coy Mc-Coy. My feet hammered his name. Somehow Emerson had heard about him.

Keep your friends close, your enemies closer. I didn't need my grandmother to remind me of that old quote. Emerson had. The way he'd held onto my hand last night and kept me near instead of turning me loose to mingle on my own. I understood it now.

"You're doing that thing you do again." Frank pedaled his bicycle from behind to alongside me. "You know…"

"I know." The two words exploded, sounding ugly. I stared straight ahead as I ran. "I didn't mean that the way it sounded. Sorry."

Bits of asphalt and dirt crackled beneath Frank's tires, a sound I normally liked. When I added the beat of my breathing along with *Mc-Coy Mc-Coy Mc-Coy*, a symphony resulted.

"That's better. Sort of. How about I go a little faster and you put your energy forward into keeping up?" Frank asked as he inched ahead.

I watched his bike. I could take up cycling instead of running. I could go farther faster, be gone a whole day. No one took jogging tours, but anyone could take a bicycle tour.

"Faster." Frank stretched in front of me. I could see the strength of his back, the muscles in his thighs. The light pumping motion he exaggerated so I'd do the same with my feet. Light, not hammering. Forward, not grinding down to the center of the earth where my family should be, by the look on Emerson's face last night.

"You're doing it again. I can hear your feet, and I couldn't a second ago," Frank called without looking back.

"Frank." I lengthened my stride and came alongside him.

"What are you doing?" He swiveled his head my direction. "And you claim you couldn't win. Want me to go even faster?"

"Frank." I kept my arms close, my fists pumping me forward. "You've been around here for several years."...*and you live with Jill, who involves herself in more than she should...* "Tell me, is there talk going around...about my grandparents?" In the silence I could hear the crackling beneath his tires again, hear the breeze in my ears, see the tunnel of trees, houses, and cars we were working our way through. "There is, then." I said it for him. It was probably Dietrich's fault. Or the army's. My feet drowned out the crunch of Frank's tires. I lightened my stride before he could change the subject to how I ran. "So what are people saying? That my grandmother has some crusade that makes no sense, in a bookstore where love stories mean nothing?" Please say that's it. Please don't say it's *Mc-Coy Mc-Coy Mc-Coy.*

"Are you kidding? Love story is all over your grandmother's store, according to Jill." He grinned. "That's why I don't go in there."

I ran on my toes, listening and waiting for Frank to

correct himself. Correct Jill—something I would enjoy. "There's no love story there."

"Cate, surely you see that. Everyone does, according to Jill. It's just not the normal type you read about, or something like that, but it's love."

Everyone saw love? Because Grandpa really did bring it to their door? But he was never in Non Bookends or even at Grandma's side. Or maybe everyone saw it because they hadn't lived around the two of them and been blinded by experiences that spoke of war instead of love. I dropped from my toes and stopped. I stood where I was, propped my hands on my knees, and looked up, soaked strands of brown hair clinging to my face. "People...or Jill...really think Grandma's crusade is about love?"

Frank looped his bicycle in a circle...again...and wheeled to a stop in front of me. "They evidently do. Jill's usually right."

I dropped my arms to my sides and straightened. Sweat dripped from tapered ends of my hair, trickled down my face, my neck, and into my already soaked shirt. "But...but..." I frowned. "Never mind. How about Grandpa..."

"Your grandfather is..." Frank lifted a hand and rubbed his chin. "Wounded."

"That's all?" *Mc-Coy* hammered in my head. The look on Emerson's face, even in the shadows when he had wedded McCoy's name to my grandfather's, said more than wounded.

Frank glanced at his watch. "He ever tell you about his injuries?"

The limp and the long sleeves. I shook my head. "He won't talk about the military." Except to the army officials, and to someone who must have told Emerson about McCoy.

"Well, might be he's embarrassed, maybe about his long legs getting him in the way of instead of out of the way of whatever happened. Jill suggested that once." Frank looked from me to nowhere, fidgeting with his handlebars. This wasn't his sort of discussion, racing was, unless he could quote Jill. "Is it your running that's really got you upset? Not this drivel about your grandparents?"

I was looking for a runner. But it's not you. "I told you, I don't run to win, so there's nothing to be upset about."

"I know, but your fiancé does, and I hoped it would rub off on you. You ready to get back to running before you stiffen up on me?"

Frank was right. Emerson was running, and doing it to win. Stretching forward and wanting nothing to weigh him down.

"I think I'll just jog over to the high school track and take a couple of slow laps, then call it quits for the day." I flung my arm the high school's direction, a block to my left.

"Suit yourself, but I think you should keep going." Frank hoisted himself up on his bicycle seat and set a toe on one pedal. "Don't wear yourself out worrying. No one's talking about your grandparents, or Jill would have told me. Call tomorrow. We'll run again. Or, you will." He turned his front wheel hard the direction of his home, squared fully on his seat, and was gone.

Someone was talking, and Emerson was listening. I started forward, to the right instead of the left. I had a soldier to run down. McCoy.

Chapter 28

Cate made a much better runner than Catharine would. Dietrich watched from his car while Cate talked to a man on a bicycle who wasn't her fiancé. Dietrich never sat like this, he never just watched... Her form was good, though, her step muscled, her body posture exposing a trust she didn't have with Emerson.

The bicyclist pedaled away. She stayed behind, pumping those too-short legs. Too short to be a real runner, too nice to be crushed like she probably would be. He latched onto the keys. Only hacks sat in parked cars. Her arms bent, her fists clutched tight. With her head high and brown hair waving, she took off to her right.

He folded the notes he'd taken about McCoy, what he'd been reviewing when she'd happened by. He started the car when she was out of sight. This was the perfect time to visit Non Bookends, the opportunity to speak with the grandmother alone.

****

The bells tinkled as he eased the door open. He drew the jangle out so Cate's grandmother would hear. He stepped inside and fell into the flow of the other customers, hugging tall shelves, plucking novels from tiers, scanning titles and authors as he went.

He took a book from its shelf and let the cover fall open. He glanced at the title page, at the date of printing, the edition. He closed it and took the one next to it—no similarity, not the normal bookstore order. He rounded the shelves and plucked down another.

"May I help you?"

"Just browsing? Is that how you say it here in the US?" He slid the book back into its slot.

Cate's grandmother watched him as he studied her, doing what he did so well—unraveling what he saw to find what was hidden behind it. He saw teetering. The expression beneath Cate's grandmother's taut exterior was teetering—between excitement and anger.

"Browsing for what?"

"Your granddaughter told you, maybe...I write. And I research what I write."

"I thought we didn't carry what you wanted."

"Because you are a fiction store..." He smiled and shook his head. "We would be fools to think fiction authors weren't writing their own truths. And we would be liars if we didn't admit our truths were in their stories we read." He faced Crawley's wife, her matronly veneer marred, likely by some Amabile.

"Nonetheless, researching in a fiction store would be nearly impossible unless you..."

"Knew exactly what and who you were looking for?"

Her veneer tightened.

He looked at her unique array of shelves, her homey seating, the odd assortment of framed glass all around the tops of the walls. He slid a hand into his pocket, felt the charred lump as his gaze stopped on the nearly black frame. Rounded corners at the top, one lump attached below one of those corners. He clamped down on the charred lily in his pocket. No, it was impossible. It couldn't be.

"You know what you're looking for. Or whom." She watched him watch the dark frame. He felt it.

He was looking for another author besides Erika, and that author's fictional cad. Not Crawley, his connections to Amabile were too loose…except for what hung above Dietrich's and Crawley's wife's heads…and the unanswered questions about McCoy…and the photograph. He was looking for truth. And he was afraid.

So was she. Dietrich saw it in her face, the horror of relief. He knew, without seeing his own reflection, horror was in his. Monika had carried an Amabile, an original straight from the author's hands. And Oma, most likely by coincidence as an admiring author, had Amabile also, not to mention a lump of burnt wood. He looked up at the lump on what resembled Amabile's mirror. On the wall of a bookstore run by a woman who'd ordered an Amabile, and whose husband had possibly run.

Chapter 29

These weren't faces I wanted in my photo display, nor were these hands I would ever admire. I centered my camera above the opened book, focused on the black-and-white photo of an army lieutenant, and clicked the shutter. A brief dry snap broke the library's quiet of pages and thoughts. Click. I took another. I zoomed closer on McCoy and took another.

My camera dangled around my neck as I turned pages. Picture after picture went by of US Army men before the war. The New York Library hadn't stopped me from bringing my camera in. *It's for research,* I'd said, rambling on about my photo display and the faces I wanted.

I watched for Grandpa's face as I flipped page after page. The reference librarian had suggested microfilm, but through my camera was how I saw best. Another of McCoy appeared, none of him alone with Grandpa, a few of their whole unit, faces that were tiny blurs, all looking the same. If it hadn't been for names beneath most pictures, I'd never have paired Pvt. G. Crawley with Lt. S. McCoy.

I exhausted the books, my camera heavy with pictorial histories of Grandpa's military days and Grandma's war. I needed specifics. The librarian was right. I needed articles about McCoy…what he did, what he didn't do, why he was being investigated. I returned the volumes to the reference desk in the strange atmosphere of nonfiction, the odor of facts. Real facts, not fictional confessions through the mouths of artificial characters.

"Thank you," I whispered as I slid the military information across the counter. "I think I will go search through microfilm after all. Some faces in there warrant stories," I lied. "That way I know how and if to insert them into my display."

"Certainly." The librarian smiled. "You know where to find the microfiche area?"

I nodded, gripping my camera in case she suggested I store it with library security. She eyed the camera and my hand but said nothing.

She slid the books I'd returned off the counter and set them behind her. "There was a gentleman asking for these. I'll hold onto them for a little bit. He must be browsing somewhere." She scoured the room behind me.

I glanced over my shoulder and scoured it with her. This was New York. It could be any of thousands of men who wanted to see the same books I just had, for any of a thousand reasons. The room was littered with people, some standing, most sitting, a few crossing the area on missions of their own. I scanned the room for tall. Tall with black hair and then tall with a corduroy jacket. There was no Emerson. And there was no Dietrich either, but he wouldn't know about McCoy or even care.

"Thank you," I said and stepped away. Emerson wouldn't spy on his future in-laws in a public place. And Dietrich hadn't paid attention to any of the other suggestions I'd made—such as hopping on a plane and putting an ocean between us—so surely he hadn't come here requesting a book.

****

The sharp smell of developing fluid was home to me as much as yellowed pages and cups of tea. The red-lit darkness of the film developing lab I was allowed to use at the local college felt comfortable. More comfortable now than the one Grandpa had set up for me in their basement would. I couldn't bring McCoy to Grandpa's house and hang his face from lines while Grandpa whittled sticks upstairs.

I watched McCoy's expressionless features wobble and swim beneath the fluid. Diligent. That's how Grandpa had described him. Efficient. That's what the microfilm articles had said. Lieutenant McCoy had efficiently managed his unit of men overseas—spreading them from France to Belgium to Poland, men stationed in several countries, strong efforts to thwart, but ultimately to prepare for, war.

I lifted McCoy's face from the chemical bath. His hair may have been brown, but it was nearly impossible to tell. His face could have been anyone's—average features, average coloring, regular military pose and style. Stiff and rigid, with a highlight of energy my camera had captured. I felt it as I hung him to dry.

Grandpa was in France. He'd been in Poland too, but briefly. My hands worked through my film and the photos while my mind reviewed what I'd read and the names I'd written down…men who were in France with Grandpa. Men who were probably also being contacted by the army about McCoy. Names I'd contact if I had to.

I finished hanging the last of the photos, McCoy's

history having traveled through my mind several times—his time of enlistment, becoming an officer, where he'd been stationed, where he'd been before, during, and after the war. Nowhere near New York, never affiliated with Grandpa alone any of those times except for that brief time overseas. Grandpa must be nothing more than a faint thread of military hope in their investigation, making Emerson's apprehension unnecessary. I glanced at Grandpa's photo, a recent one, lying nearby. There was no faint thread of military hope in his expression. It was more the look of someone too tired to run and always on trial.

I closed my eyes. Grandpa never ran. He wasn't the one on trial.

I needed something more. Like Governor's Island. It was the Coast Guard's now, but it used to be army. I retrieved my camera and its case—my ticket to anywhere—left my pictures to dry, and went to find old army records. Ones where Grandpa didn't look like Emerson's doubts or Dietrich's lies.

Chapter 30

My photo display, black-and-white snapshots of faces along with old and young hands, was telling a story. A real story. I stepped back, scanned the array of profiles—bent heads, distant glances, deliberate grasps—the photos of my grandfather overshadowing them all.

Governor's Island had been the right place to go... yet so wrong. From there I was led to other sources of military archives, pictures of a young and broken soldier coming home, discharged by duty papers issued by McCoy, scanty information about his leg and an explosion. Like the eruption in my gut when I'd managed to find two of the soldiers who'd been sent to France along with him, their stories identical—sorry and surprised. Sorry a man so gifted with his hands and legs had been hurt. So surprised those very legs hadn't been able to deliver him farther and faster from danger than they had...like Jill had thought...he being by far the fastest man in their camp, probably even with the pain medication he was on.

No runners in our family. I'm looking for a runner...you're so small yet surprisingly fast. Dietrich couldn't be looking for Grandpa. Grandpa hadn't been fast enough, and neither had he been in Germany, where Amabile supposedly was.

I thought of Grandpa's wrists and hands, what little

I'd seen of the streaks and blotches of unnatural skin jutting below the long sleeves he always wore. *I got rid of everything pertaining to the military because it bothered my wife.* I looked up from the photo arrangement. That would be why Grandpa suffered with long sleeves in the New York summer heat and humidity—for Grandma. That would be why he never used his cane, why he struggled to walk as if he had no limp—for her. Grandpa was a man broken by losing all he knew—gifted hands, fast legs...and his wife. How dare the army come back and drag him into affairs Grandpa had intended to erase from his wife's life.

I grabbed my camera bag and car keys, locked my photo lab's door, and hurried to my car. It was time to be candid with my grandfather, burst that shell he was stuck in by telling him I understood what he had been trying to do for Grandma. The carved lily in his workbench was just a coincidence, only evidence of the talent Grandpa'd once had according to his military companions, or something he admired as an artisan.

I unlocked my car and set my camera bag in the back seat, then climbed into the front. I inserted the key, felt the roar of the engine, and stared through the windshield.

At paper, yellowed pages pinned beneath my wiper. I opened my door and stepped out. Sheets torn from a small book had been put there.

The mirror was her companion, her window to the world. It was where she saw him as she lay still, dowsing the fire that raged over her skin, through her heart. She kept it close, what was left of it, so she could see his fair hair, the length and strength of his build. The smile, even when it was only the back of him she saw, the look that promised he'd always be with her and be hers. And he was. In the mirror.

I dropped back into the car, the pages falling onto my lap. My heart hammered louder than voices, footsteps, and other vehicles as they passed. I glanced down at the printed words.

She saw what little there had been, salty tears searing cheeks that were tender with pain. She saw his hands over her mirror, adorning it with thoughts, feelings, little carved ornaments he said were for her. She saw his face alongside hers, though his much higher with his height, the promise and oneness in his eyes that his words couldn't convey. Not from his language to hers. Their communication within. That was the language they understood. The vision of the two of them in the mirror, the life together they held.

She saw also what would be, even with her broken body and his absence screaming what would have been, instead. The mirror itself, even in its scorched and burned state, its battered frame with his two surviving carvings discolored by ashes, spoke of now and tomorrow, its smoky glass revealing the life that was theirs. Their hands woven together, a life in a city foreign to her, his visits to this, her city, foreign to him. He ran. Faster than ever. And she wrote. Better than ever. She saw him win. She saw herself spreading the love she'd only imagined before on pages for all to see.

She rested, the heat and the brokenness less when she saw the two of them in the mirror's glass. It silenced her heartache, its own destroyed state silencing questions she didn't want to hear from visitors she didn't welcome. Interrogations, queries suggesting blame. Eyes dismissing the mirror, seeing only something that wasn't whole.

But it was. It preserved him, the two of them, the visions she saw. That's when she knew the mirror must go to him. It and its seared frame, along with only one of the two surviving lilies attached, the other to be hers forever. It would remind him of what they'd seen.

I folded the pages, creased the runner and the writer until only the back showed, where someone had written—*Amabile.*

Chapter 31

Dietrich watched the little runner read Amabile's story. He was going to take down that black frame from her grandmother's wall, and Cate needed to be ready. She'd need to understand, be prepared to move forward through the pain…like he may have to.

Brown waves fell around her profile, hiding her expression. She had a pleasant face, though it wouldn't look that way now.

He turned and left the little runner to her thoughts. He had his own to contend with—the even faster race Oma's conversation had thrown him into the night before.

Guten Morgen. Dietrich had called Oma when he knew she would be up and starting her day.

Wo bist du? she'd asked. It was standard conversation for them. *Where are you now, where have your travels taken you this time?* It had only been a week, but she would be ready for him to return. He was too often far away, keeping near through phone calls and postcards, sometimes letters if he was gone long.

Amerika, he answered. *New York.* He waited for her usual comment or question about what he was doing, especially since he'd said little when he left. But Oma was silent. He filled her silence with lies…fiction…about this trip and the article he pretended he'd been assigned. She was listening, and he caught her intake of breath.

Wie lang? How long? It wasn't the question that caught him off guard but the way she asked it.

Long enough to finish the article…short enough to get back home…soon, sooner than he'd expected.

Mehr Zeit. Not long, he said, and more silence was her answer. He needed to hurry. His employer was impatient, and maybe Monika was the same. Maybe she'd gone to Oma's house and said things that stunned the poor woman. He apologized for being so far away and asked if there was anything he could do, anything she wanted.

New York, she'd said. She'd wanted a ticket to join him. Oma never asked to join him anywhere. She never left her home, her quiet Berlin suburb. It had to be Monika, her silly fantasy driving Oma here to Dietrich for comfort…or to the "he" who could be Monika's father.

His pace quickened, his feet rushing down the sidewalk toward his car. He wasn't a runner. He came here to deny a runner, prove such a person never really was. And yet, there was a runner, one he couldn't deny—the little runner.

Chapter 32

Grandpa's car was gone. Again. I parked on the street instead of in his drive and stared at the quiet house, glad for this moment before I talked to him about his good record of service, burned arms instead of burned lilies, about holding our family together while that German and rumors that alarmed Emerson tried to take it apart.

I left my car and went to the garage, let myself in the side door, and fumbled for the light. A harsh fluorescent glow flooded his bench where everything looked the same. Nothing had been touched, nothing new created, just as he'd promised.

I walked to the last drawer beneath his workbench's top. I slid my fingers through the handle, felt the gritty sensation of who I knew him to be—or maybe used to be—and pulled.

The drawer opened to his row of carving tools, all neatly in a line. I swept my arm to the back, to the carved flowers, and dragged the three of them forward. Two roses and one lily. I'd looked up pictures of lilies to be sure, praying I'd been wrong, but I wasn't. I laid the two roses on the bench top and studied the flower Amabile had called herself, the type of flower that hung charred to her mirror. This wood was aged and dry, almost splintering at the lily's ridges and peaks, but not burned.

Returning the roses, I tucked the lily into my pocket, jiggled the drawer closed, turned off the light, and left the garage. I took the steps up to his porch, dropped into his rocker, and waited. I watched the quiet street, listened for his car, and felt the breeze that normally swept away his whittled nothings.

I ran a hand into my pocket and wrapped my fingers around the carved lump. I pulled it out and wallowed it in my hand, glancing down the street both directions, then at my feet, at steel gray paint on the porch floor, clean and free of shavings.

I stood, walked to the porch's edge, and leaned over the side. No shavings there, either.

Stuffing the flower into my pocket I stepped to the door. It was locked. I ran to my car, fished my key out of my bag, and darted back to the house. "Grandpa?" I opened the door and barged into the silence. An empty silence, one where even the smell of Grandpa waned.

"Grandpa?" I ran into and through the living room, to the kitchen, his bedroom, and the rest of the house. "Grandpa?" I called down the basement stairs, leaning through its door. I turned on the light and hurried down the steps, the odor of developing fluids growing stronger with each one. "Grandpa?" I stopped in the space he'd built for me, the place I stood to peel life off of film.

Cate.

The note lay next to the first tray. I recognized Grandpa's handwriting even though I'd seen very little of it my whole life. My hands shook more than the quiver I saw in my name and the way he'd written it as I unfolded the note.

I told you a man is always on trial. He is when he

lies, and sometimes even when he doesn't. I lied to you, my dear. I'm going now, not in October, for the investigation. And if preliminaries don't fare well, I'll have to stay. Don't lie to your fiancé. Tell him. Lies are a grip on what should never have been held to begin with. Grandpa

Chapter 33

Tell Emerson. Don't lie. I trotted alongside my fiancé, my pace slowed to his, a half-mile trot so he could smile and wave at his public. Frank would be waiting at the end of our half mile, and then I'd run. Really run, hammer and re-hammer the conversation I had yet to have, while Frank pedaled around me telling me to lighten up—go far, not deep, light foot, not heavy. Things he should probably say to his wife.

"I have another function this weekend," Emerson huffed at my side. His arms were pumping windedness into his words. "It's casual, but I'd like to get you another outfit. Maybe this evening?"

He glanced my way, a strand of black hair dangling over his forehead, an unusual but attractive sort of casual for him. My heart beat a little faster. I'd made a commitment to that hair, that face, the man running alongside me. A commitment I trusted he had made, too, far above the one to his campaign, one that honesty wouldn't break.

"This evening." I added breathiness to my words for his sake. "That might work."

We trundled along in jagged silence, broken by choppy breathing, the occasional hello and wave from Emerson to people we passed, and the truth reverberating in my head. I took a sudden turn toward the college and veered Emerson off his normal course to where an old track lay without use.

"Catharine?" He followed, and I led him to the broken oval, a secluded place we could continue our trot.

"I need to talk to you," I said at the first curve.

He tucked his elbows closer to his ribs, knotted his fists into tighter clenches.

"It's about Grandpa."

"I know." Emerson pulled ahead. Not much, but enough that more of his hair came loose from its plastered style, enough that more of a glistening appeared on his skin.

"You know? How much? More than before? How do you know?" I breezed alongside him.

"Miles. He does a good job of surveying the landscape. He's kept me informed of what your grandfather is going through." Emerson stopped, clutched his sides as he watched me.

I powered three steps beyond him, stopped, and turned and saw what I hadn't before. The mirror of Miles' cool detachment in Emerson's warm affections, the slight crispness of the times Miles had smiled down at me. The worry I was an enemy instead of a worthy wife, that one or both of them had mistakenly chosen someone who might drop the baton in Emerson's race...the bad and ugly they didn't want.

"You know my grandfather is gone?"

Emerson didn't close the three steps between us. "I know he's not far. Not geographically, anyway."

"What else?"

"What else? You mean besides your grandmother, now that I know that too? At least people seem adjusted to her, from what I'm told. Or maybe you mean what else besides a possible criminal investigation regarding your grandfather? A possible court martial? Aiding the enemy? Do you realize how serious that is?"

My mouth fell open. My gut roiled. Things couldn't be that bad, not as ugly as Emerson said. Surely not as ugly as Dietrich made me think. "No! That investigation isn't about my grandpa, it's about Lieutenant McCoy. You know that. And I should have told you about Grandma, but since she's so peculiar, are you sure you want to marry me? Or do you want to break the engagement because you believe we are tied to an enemy?"

Emerson faltered, then hurried forward, destroying the three steps between us. "Catharine, no, I'm not breaking the engagement or accusing you. And I'm not entertaining stories against your family. I'm trying to manage what's out there, and what's being said. Miles is too." He reached for my arms, to hold on so three steps couldn't happen again.

Court martial? Aiding the enemy? "Grandpa wasn't even in the service when the war began." I twisted away. "We didn't even have an enemy back then."

"Catharine... You can't blame Miles for..."

"I don't. I blame you."

"Blame me? I've done nothing more than trust Miles to handle my image." Emerson's hands rose again and then dropped. "Look, I'm sorry. Maybe I should have asked you, or at the very least let you tell me what you knew before I listened to him. You can tell me everything you know, even things from your childhood we've never talked about, so nothing like this happens again. How would that be? Complete honesty for us and my campaign, beginning now."

I saw Ibsen as I stared at my fiancé. Nora's husband, Torvald, trying to trap her into the doll's house that suited him more than her. Maybe Grandma felt like a Nora of sorts, so she escaped to Non Bookends. Where stories went on and on until at last she found the answers she needed. "Maybe over dinner tonight. I can't now." Even if I could, I couldn't now.

The style fell out of Emerson's hair, the wind shifting the black into a disarray that made him human instead of a man running a campaign. "After we shop for the outfit you'll need for this weekend. I'm all ears after that. Let's get this cleaned up and behind us so I can keep moving senate responsibilities forward."

I glanced at my watch, stared at its hands instead of Emerson's hair. "I need to keep moving also. Frank is waiting for me. My marathon's coming up shortly."

Emerson wrapped his fingers around my arm. "Wait, Catharine. Don't go run. You weren't interested in winning anyway. Let's talk now instead of later. You need to get everything out in the open, and I need you with me this weekend. We'll get through this. After all, it's only an investigation. Pretrial, mostly."

It was wrong to love an enemy. It was on Emerson's face no matter how hard he tried, no matter how casually his hair tossed with the breeze. I put a half step between us. "Maybe you want to wait and see how this investigation turns out." He let go of my arm. It *was* wrong to love an enemy, and it was just as wrong to be seen loving one. I turned and ran, feverishly, leaving the plea of *Catharine* fading behind.

Chapter 34

Cate appeared from between two buildings and disappeared in a solid run down the street. Dietrich stopped. Their paths had nearly crossed. He stepped back and veered toward the campus. He was here to relax, let the myriad of data stored in his mind realign and fall into place.

He stopped again and glanced back at the empty sidewalk where she'd run. Where her fiancé appeared, stepping out from between the same two buildings she had. Emerson turned the direction she'd gone, but he walked instead of ran. "If you really want to catch her, you need to try," Dietrich whispered. Even he knew that much. Emerson's senatorial clip was a halted walk now, one that stayed well behind his fiancée, one that would be easy to trip up if Dietrich was so inclined. Dietrich watched Emerson go. Cate had enough to contend with. Enough.

Dietrich glanced at his watch. Time was ticking away. Crawley was gone, a complication that would slow Dietrich's plans, walking into an investigation that had been going on in pretrial conferences before Crawley officially knew. McCoy had diverted the focus elsewhere as the army pried into his activities before and during the war. Journalistic collaboration, often not honest, gave Dietrich this much information. A traded favor with a contact in Washington who fed him the background on McCoy and the investigation in exchange for the sole right to publish the story himself when it was done. Randall Templeton. Dietrich had agreed to Randall's terms because Randall was ruthless, quick for a kill, and Dietrich needed quick. If Crawley had committed some crime, really had run the Olympics under a false name, had been in Berlin, then...

He hurried to his car. Crawley's trial wasn't far away. He'd use his journalistic privileges to gain entrance. It was time to see the little runner's grandfather.

Chapter 35

"I'm family," I told the soldier at the door to what must have been a courtroom of sorts. I'd never been in this part of New York and certainly never to this building. It reeked of age, high ceilings, and plastered walls cold and stiff from solemn procedures. "Can I go in? George Crawley's my grandfather."

I tried to hear through the heavy doors behind the soldier, his erect posture a formidable barrier I needed past.

"This isn't a public hearing," he said, his lips barely moving.

"I told you, I'm not public, I'm family, and this is not a hearing. It's an investigation, and my grandfather is not on trial. He's a witness, so please let me through."

"Charges have been preferred," he said, still barely moving.

"Charges? Preferred?"

"I'm not at liberty to discuss the pending case. You may wait out here while the judge is in conference." He nodded toward benches lining the hallway.

I hedged, then marched to where he'd indicated, the creak of the seat and my purse hitting it creating a dull echo down the hallway. Everything was muted here, even the paint, the color I imagined bile to be if it had years to fade.

I set up a drum roll of fingernails on the bench's wooden armrest, a steady rat-a-tat-tat to annoy the mummified soldier blocking the door. Preferred. He should speak English.

I drummed louder and faster to resurrect him so I could go in. Another beat arose along with mine, farther down the tomb, a slower, steadier cadence that grew even louder than my own.

"Officer McCoy."

Three army officers appeared in the hallway to the left, pausing at the juncture of an intersecting hall, speaking to what looked like another guard. I quieted my fingers as the military footsteps resumed, their steady rhythm becoming stronger as they neared. I eyed the man in the middle. McCoy—much older, but still stolid.

"Excuse me." I was on my feet and in front of them, the two escorts each taking hold of one of McCoy's arms and steering him around me, until they stopped in front of the lifeless soldier who blocked me from Grandpa.

"Lieutenant McCoy," one of the escorts said. The mummy nodded and opened the door behind him. I scurried to steal a glance into the room my grandfather was surely in, a room that resembled a square of this hallway—the same drab color, vacuous atmosphere, nothing photogenic at all except for the backs, the shoulders, and the few stern faces I caught glimpses of before the mummy shut the door and McCoy was gone.

"There are a lot of people in there," I said as the soldier settled back into his posture. "Why can't I be in there? I could sit in the back with the others."

He glanced at me, a tiny glimmer of humanity

there and gone as he shook his head. "Not while the lieutenant is in there. He's preferring charges."

"What do you mean by preferred charges?" It wasn't my store voice.

He glanced down the hall to where the other guard had been when McCoy came through. "In an army court, a commander can prefer a charge against anyone he knows has done wrong. It's initiating a charge against the wrongdoer."

The temperature of the hallway plummeted, and my own body warmth went with it. I opened my mouth and stood there with it agape. *This was against McCoy, not for him. Against him, not for him.*

"If you would like to wait…" The soldier nodded to the bench where I'd been.

I took a step backward. If only Emerson were here…an attorney, a potential senator…more than family, the way he offered… I inched farther until the wooden seat bumped the backs of my knees and I dropped into the spot where I'd been.

My hands lay blue in my lap, my fingertips white around arcs of red where I pressed them together. The hallway became my morgue, the mummy of a soldier my only companion, the tomblike silence hammering my ears.

So this was how a grave would feel, how furtive could go away, and how cold could make a person unable to care. I heard a click and I cared again, even the mummy moved. The door behind him opened as he grabbed its handle and swung it wide. McCoy marched back out between his escorts, quicker this time, his face everything I'd heard Grandpa say in his living room. Diligent, a solid force that never wavered. I was invisible to them. They whisked past in step, marching to a drumbeat that kept them in time. They rounded the corner into the hallway they'd first come from, the guard there ushering them forward with a "Sirs," and they were gone.

The door clicked shut as the soldier in front of me pushed it closed. I felt him looking at me. I felt his pity—as if I'd just been run over and there was nothing he could do. I rallied to stand and to demand he explain what had gone on behind the door, but a tap from its other side bent him to his duty. He latched onto the knob and drew it open. Two men appeared, one tall, the other even taller. Like Grandpa. I tried to stand. Blond hair. Hazel eyes with blades of gray looked at me from the doorway, surprised eyes above a corduroy jacket.

Chapter 36

Dietrich's fingers wrapped around my arm and raised me to my feet.

"Come with me," he commanded.

"I will not come with you." I wrenched at a grip that didn't let go.

"You won't be able to see him." Dietrich looked down at me. "And he won't want you to."

"You know this girl?" His friend, nearly as tall as Dietrich, snorted a surprise.

I shot him a glare. I wanted to ask the mummy if it was true I couldn't see Grandpa and that he wouldn't want me to.

"Crawley's granddaughter," Dietrich explained over my head.

Another hand latched onto my other arm. I felt like McCoy as Dietrich and his darker haired friend half led, half carried me down the hallway toward the outside.

"Let me go." The main door opened and fading sunlight hit my eyes. My two escorts toted me down the front steps as I blinked against the light. "I said, let me go. I will talk to my grandfather."

"Fat chance," Dietrich's friend said. Another snort.

"That's her car over there."

"How do you know what or where my car is?" I found my footing and tugged free from Dietrich and his snorting friend. I wheeled and faced the two, the word

PRESS greeting me from their jackets.

I knew my grandfather and how he had probably looked in that investigation room…charging room…but the picture two unscrupulous reporters would paint of him was much uglier—of Grandma, too, and Non Bookends—the sort Emerson would dread, and Miles be wary of. "So much for truth and facts. You're nothing but a two-bit reporter." It was a screech. I'd never screeched before, but I'd never been engaged before or had enemies turning my fiancé and family into foes.

The gray lines in Dietrich's eyes sharpened. "You have no idea what you're talking about."

"You don't know who he is?" his friend asked me without a snort.

I looked to Dietrich's friend, lanky in lankier clothing, ignoring the hand Dietrich raised to silence him.

"That's no reporter." The friend nodded at Dietrich, then backed away. "Come on, Dietrich, I'll give you a ride back to your hotel."

I knew who Dietrich was. He was my enemy, my whole family's enemy, that I had disliked from the first time I met him.

"Go on." Dietrich waved to his friend. "I'm riding with her."

"You will not be riding with me," I announced as Dietrich ushered me by my elbow toward my car. His friend shrugged and sauntered off, a pen pointed toward me, a roll of his eyes to Dietrich.

"Who is he?" I imagined a target on his friend's back.

"Let's go, and I'll explain what's going on." The

loll of his accent made his words sound softer, an offer to help, a chance to escape…the rain, like in Amabile. I glanced up, counted the spears in his irises, then looked back at the building my grandfather was still in. "They won't let you see him. I can tell you why."

I fumbled with my purse as I stared at the cold concrete steps. My heart was bounding up those stairs while my enemy stood near my car. An enemy offering to tell me why.

I was betraying my grandfather, denying my grandmother. I slid into the car's seat, stretched to the other side, and unlocked the passenger door.

"Let's go," Dietrich said once he was inside. His long thighs stretched to the dash, his knees butted against the glove box. Emerson fit there. The seat was fine for him…if he had come…and for Grandma, also…if she had. But this man was too much. He overpowered my car with his legs and his presence. I rolled down my window for air, started the engine, and drove.

"Charges were brought against your grandfather." Dietrich's words rose above the road's noise. "His lieutenant charged him with conspiracy with my country before the war."

I raised a hand, and Dietrich paused. I opened my mouth, but nothing came out.

"Anyway, Lieutenant McCoy said your grandfather attempted to pass US information to the German military in Berlin in 1936. There were deaths because of that information, and the trials and convictions in my country have now spilled over into yours."

I shook my head. My grandfather was never in Berlin. He came home a hero of sorts; he came home wounded. He came home from Poland and France. I stared at the road in front of me, a long thin ribbon of pavement that dropped off the edge of the world.

"In your army, a commander can make a charge if he has enough evidence."

Evidence. My heart thundered. Grandpa, silent about his military days, refusing to talk about them, destroying everything from them. Even hiding his wounds left over from them. For Grandma. *Not for me, because of me.* I glanced at a passing sign. We'd gone five miles, and I had no idea how we'd made it that far. I stared at the road in front of me, at the nose of my car plowing forward.

"Your grandfather was assigned a defense attorney, although he can hire a civilian one also, if he wants."

He's not the man I was engaged to. Had Grandma been right all these years? Had she been forced to harbor a criminal, and only she knew? I shook my head. No. She didn't know about the army coming. Grandpa wasn't a traitor, he wasn't some woman's fictional lover. He was a wounded soldier with a dissatisfied wife.

"My grandfather was not and is not a criminal." Not my store voice. I reeled to the side and glared at Dietrich, caught by a look that mirrored the distress I felt, but I slapped my palm on the seat between us anyway.

He glanced from me to the road my car was barreling down. "Maybe drive with both hands."

I stared ahead and set both hands on the steering wheel. "Why are you here? It was bad enough you were in my grandmother's store." I turned to him again. "Where did you come from, and when will you leave?

Who are you? What in the world are you doing?"

He looked from the road to me, splintered gray spikes scattered throughout the hazel. "I told you. I was looking for a runner. I need to know if you knew any of this about your grandfather."

Chapter 37

Dietrich waited for the runner he hadn't expected to find on his mission to the US to answer him.

"My grandfather was never in Berlin. And he was never a runner. I'm the first in the family. He doesn't even like running. In fact, he's always trying to get me to…" Cate's knuckles whitened as she leaned into the road.

He watched her profile, the fragile sharpness as she stared straight ahead. The army was suggesting what the picture had indicated to Dietrich but he still wanted to disprove—that there really had been a tall, lean, fast American in Berlin around the time of the war. Amabile's lover, who couldn't be, wouldn't be Erika's lover also. If he could clear Crawley, he would be satisfied there wasn't such a person. If he could just get past the brown waves beside him framing Crawley's granddaughter's brittle profile… He should have gone home when the three US Olympian names he'd come here with didn't match. He should have gone when Marvin Shanks seemed to be George Crawley. If Dietrich hadn't been such a stickler for detail, he could have returned to Germany quietly. He could have if he hadn't met them—Cate and her grandmother. Now Cate was a complication.

Dietrich never allowed complications. He turned to the side and stared out the window, at the window, at his reflection, a thin sheen on the glass. She was there, too, the little runner. Soon it would be Cate alone in the reflection, if what looked like a mirror on Non Bookends' wall really wasn't.

Cate was leaving other cars behind, the way thoughts and faces raced past in his mind. McCoy had claimed Crawley was passing information, a list of names, to a German in Berlin, possibly a girl, a part of a German spy ring used by the German army. Dietrich had nearly come to his feet, his face and hands white like the little runner's now, when a woman was insinuated into some traitor's scheme. That traitor Crawley, according to McCoy...which complicated Dietrich's situation even more. He would call Randall from the hotel tonight and make sure he maintained his pass privilege to the trial, even though it would go public quickly. In the meantime, Dietrich would make sure he and Randall did more legwork than any army attorney. He had to get his hands on that mirror. The filthy aura had to be off his family—a traitor and an enemy for a lover. And he'd do what he could for Cate...

"Just leave us alone." Cate was turned his way as he faced her.

"I can't do that. You need to tell me what you know. About everything. Think hard." He understood the ugly bond between fear and anger. He felt it now, and was responsible for what he saw of it on her. But sharing Amabile had been right.

"I said leave us alone."

Cate would be facing a lot of alone with what Dietrich had to do, what her grandfather may have done, and with a fiancé who had chosen a slow walk toward her instead of a run. "This will be difficult for your fiancé."

Cate clenched tighter to the steering wheel.

"He knows," Dietrich continued, "that 'The race is not to the swift.' "

"Emerson is none of your business, and I only speak 'literary' with my grandmother."

"He can't outrun what is happening to your grandfather. Your man has to stand on his own values and keep the focus off the negative going on with your family."

"Are we close to your hotel?"

"Not yet."

The car veered to the right, a chorus of horns protesting the maneuver as she yanked to the street's edge and braked to a stop.

"Get out."

"What?"

"I said, get out!"

He opened the car's door and stepped outside. She was back in traffic as quickly as she'd pulled out of it, horns blaring their protests again. Then the little runner was gone. Fast.

Chapter 38

Emerson had excellent values, values he'd assumed were mirrored by my grandparents. Values that included family, didn't just let them be… I stared at the street ahead of me. I hit the gas and hurried to my grandparents' house.

Who was that German man, anyway? How did his search for a runner keep appearing in our lives? Amabile—she was a ridiculous story, a coincidence at best, pure fiction, proving again Dietrich was a liar. I slammed the heel of my palm against the steering wheel.

There were two places an army attorney would probably search eventually—Grandpa's home, and Grandma's store. I wheeled my car into Grandpa's drive, climbed out, and scurried to their house. There had to be something in there. Something of the military he'd failed to throw away. For her.

The living room seemed to sigh with relief as I entered and closed the door behind me. Like the house had worried the last of the Crawleys had finally gone. I pulled all the drapes and turned on enough lights to see as I sorted through every drawer, every cabinet, and every closet I could find in their house.

The main level produced nothing. Upstairs they had a gabled loft they used for an attic, where a string to a single ceiling bulb exposed boxes stacked around the edges, a thick layer of dust telling me no one had been up here in ages…until now.

I disturbed the dust on every box, pawing through the Crawley history, producing a stack of family letters and pictures but nothing from the army. I scooped what I'd found into a pile and took it downstairs with me.

The basement was mine, but I checked it anyway, the faint smell of acid making me melancholy for the grandfather I had always trusted. I turned on the lights in the little photo lab he'd built, checked every nook and cranny, and found nothing there or in the rest of the basement, either.

"Good luck, McCoy," I said as I carried my stack of envelopes and pictures from the house. *Good luck, Grandpa,* echoed behind me.

I deposited what I'd found in the passenger seat of my car. Where the German had sat. I slammed the door I should have rolled him out of.

There was one more place to look—Grandpa's garage. I entered and toured the perimeter, running my hands and fingers along the wall, checking boxes, cans, any sort of crevice I could find, as I inhaled the quiet scent of the man and touched what he seemed never to touch himself.

"Why, Grandpa?" I whispered to the absence of him, that spot he'd been in but never filled. "Why is everyone attacking you?"

I walked to his workbench and breathed in what was left of him. He had values. Values Emerson could stand on. Dietrich was a liar and Amabile was fiction, written long ago and far away in a place Grandpa had never been. I ran my hand along his seldom-used bench, touched the surface, his jars of screws, the few tools on the top, and the handles of each drawer.

Hold on, and don't let her go. That was Grandpa's value. That was the sort of man he really was. He held on. He was telling Emerson to do the same.

I ended with the drawer where his carved flowers were, the roses I'd left behind. I gave it a tug. It caught, then popped loose. Something hit the floor while the roses and tools rolled and scattered. I straightened Grandpa's drawer, then bent to the floor. Papers lay there, not just papers, but envelopes, white and yellow, legal and large, all bordered by tape that had come loose. I knelt beside letters to and from the army, some old and some recent, and three bulky envelopes I'd seen before, all open. Each one trembled with the hand I slid inside. So did the books...the three small books I fished out...one Moliere and two—Amabile.

Chapter 39

A heart knows what a mind doesn't. She knew, even though everything about him said he belonged to another world, that he didn't. That erect posture that said service, that flush on his face that said energy and speed, that American boyishness that said stateside, all were hers and gifts to her. Foreign gifts he brought with him the next day.

"You write?" he asked as he stood at her desk, his accent strong, his words slow, smiling at her and laying a finger on her stories. Stories she'd written for the Games. For the competitors, to entertain them in the evenings. Simple love stories at the bottom of the pile, something more radiant at the top. What she'd written almost overnight since meeting him.

"Write, yes, but live, more." She set a finger beside his, on the story she considered his. She said it in his language as best she could, then looked up into that blue-eyed smile and asked, "You run?"

The flush that said health, the lightness of his hair that said vigor, answered for him, even more than the "I win" he stated as best he could in her language or the "Read to me" he said in his own tongue.

"Win for me."

He smiled. "I already have."

I closed the book I'd closed once before. The same one I'd read in Grandpa's bedroom while the army officers drilled him in the other room. The one Grandpa said he'd burned, but he hadn't. Not this one and not the other one Grandma had received that day. Not Moliere, either, but his was inconsequential…to me at least, although maybe not to Grandma. I stared at Amabile's books Grandpa had kept when he said they weren't Grandma's type.

Grandpa was a good man…

For her? Because of her. Because of which one?

I slid the book aside on his workbench and stared at its cover as I scooted the other one in front of me. This one looked just as old, just as simple, a thin hard cover with faint ridges where something had been embossed long enough ago it was no longer visible. I could feel it with my fingertips, running them over the indentations and ridges, the title, and Amabile.

The book creaked as I drew it open, yellowed pages fanning past with the same odor of dusty prose that permeated Non Bookends. These books looked like the sort Grandma would choose, but they weren't. *Oh, Grandpa.* I thumbed toward the back and read what Amabile wrote.

"There's more," he said. He laid within her fingers a small gift too dark to see. The lights of the village were behind them, the place where he and others like him stayed. She'd read for them, shared the heart of a German woman in her language while others translated to theirs, a harmony of voices and accents telling her and his love story in a thousand different tongues.

They had clapped, a tidal wave of applause as each translator finished and the story was done. She flushed in the evening warmth, the heat of what she felt for him on their faces.

"Come with me." He'd taken her hand and whispered as in a myriad of languages the village asked for more. He faded back and waited as she was told to read again. She did. Her voice solo at first, then others following, another symphony of love in a multitude of languages blanketing the night.

"You inspire me," he said when they were alone at last. He was so tall, his stride one step for every two of hers, his fingers so long they could have wrapped twice around hers. She laughed in the language they both understood. One that brought her into his arms and her face against his heart. It beat with the pace of a runner. Fast, strong, steady. She felt the breeze as he took the two of them away, felt the strength that held him straight and strong.

He pressed his gift into her hand again. "Another thought," he said, "the only way I can write it."

She lifted it close, ran her fingers over its wooden ridges and smoothed surfaces.

"This one is for the thoughts I have of you that spill around in my head in your language. Words I don't know, yet understand. I carve them there." He pointed at the gift. "They come out the same every time. Amabile. My lily."

My heart raced more than her lover's ever could. More than mine did when I trained with Frank or fought with Grandma. I stared across Grandpa's bench, at the untouched tools, the stack of wood he let sit. Lily. Everything else he worked on, he worked to nothing, whittled it to dust.

"You made this," she said. She knew he had. He was an expert with his hands.

"I will add it with the other to your mirror. There

will be more. More thoughts, more lilies, more to share with you."

Her mirror. She thought of it hanging near her desk, a solitary lily attached at one corner. And now, another. And soon, more. More lilies, more thoughts, more stories for her to read to the athletes before they went. Except for him. He would stay until they could leave together. They saw it in the mirror. Both of them. Forever. A crown of lilies capping their love.

Chapter 40

Randall grinned. Dietrich's journalistic accomplice had uncovered more information than the military attorneys had…than Dietrich had either. It was on Randall's face, and he'd done it for a price, not the sort of price hacks asked for, such as a setup with a girl, or even a bottle of expensive liquor. Randall wanted to know why the hurry, why staying one step ahead of the military was so important to Dietrich, and he wanted all rights to everything he found for an exclusive, including Dietrich's reasons. It was a gamble for both of them, but especially for Randall. That's what drew the line between good journalists and bad. Good ones were willing to lose. The bad fabricated sensationalism to fill in for their losses.

"Crawley was in Berlin." Randall leaned back in his chair. The air was brisk, but they'd chosen an outdoor café far from Dietrich's hotel, Non Bookends, Randall's hangouts, and the little runner's normal routine. The steam above their coffee cups vanished with the breeze, the hot black pleasure disappearing with it. The smoke from Randall's cigarette did the same, the thick thread at its fiery tip dissipating instantly into a vapor no one could see.

"When?" Dietrich asked. He did it casually, with the practiced mien that kept him from fidgeting with his cup. So Crawley really was there, likely as Marvin

Shanks, possibly as Amabile's "he." But surely not as what the military said. If that was the case, Oma would no longer be innocent; she could be Germany's enemy, and their enemy's discarded lover. And the US would label her a spy. Dietrich wrapped both hands around his cup.

One corner of Randall's mouth kicked up as he wound the tip of his cigarette on an ashtray's edge, skimming off burned residue, sharpening the flame the way Dietrich sharpened pencils. "August," he said, focused on what he was doing. "Nineteen thirty-six."

Guilty. The time period of Amabile's fickle runner, also possibly of America's fickle soldier.

Randall concentrated on the fiery ash and returned the cigarette to his mouth. Dietrich hated the stench of stale smoke that marked too many reporters' clothes, cigarettes being common props most of them used. But fresh smoke, such as what escaped after Randall's long drag, Dietrich craved. Smoking was also a thinking man's habit. The sort that let facts and details fill the white cloud Dietrich watched vanish too quickly, and with it the words Randall was holding back—how he knew and how sure he was. It was part of the game, part of the win and lose. It could have been the same picture Dietrich had found, but likely more. Dietrich wouldn't ask and Randall would never tell.

"The man we saw in court isn't designed for on-the-front-lines espionage." Randall looked at Dietrich. "Crawley isn't built to handle guilt. Not that kind." Randall spoke into the air, his eyes and thoughts at work, his brilliant mind fitting broken fragments together. "Something else broke that man." He balanced the cigarette on the ashtray's edge and leaned back. "A woman."

Dietrich let go of his cup, avoiding any falter Randall would notice as he did. Randall was Dietrich's closest competitor for journalistic skill around the world. Closest, and razor sharp, but not the same. A woman. Randall could be thinking a lover or a spy, or both. Dietrich stared at the cup, tapped a finger on its handle to keep from throwing it to the ground.

"That girl you went off with doesn't know anything." Randall righted in his seat. "She's got that unsteady look like someone far enough away from the epicenter of a quake they think it's their fault they're off kilter, too much caffeine or something."

Oma and now Cate. Randall was circling his prey. Dietrich wasn't here to take care of Cate; there wouldn't be enough time. He was here for Oma, his family, his reputation. Randall was doing his job, fast and thoroughly, as he was known for, and Dietrich needed. There'd be no distracting him and no thwarting the army if there was a woman tied to Crawley who was a spy. He wanted to curse; stop Randall and tell him to hurry all at the same time. "Crawley's love life—if he had one—is incidental." Dietrich leaned back in his chair. "Like I told you, I'm here on another lead I thought Crawley and some others may be tied to. I've talked to everyone else, but not him, and the army had him at the trial before I had a chance to. If he's guilty of something big like this, that changes him as a resource. *Der Spiegel* is breathing down my neck, and I want to know his chances of being convicted. Fast. Skip any illicit lovers and his personal life. Help me get where the army's going before they get there, and you get the story." It was a lie, and it was the best he could do to divert Randall.

Randall balanced what was left of his cigarette on the ashtray's edge and fidgeted with it. He was thinking, but with that invisible awareness Randall had. He was scrutinizing Dietrich, watching him as he cleaned more ash from the tip and returned the stub to his lips. Oma wouldn't escape Randall if she was there, either as a lover of Germany's enemy or as a spy. Dietrich could read the growing story with each of Randall's movements—a military crime, an illicit affair, or both.

Dietrich wrapped both hands around his cup again and squeezed, gave a pretend shiver. Cate couldn't handle someone like Randall either. "I know what you're thinking. It would make things easier if the girl knew something about her grandfather's military days. Or his private life," Dietrich said. "She might be angry enough she'd spill some little hidden tidbit if we pushed. I already tried that, and there's nothing there."

"Because she doesn't like you." Randall snorted, grinding out his cigarette. "She clearly doesn't, but you're right. People talk when they've got something in their craw, even if they don't know what it is. Give it the right ignition, and out it comes. Tell her you love her." Randall laughed. "I checked her out. She's got a fiancé running for office. The news splash of an illicit affair that could cost him his election—that ought to make her spew something. Anything."

"More coffee?" The waitress was smart enough to bring two fresh cups rather than a pot to top off the ice-cold coffee they had. They both nodded and watched as she traded the fresh cups for the old, whisking away the paraphernalia Randall had littered the table with. They watched her retreat inside.

"Pretty thing," Randall said in the quiet.

Dietrich stared at the closed door the waitress had gone through. He could have drawn her face, never missing a detail around him. But pretty? He hadn't looked at the picture as a whole, only the details.

"Parents moved across the city after family problems, takes pictures, helps out in her grandmother's strange bookstore. Likes to run." Randall tapped a finger on the table.

Dietrich continued to stare at the door. He fought a blush at Randall's sudden reiteration of Cate, defied the warmth crawling inside his collar at her name. Randall was watching for that flush. He was still fishing, and in Dietrich's private pond.

"The granddaughter's irrelevant. And like you said, she's off kilter. That fits with her knowing nothing when I asked. All I ask is that you keep to our original agreement—you find out what you can pertaining to the army case before they do." Dietrich squeezed harder, the fresh hot cup burning his palms. He glanced across the table at his cohort and competitor.

Every journalist knew that when you stirred the pot of a man's crime, sludge came up. Randall was stirring, and Dietrich had to keep Oma from rising in the swirl...Cate, too. "Focus on the case before you go digging around in the dirt, so I can get done and head back to Germany."

"You'll get what you want." Randall grinned. "And so will I."

Chapter 41

Curled up in my living room chair, I stared at my and my grandparents' background I'd taken from Grandpa's house.

There were envelopes within envelopes of my mother's letters, the innermost ones unopened. Sent back, and sent back again as my mother's and grandmother's war raged. Some, addressed to my grandfather, had never been opened and never returned; whatever my mother had tried to say pressed flat and invisible within. Maybe he'd never seen these letters. My grandmother was the one who should be on trial. Surely she had tampered with her husband's mail.

I picked up Grandpa's military correspondence: stilted jargon, which read the way the three military officers had spoken in Grandpa's house that day. Nothing personal or personable, the most recent being dates, times, and words like "charges" and "preferred" such as the mummified soldier had used.

You are hereby being notified...

I read each one, understanding little, but enough. I needed Emerson, really needed him. I glanced at the phone. He was the one man who could step in and hold onto me while he set Grandpa free like he surely should be, and tout Grandpa as a hero instead of a criminal, like he'd promised.

I set everything on the floor and stood. I lifted the

phone and dialed, listened to three rings before he picked it up. "Emerson?"

"Catharine. Can I come over?"

Tears came, and I nodded a muffled yes.

"Be right there."

I set the handset in its cradle, hot tears cooling my face. I walked to my bedroom and stared at my reflection in my mirror.

"I will add it with the other to your mirror. There will be more. More thoughts, more lilies, more to share with you."

Her mirror. She thought of it hanging near her desk, a solitary lily attached at one corner. And now, another. And soon, more. More lilies, more thoughts, more stories for her to read to the athletes before they went. Except for him. He would stay. They saw it in the mirror. Both of them together. Forever. A crown of lilies capping their love.

Loving an enemy. Done so wrong. Written so right.

Chapter 42

Emerson's knock brought me from my mirror. I brushed Amabile away, pinched my cheeks, ran my fingers through waves that coiled back exactly where they'd been, and walked to the door.

"For you…" Emerson stood behind a handful of hangers draped with shimmering bags of thin plastic. "I found three outfits that will be perfect."

He appeared around the plastic as he stepped into my apartment, a smile and a face that could get elected on their own merit.

"You…you shouldn't have."

"Of course I should have. For you." Emerson draped each garment over the back of my small sofa, smoothed the plastic, and stood back. "That won't do." He slid the plastic up off each one, bunching it near the hangers. "What do you think?"

I shouldered close to him and stood near enough to share his view of the brown slacks outfit, the maroon dress, and the casual jeans with a jacket—a corduroy jacket. I edged closer until our shoulders touched.

"You will look beautiful in these," he said, his arm sliding around my back. I fell into his embrace, relieved tears ready to wash away all that was wrong. "Let's see how you look in them."

Letting go of me, Emerson bent over my sofa and gathered all three hangers into his hand. He smoothed the outfits, bunching the plastic tighter at the top.

"Emerson…before I try those…"

"There is no 'before,' Catharine. We have now. We'll start fresh. Let's see how these look."

"Really, Emerson, I want things to be that easy, but…"

He re-draped the garments over my sofa, smoothed them with a hand, and left them be. "I'm sorry, Catharine. There is a 'before,' and I'm sorry for how I was to you about your family."

Your fiancé will have to stand on his own values.

Emerson understood that. And whatever running or standing he was doing, he was doing it with me. "I was confused. I have so much on my mind." He inched my way, the face that never cracked under pressure hesitated, no longer a candidate but a man.

I closed the last of the distance between us and fell against his chest. I held on, my arms tight around him, my ear against him, listening for his heart. His arms rose, they found their place around me, and I squeezed tighter. Everything would be okay.

We stood in a quiet different from Grandpa's house. This quiet breathed. It sighed a different sort of relief, like a gasp of hope. This was how a relationship should be. This was love.

I tilted my head back and looked up at the man I was to marry. "Thank you for the outfits. But more than that, thank you."

I'd forgotten what it felt like to kiss Emerson. It had been so long, affection so hurried between his agendas, so lost in my chaotic world. His face bent close, his breath and mine mingled.

I stretched to my toes, pressed through the small

space, pressed beyond Miles' opinions, the pressure of Emerson's race, beyond Grandpa, the army, and Amabile.

Emerson's lips softened. My kiss was returned, and his hold became a squeeze. "We'll be okay," I said. "With your help, the two of us will be fine." I locked my fingers behind his back and smiled up into a face I would trust.

"Yes, everything will turn out fine." He eased back as he said it, bumping my emotional clutter with his foot. "What's all this?"

"That? That's my history, actually. Or my family's. And some of Grandpa's present." And Grandma's, if I counted the enveloped books I'd left to the side. I latched onto one of his hands as he swiveled in place, staring at the piles arcing in front of my chair.

"His present?" Emerson frowned at the envelopes at his feet.

"You know, the things Miles told you about."

Emerson cocked his head, studying the military pile. "He's going to be okay..." He glanced back at me. I saw and heard the question in his statement.

"I hope so. Especially if you help."

He can't outrun what is happening to your grandfather. Emerson's fingers moved within mine, his thumb racing across his fingertips.

"Shall we see if these outfits fit me?"

Emerson let go of my hand. His focus left the piles of letters—my life and my grandparents' lives—behind, like Dietrich said he should. Emerson retrieved the hangers and nodded toward my bedroom.

I led him to where I'd stood minutes before, to the mirror where I'd seen my heart. My reflection was there, and I looked for his behind mine: for black hair and black eyes, but I saw his heart instead—dangling from his fingers.

Chapter 43

The bells above Non Bookends' door tinkled. Dietrich listened for Cate's grandmother as he closed the door. Fiction created a different atmosphere than nonfiction: too full, too many ancient words on ancient pages, too many hearts printed for everyone to see.

He moved into the store, Non Bookends already alive with reading and browsing. The grandmother's voice could be heard near the table she worked from, so he stayed to the perimeter, her tones telling him where she was, and how she felt.

He slid a book from a shelf, pretending to flip through its pages as he strolled on. He needed the mirror, a good look at it, or an answer from the woman working below it. He closed and patted the book against his palm, glanced at the shelves next to where he stood.

Men prize the thing ungained more than it is. Shakespeare

He stared at the handwritten words, saw Crawley's bent form and the spear aimed at him. A woman, according to Randall, but in all honesty, there could be more than one. Revenge was this mistress's passion. Dietrich retraced his steps and thrust the book back into its space.

Fictional revenge was suffocating, too many words like clubs to the backs of the guilty when facts made a much quicker and cleaner end.

Sunlight, ceiling lights, and low lamps reflected on the ring of frames above the condemning prose. He squinted at the glare. At the single gem of fact crowning the hostility.

One frame, one sheen, the ugliest and the oldest cast a different sort of reflection within its arched rectangle of charred wood. He needed that fact to settle Amabile.

Chapter 44

I stood in my grandparents' house listening to their phone ring.

I had hoped Grandpa would be back, his face worthy of another picture for my display—content this time, relieved, whittling sticks to something because this was his life, his world, and it suited him.

Because Dietrich and the army were wrong.

I stood in the silence where sticks became nothing. Where there was no life, no world, no Grandpa.

"Mama..." I said when I finally answered the second round of ringing. I wanted to ask if she knew Grandpa may have done something to be considered a spy, if she'd ever heard of Amabile, but she dove into wedding plans for me, plans suitable for an upcoming senator, as if she'd called my house instead of her parents'.

Clearly Mama didn't know, as she spilled elaborate plans at her frantic speed, never asking why I'd answered Grandpa's phone, never sensing there was an enemy I hated and that she should hate too. Hate for what he'd brought to us, and what he'd shared after the hearing.

As I put back everything I'd taken from Grandpa's house, except the books, I wanted to ask her if she knew her letters had never been opened. The letters still weren't opened. I couldn't. But Grandpa could, and someday he would, and Mama's frantic running would slow down enough to know.

Chapter 45

I slipped into the back of Non Bookends, enemy territory and a home-away-from-home all in one. I dropped my camera case and purse in Grandma's little nook, glad she wasn't in there, just the aroma of her—books, coffee, and stubbornness.

"New books just came in." One of Grandma's regulars met me as I stepped from her door. "Your grandmother ran out all of a sudden. For more price ribbons or something. She left me in charge when she went."

I was always the outsider in Grandma's crusade. It was in her customer's tone and the way she looked at me. I was family, but an outsider. "You want to open the packages?"

The woman's eyes rounded. "Could I?"

"Sure." I followed her, nearly running to keep up, to Grandma's table. To a stack the woman swiped to the edge and butted against her hips, now a crusader instead of a mere crusadee.

I walked to the far side where Grandma usually sat, pretended to sort and organize tags and pens and whatever else made the woman trust that I was trusting her...even if Grandma wouldn't. I spotted two notes in Grandma's hand, messages from Frank telling me I was behind in my training. I dropped them into the trash and watched the woman open the first package, listening to hear if some chant was involved. With all of the regality of the Oscars, the woman withdrew the book from its package as I dropped into Grandma's chair.

"*Mutiny on the Bounty*," the woman whispered. "W." She set the book aside.

I stood and walked behind some shelves, listening while she opened the next.

"*Forever Amber*."

I came back to my seat, dusting my hands.

"Hmmm, H maybe." The woman set the book in its own spot.

I bristled, one of my favorite literary phrases, that this nonfamily person was privy to Grandma's system.

"*The Scarlet Pimpernel*. A."

"We already have one of those, and that title belongs under W," I corrected her.

The woman stared at me. "You're wrong. There are two reasons for this book, so it belongs in two places. I'm certain that's why Mavis ordered a second. A." She clapped the book on Grandma's table.

My non-store voice teemed with retorts of *Get out...leave my family's bookstore alone*, ready to explode as beige corduroy flashed across a narrow gap between shelves. *Get out...leave my family's bookstore alone*. I stared where he went, then stepped away from the table to the nearest tier of books and slid around the edge.

I eased to the right as the woman opened and announced the next book's title, pressed my back against and peeked around the shelves. He was there, standing in a gap several cases over, staring toward the ceiling over my head. Maybe Germany didn't want him back. I couldn't blame them. I stole one more peek to see if he'd moved. He hadn't. He was still focused far above my head.

I looked up, straight up, at the frame that was older, longer, and uglier than all of the others. Burnt looking, a fragile structure of ash and wood, with a dark lump dangling near its top. Moving from the shelves to the wall, I slunk to the back to Grandma's room and fished my camera out of its case. Staying out of sight, I made my way between where Dietrich had been standing and where I had been, until the frame was clear in my view. I raised my camera and brought the old frame into focus. I zoomed in to the blackened wood and the shattered silver behind the glass. A mirror. I clicked the picture. Then I zoomed in farther for the lump. I steadied my hands, the darkened wood piece weaving in and out of focus...something carved that was attached. I clicked again on a shape far too familiar.

Chapter 46

The little runner's camera was louder than the woman spouting titles across the store. Dietrich was used to verbiage and let it roll past. It was details he was honed to, and a camera's click was one.

"Another A," the woman gushed as if surprised. Dietrich wasn't. A was for adultery. Mrs. Crawley's system was simple. W for war…the type of war she knew, and the type the author apparently did too. Not the strategies of war but the consequences, instead— hearts ravaged by battle, crushed and left behind.

Cate stared up at the frame he planned to take down. Seeing her photographs would be easier, especially blown up and close. If it was anything like Amabile's mirror, it would be coming down for good. And he preferred his hands be on it instead of hers.

She backed away from where she stood and slipped to the rear of the store. He ducked into the sole restroom and closed the door. She would leave. She would go develop that roll of film even if those were the only pictures on it. He was sure. Because that's what he would do.

He waited longer than she would need and then waited more. He flushed the lever, ran water in the sink, and stepped through the door. No Cate, no grandmother's voice; he walked to the main table where the woman was now aligning her stacks of books.

"New arrivals?" he asked, exaggerating his accent.

"Why, yes, they just came. I'm getting them organized for Mavis...I mean Mrs. Crawley. She left me in charge while she stepped out."

"She has very good taste." Dietrich tilted his head to read one of the titles. Close enough to pretend admiration, but far enough to stay out of this watchdog's territory.

"She sure does." The woman neatened the stacks, owning them.

"Beautiful store." He ran his gaze over the shelves, the nearby furniture...and a finger over the smooth tabletop.

"Very comfortable. Non Bookends is like a home."

"Even the decorations." He pointed to the rim of frames above their heads. "I noticed them immediately. A couple remind me of my home. Germany. Where I'm from."

"Germany," the woman said it with too much breath. "I knew your accent was from somewhere over there."

"Germany is beautiful. You should visit us sometime."

"Oh, I've never been out of the country. Heck, I've hardly been out of New York. But you can find a little of everywhere here. New York City has people from all over the world, you know."

"And relics, too. Like that one." Dietrich pointed upward again, directly at a picture. "That is German, I'm sure."

She followed his gaze, cupping her hand over her brows against the glare on the glass. "I can't even tell what it is."

"I believe it's an Emil Adam painting." Dietrich cupped his hand also. "An original, possibly."

"An original…" The woman moved closer, then farther, straining to peer where he pointed.

"It's worth a lot, in either case, but especially if it's an original."

"I'm not sure…I can't tell."

"It's the way he does his mountains that makes me think so. Horses were his specialty, but from here I can't see the details…" Dietrich stepped closer and bent his head back. "I've never seen an original."

"Should we check? What if Mavis doesn't know what it is?"

"That would be a wonderful surprise. She looks like she could use some good news."

A series of tsks ratcheted from the woman's mouth. "You have no idea. Yes, let's look at it for her. There's a ladder in the back. A small one, but you're plenty tall enough to see, once you're up there."

Dietrich unfolded the stepladder she found and worked his way to the top.

"Be careful." The woman held the sides, making his climb more treacherous.

Dietrich stretched and stared at the picture he'd called an Adam, one he knew from the floor really wasn't. "No, now that I'm close, I'm sorry to say it's not one of Adam's paintings. An imitation, likely. That happened to the true artists. Very sorry. And I'm not close enough to see the name of who did it." He feigned a stretch.

"Darn. That would have been wonderful if you were right. Well, come on down. I'll hold the ladder while you do."

"Yes, it's too bad." Dietrich set a hand on the wall as he maneuvered to step down. "This old frame next to it is falling apart. I'm surprised it hasn't dropped to the floor."

"Which one?" A hand cupped her brow again as the woman squinted where he pointed.

"This old one. It looks damaged." He stretched a hand and tapped the wood with a finger. Burned. At the top, a charred lump like the one in his pocket—the one from Oma's attic. He leaned close to the wall. It couldn't be... "It's barely holding together."

"We don't want it dropping on anyone. Bring it down. Mavis can get it fixed or replace it."

"Looks like a simple fix. I can have it sturdied and back on the wall before she returns." The mirror was old, it was burned, and it wobbled with the tremor of his hands when Dietrich ran them behind the bottom as he lifted it off its nail.

Chapter 47

The fifth lily, the one he placed on the mirror's left side beneath the first and third, changed what they saw in the mirror's glass. No more of the past, no more of the present, but more of the future. A place unknown to either of them, they knew it was home as their hands locked and they saw themselves standing in its midst. It was an ethereal home, unlike any place she'd ever imagined, one woven by dreams, where all was perfect and love never faded.

"Yes," he said, as he stood beside her, gazing into the glass. "That is how we should be, how I imagined us to be." And as he turned her direction and looked down at her, his face in the glass stayed the same, peering out at her with a promise—he'd always be with her, just as she saw in their reflections.

The fifth lily. I stared at the two photographs I'd developed from Non Bookends, Grandpa's basement closing around me as I did. That lump on the charred frame was on the left, beneath what looked like two dark holes. I let the picture fall to my lap. Surely this was a dream. A nightmare Dietrich had brought.

Maybe I had been running too much. No, that couldn't be. I hadn't been running at all lately. Maybe I'd fainted while running and I was lying in a hospital somewhere unable to wake up. I pinched myself. I pinched hard, wringing the skin until it flared red. This wasn't a dream. And it was worse than a nightmare.

I closed the door to my developing lab and carried my photos and Amabile's book upstairs. I went to Grandpa's phone and called Emerson's office.

"Any news?" I asked when his secretary put me through. Emerson paused on the other end, and in the quiet I imagined that readied look he always had—that I needed him to have. *Please, God, please don't let Emerson let me down.*

"Catharine…" He was tapping: I heard it in the dead air space. "Yes, there is some news."

"What is it?" I tapped my foot, trying to catch his rhythm.

"Miles found out Mr. Crawley…I mean your grandfather…is being kept there. The investigative stage is done and probable cause is being established. Then the trial. Your grandfather won't be allowed to leave…for an unspecified amount of time."

I felt what Emerson wasn't saying. *Your grandfather won't be here to walk you down the aisle. Your grandfather can't possibly walk you down the aisle after this because of the tainting and guilt…we can't allow that. I can't tout a hero who really wasn't one.*

"Can he have visitors?"

There was a pause again. "He can. It's not like being held in a prison; he's just being held there for the hearings."

I wanted to laugh, explode with a brief ecstatic moment I desperately needed. Something Grandpa would need also. "Will you go with me?" Please…

The tapping increased, the bounce of a solitary pencil on Emerson's desk. "I can't…you know I have obligations…a packed schedule of appearances. Miles represented me to your grandfather, though. He gave him my best."

The silence was mine, this time. My tapping stopped. "Miles went there?"

"Of course. Miles is very thorough. He does his job well, and he spoke with your grandfather kindly and encouragingly. Thanking Miles would be the appropriate thing for you to do."

I tried to grasp what I would thank Miles for.

"Catharine…you're not really thinking about going, are you?"

"Of course I am." Not my best voice.

"Listen, Catharine, this is about us and my career. As well as your grandfather, of course. But his choices could affect us…"

I glanced down at the pictures still in my hand. At choices someone made and hung on Non Bookends' wall. That someone couldn't be my grandfather. He didn't live by fiction, and he never went in Grandma's store. "I have to go see him, Emerson. If you don't, that's your choice."

Chapter 48

"Well, so there you are." Frank straddled his bicycle on the sidewalk in front of my apartment. "You don't look dressed for running."

"I'm sorry. I can't run now. I'm on my way to…" I was running. But to my grandfather, just like I always had. The sort of run that wore me out more than five miles did. "I have something to do."

"The marathon's almost here, you know. Twenty-plus miles is a long run."

The photo display was due shortly after. I tossed my purse into my car and stood in its opened door while Frank bent forward and rested his elbows on his handlebars.

"I'll be ready."

"You're good, Cate, but you've got to work hard if you want to win."

"Frank, I've told you a thousand times I'm not running to win. I run to run." And the farther, the better.

"If you want to run well, run to win. If you don't have a goal, you'll just pound the pavement." Frank straightened on his bicycle, legs angled to the sides, his weight leaning back on the seat. He glanced over his shoulder as a rhythm kicked up in the distance, a blur of movement I followed his gaze to see. The dark blur became larger, taller and lither, as it advanced our way. The rhythm had a cadence, a beat that hailed the approach of a winner.

"Cate! Hello!" Jill circled around her husband, long legs slowing, arms pumping and close to her sides like they should be. A ponytail swung behind her head. Jill's runs were frolics, happy prances to a finish line instead of frantic hammering escapes. Looking at her was like looking at high school again. From behind, when I'd seen her back sailing over the finish line ahead of me.

"What are you doing?" I closed the door on my purse and marched to the sidewalk.

I could hear the rhythm of her feet. Tap-tap-tap, faster than I could think. "Running." She grinned. "Training."

"With your husband?"

"I never thought training with him was necessary, or a good idea. Until now." She smiled at Frank. "He wins if I win."

"You can run along with us." Frank grasped his handlebars, his fingers splaying and unsplaying over the brakes.

"I can't." I wouldn't. I'd never run against Jill again unless I actually wanted to win, and that included their idea of casually running with her. "I have to be somewhere."

Jill continued to bounce in place, prancing like a racehorse, ponytail whipping behind her. "See you at the start line, then?" She smiled. I knew what she meant. At the start but not at the finish line when she crossed it well ahead of me.

I walked back to my car, keeping the run out of my steps, Jill's *Let's go,* and Frank's *Right behind you,* making me want to vomit. Frank knew I needed that marathon for reasons of my own, and I didn't need their imposed finish line choking those reasons. Jill should have known I'd never run it with her there. They were supposed to be my friends. Friends were supposed to love. Enemies were to hate.

****

Grandpa wasn't being kept in a cell, just like Emerson had said, but he was staying in some army-quality living quarters, everything about the building shouting "military" with its starkness, invisible colors, and straight lines. Grandpa could die of boredom in there.

"Grandpa?" I tapped at his door, barely feeling the tenuous attempt. "It's me, Cate." I listened for his stilted step. "You there, Grandpa?"

The door eased open, a sallow eye appearing at its edge. "Cate? Why are you here?"

"Let me in, Grandpa. I'm here to see you."

He hesitated, *Is she with you?* in the eye that peered behind me. "Not the best time for a visit."

"Just let me in. Please." I stared at the eye and the door until the eye disappeared and the door eased open, a gaunt, bent Grandpa behind it. "Thank you."

I entered a room just as sterile as the rest of the building—square everything, no rounded edges, no soft corners.

A solitary cup sat on the lone coffee table near a worn chair, a fine ring inside like a start line above where the drink was evaporating.

"What's going on, Grandpa?" I turned to a long thin arm braced on a cane, his other indicating the only other seat in the room. I wiped a hand across the sofa's worn cushion and sat.

"Tea or coffee?" Grandpa asked.

"Grandpa…"

He angled himself in front of the chair and eased, almost fell, into the seat, so unsteady and halted I was sure he couldn't get up.

"Why are they doing this to you, Grandpa?"

"I'm accused of trying to leak US information to the Germans. Before the war."

"Did you?"

He stared at his knees, legs so thin he could have fit both into one side of his trousers. "All that matters is what the judge decides."

"What does that mean? The truth is what matters."

Grandpa looked at me then. "It does," he said, and started to say more, but stopped and stared at his knees.

"I'm coming for the hearing, and nothing you or the army says can stop me. I'm family. And I'll do whatever it takes to see you walk away from this, free and clear." My tone was rangy, my words quick and sharp in the bare box of a room. "You must have something, some sort of proof you're innocent."

I kept nothing from my military days. It bothered my wife. I tried not to think about the mirror, its charred lily, the whole one I'd found in his workbench drawer. "Something, Grandpa. Anything…" The same thing Dietrich had asked from me. Except he didn't care.

Grandpa shook his head, the travel of his gaze from his knees to the wall in front of him giving me hope he was pondering anything there could be. Could have been. Anywhere. The slow wag of his head told me he had come up with nothing. Or maybe he hadn't tried.

"You have nothing left from your service days that might help? Even a friend who could vouch for you?

Any proof you were never in Germany?"

"What I have left of the service is in plain sight."

I stared at him, at the fragments left from a military man. At the scars peering from the cuffs of his sleeves, at the cane he kept a hand on.

"What happened, Grandpa? I want to hear it from you."

He ran a hand down the leg of his pants, wrapping long fingers around what little there was of what had been broken. "Fire. Everything that mattered got burned."

Burned, like his arms, like everything else he'd gotten rid of...or nearly got rid of. Burned like the mirror in Non Bookends—and all of the lies if Grandpa was never in Berlin. "And your leg?"

"An accident," he said, letting go of it and straightening.

"Why has Grandma been so angry all these years?"

The answer to my question never made it to his mouth, not in an argument or an agreement. He was letting her choices stand...like the judge's. I came to my feet, bringing my purse with me. I stared at him, at the back of his head as he studied his lap. "Grandpa, if you won't explain thoroughly, how can anyone know what's true? How can anyone help you?"

" 'Not to the swift, the race; not to the strong, the fight; not to the righteous, perfect grace; not to the wise, the light.' "

He sounded like Dietrich. And like Grandma.

"I'm fed up with hiding behind other people's words." I slung my purse over my shoulder. "Grandpa, tell me this...were you a runner?"

"I wasn't fast enough." So I'd heard.

Chapter 49

The mirror's charred frame and ragged silver ran through Dietrich's mind. Cleaner than expected as he'd pretended to sturdy it before returning it to the wall. He twirled the note on his hotel suite's table that Randall had left for him. "Trial at 1:00 p.m. Thursday." Tomorrow.

"Hello, Oma." He hid his relief when she answered. This was his third call, Oma not answering the first two, sending his thoughts running their own race at what may have happened to her, whether Monika had visited Oma, or whether Oma may be on a plane heading to New York.

He fished the burned lily that matched the one on the mirror from his pocket, set it on top of Randall's note, and spun both.

"No, Oma. I haven't had time to check flights. I won't be here that long anyway. How about Spain? It is beautiful. Warmer right now than here. We can go there as soon as I return." Since he'd likely be jobless by then anyway.

His grandmother had never asked for anything. Never argued or put up a fuss. He spun the lily harder, sending it near the table's edge. The last place she needed to be was in New York near a trial suggesting a young German woman loved an enemy, or worse, was a spy.

"I've decided to start writing again." Oma was coming here after all, but through her words. Curses stirred inside, English curses. They sounded uglier than the profanities he'd grown up with.

He glanced across the bed to the other side of the room, at the table and lamp where he kept Amabile's books.

"What sort of story?" He stared at their dark covers, simple wrappings around stories that needed to end. *Please say "silly romantic tales that couldn't possibly be true."*

"The words aren't strung together yet. But I feel them."

"Erika Müller has returned?"

She said nothing. He strained to hear Amabile in her silence.

"I will edit for you. Proofread. As soon as I get back. We'll do it on the beach in Spain."

There was almost a laugh on her end. "You are a masterful writer, courageous for truth, but you lack the sort of heart it would take to edit what I say. You write marvelously what you know in your mind. I write what I know from my soul. Beneath every great and even darkened mind there beats a heart. What the mind can't unravel, my stories sometimes can."

He touched his face. It felt cool, likely pale. Someone's stories had done enough; for Oma's sake, he couldn't allow more. "I will be home soon. We can go to Spain immediately. You can write there." Away from Monika, away from Amabile, away from the army, and away from enemies who never should have been loved, even on a page.

Oma wished him safe travels. He could hear her

heart even in her simple goodbye.

His hand touched hers in the glass. The marred and ruined visage of a mirror nearly destroyed didn't take away the truth. Their hands still touched in the broken reflection. His and hers. Touched. Clasped. Pressed together until they were both there in what remained of the mirror. Together in an embrace that would never end.

The words roiled in his gut.

He stared at the charred flower. It could have been the one on the mirror. The mirror he'd seen two hands in, in the brief moment he'd looked into it. Hands that clasped and drew close, bringing him and her together where he could see them—Oma's and another's…then Dietrich's and…surely not.

Chapter 50

"Come with me." I'd stopped in Non Bookends before it opened. "Grandpa needs you." I needed her. I needed one of my grandparents to admit out loud any awful things that may have happened so we could face them together and make everything okay. "The trial begins at one. I want to be there early so we can get in and get close." Maybe even talk to Grandpa, but I wouldn't say that. "Okay, far. Not close," I conceded to her pallor.

Grandma looked too white in the dim light of her home-away-from-home. Noise came from the small aluminum percolator, calling her attention to the tiny stove. Gray hair hung down long on her back, strands catching on what was left of the rows and tufts striping her old chenille robe as she lessened the heat under her coffee.

"I keep telling myself to get one of those newfangled coffeepots to set out in the store—for my customers—cream, sugar, and prose. That's how coffee is best served." She poured a cup for herself and one for me. I stood from her cot where I'd been sitting and went to the small dinette that seated two.

"Thank you, Grandma." I sat on the vinyl seat and wrapped my hands around the cup, squeezing it, sending warmth to her bleached complexion.

She sat in the chair opposite me, her hands in her

lap, staring at the steam collecting above her cup. I could see the war inside—like the war in her books, except personal…close, hand-to-hand. "I won't go."

I took a sip, the coffee searing my lip, but I didn't flinch. I was still going. For her maybe even more than for him. I stood, took my cup to her single sink and washed it, then set it to dry. Picking up my purse, I stopped at the edge of her table, speaking the only language she had ever spoken to me. " 'How many times did it thunder before Franklin took the hint? How many apples fell on Newton's head before he took the hint? Nature is always hinting at us. It hints over and over again. And suddenly we take the hint.' "

"Frost." Grandma didn't look up. I squeezed leftover coffee warmth into her shoulder and left.

Chapter 51

Verdammt. Dietrich's language. I mouthed the curse as I was escorted past him and that nasty American reporter friend of his, to the front of the hearing room where Grandpa would be. Dietrich caught my eye. *Verdammt,* I mouthed the German vulgarity again, the soldier escorting me glancing down, a reminder to behave as Grandpa's sole support.

I settled alone into a row, the seat hard and cold, its back straight and uncomfortable. An enormous clock at the front of the room ticked time from past to future, from here to there, the way my hammering feet had tried to drag my grandparents for years. A door opened and army officers filed in from the right, three of them, McCoy stolid in the middle.

"Sorry, I'm a little late."

An expensive aroma swirled in the air as I whirled to the side. "Miles?"

"I meant to be here earlier. I just couldn't get free."

I glanced behind him, hoping…

"If you are looking for Emerson"—Miles' aroma came close, his head tipping my way—"he sends you his love and support and is sorry he couldn't make it. He's very busy."

I nodded and held my breath. It was Emerson's fragrance I needed.

Another door opened, this one to the left, and more

officers filed in, an elderly man in civilian clothing limping between them. Grandpa leaned into his cane as if the room was tilted. I leaned with him, holding him up with every step.

There were questions I could ask, that Miles could probably answer. His attorney posture and attentiveness told me he saw more than just my feeble grandfather limping in. A presiding officer...a military judge... entered from a solitary door and took his seat at the front, everyone standing and then sitting as he did.

Introductory statements began immediately, and McCoy sat listening, straight and alert as his attorney filled the room with McCoy's claims. McCoy was near Grandpa's age, yet somehow seemed younger. He wore full military regalia, looking like he belonged, whereas Grandpa's simple clothing made him seem like an outsider...a reject, someone who had destroyed everything military he owned. *For her. Because of her.* Maybe for another reason altogether.

Miles sat at attention throughout the lengthy presentation, never frowning as if he didn't understand the military jargon I would be jotting down and looking up later if he weren't sitting here. I stared at my grandfather's narrow back as I heard accusations presented as facts, woven into a story that was told as if it was nonfiction and irrefutable—Grandpa had been in Poland while McCoy tended to other of his soldiers in Belgium, who were aiding with the end of Belgium's elections. Paper, a list, lost in Berlin, had been seen in Poland first—handwritten secret information of US military men sympathetic to Hitler's regime. Because of Grandpa's coloring and build, he could pass as German...Aryan...seeming a natural possessor of this

216

paperwork as it was channeled through a network of undercover persons the short distance to Berlin. It took years for the espionage to be uncovered, German officials on trial finally confessing to being in line for this missing information, which was to come through a US soldier fitting the Aryan model to a German contact and then to them. This was McCoy's day, his version of what happened, him taking the responsibility for errantly trusting one of his men.

McCoy's attorney discussed Grandpa's injuries then, light statements that insinuated to me much was left unsaid. I stared at Grandpa's back, imagining the scars I'd never seen. Explosion, burns—what showed at his wrists verified both. I bounced my leg, fighting the urge to jump to my feet and ask if it wasn't enough he was wounded in duty. Maybe they could strip him to the waist and ask him to walk without his cane if they had any doubts how this man had suffered for his country.

Miles laid a hand on my knee, stilling my leg as the attorney representing McCoy reviewed the tale they'd told, spinning it so eloquently I felt mesmerized. Everyone must have, the only sound the man's voice, enchanting words over a soft hush. A novel Grandma would have kept for her crusade.

McCoy and Grandpa were dismissed, each disappearing a different direction with their escorts. Grandpa never even looked my way as the room emptied, leaving me and Miles at the front and hopefully no German behind us.

"You coming tomorrow?" Miles looked at me.

"Of course. Maybe Emerson can come then."

Miles smiled and stood. I joined him when the

sounds of people clearing the room were gone, followed him to the aisle, and turned toward the back. Toward Dietrich and his cohort, both still there and standing along the aisle. I looked down as we passed, a corduroyed arm reaching for me, latching onto my elbow, and bringing me to a stop.

"See you tomorrow." Miles glanced from Dietrich to me, then disappeared through the hearing room's door. I didn't want to see Miles tomorrow, and I didn't want to see Dietrich now.

It was Emerson who should be here, and I yanked from Dietrich's hold. "Grandpa was never in Berlin, and making a weak link to Poland is no proof he had a thing to do with any of this."

"Come outside to talk."

"I really don't have a thing to say to you." I wheeled to his friend. "Or you."

"Just me." Dietrich nodded his shrugging friend aside, took my elbow again, and steered me where Miles had gone. Thankfully truly gone as I scoured the hall for his smooth stride.

"I said I don't have anything to say to you." It was like walking with Grandpa, two of my steps for every one of Dietrich's. "You can slow down. I'm out of the marathon."

"You dropped out of the race?" Dietrich asked as he ushered me down the hall.

"I run, not race. Well, neither now, so slow down."

Dietrich kept his hold on my elbow as we exited the building. At the top of the small set of concrete stairs he scanned the barren area around us and headed for the lone tree in the center of the lot.

"Dietrich, I'm tired of asking why you're really

here." I wrenched my elbow from his hand the moment he stopped beneath the tree. "You're looking for a runner, you're looking for an old friend, you quote fiction you don't believe in, and I want you to stop dragging my grandfather and me into your schemes." I wanted to scream. How could the man who wanted to marry me be so far away and a complete stranger standing near? In a place my grandfather was being held, pasty walls and yellowed pages, all saying he was guilty.

"You understand what is happening here?"

"It's...it's a hearing."

"Yes, it's a hearing, and from what Randall"—Dietrich nodded toward his friend farther down the parking lot, leaning against a car, a cloud of cigarette smoke obscuring his head—"said, your grandfather needs some sharp defense."

"Why? He's innocent."

"His commanding officer says he's not." Dietrich leaned close. "They need the missing proof, or what your grandfather's superior claims may be the basis for their decision."

"Missing proof?"

"The list of names to be handed off to the German army in Berlin. If it can be found, that would tell a lot."

"Doesn't matter. Like McCoy said, Grandpa wasn't stationed in Berlin."

Dietrich shoved a hand in his trousers' pocket, working whatever he had in there. "True, he wasn't stationed in Berlin. But..." Dietrich removed his hand from his pocket. "Never mind that. But there is someone claiming he recognizes your grandfather from back in Poland, and that he was the soldier seen handing off the list."

I tried not to react. "I heard the army talking to my grandpa nearly two weeks ago. It was McCoy they suspected of something, not Grandpa."

"The investigation has been long running and eventually trickled down to McCoy, but then to his unit. The focus is off McCoy with his charges, and the suspicions are pointing to your grandfather instead. Your grandfather's attorney really needs that list. Really needs it..." Dietrich wanted the list, the way he leaned said he expected it from me.

"There is no list I've ever heard of. How did you find all of this out?"

Dietrich nodded toward Randall, who was lighting a new cigarette as he strolled around the car. "He's good. Almost as good as I am."

"He could have told me this. Why are you here?"

"I said he's good. And he is because—he doesn't care."

"That doesn't tell me anything, and you said you're better. So you care less."

"I care about the truth. You do too. We both need to know."

"Your friend is going to run out of cigarettes, and I'm going back in to talk to my grandfather." I pivoted and started across the pavement.

"My runner was in Hitler's Olympics. Berlin. 1936. Right before the war. Truth."

I stopped. I stared across the lot at the sterile block of a building ahead. The air became impossible to breathe.

"There was a US runner there. Unofficially."

There are no runners in our family. You shouldn't

run. "That has nothing to do with this missing list my grandfather needs." I made a half turn his direction.

"It might if it proves that runner was a soldier and in Berlin when he wasn't supposed to be. Maybe for other reasons..."

I turned fully then, my hands closing into fists. "You're looking for a needle in a haystack. That's an expression here that means you won't find what you're looking for. Not even in your fiction stories."

Dietrich walked my way. He took something from his pocket and pressed it into mine. "My runner left this behind."

He stepped back, a charred lump of wood left in my palm.

Chapter 52

The little runner was going to run. Dietrich watched her when he should have been with Randall, keeping an eye on what he found as Randall pried into the second part of the hearing that was coming later today. Crawley's part—the man who was likely guilty, proven either by that list or by the mirror. He was in Berlin, and Oma might be dragged in unless Dietrich found out first.

He'd likely be fired, no matter what, having called and declined to do the article they were holding for him. He'd never write for one of the government's journals again anyway, once the truth came out. He didn't know how to stop this trial, how to get back to disproving a simple book of fiction. Monika had sounded edgy when he'd called, defensive when he asked if she'd spoken with Oma. She hung up when he told her there may be a delay before he returned. There would be no stopping Randall now either. He wouldn't fail to do his job even if the army did.

Dietrich watched Cate walk from her apartment and glance both directions along the street. No trainer waiting, no fiancé. She bent into sloppy stretches, and began a half-hearted trot down the sidewalk. He stood in plain sight, but she hadn't looked. He watched as the distance between the two of them grew, glad she hadn't—yet watching in case she did.

****

Dietrich lingered far from the hearing room, making several laps around the complex, giving Cate enough time to get settled without seeing him. She would have seen Randall, who wouldn't stay out of sight for her sake. Randall had snorted at Dietrich's suggestion and went in early. Dietrich made one last loop, then laid a hand on the hearing room's door. Randall was where they always sat, in the back, instead of right behind Cate like Dietrich had feared the man would do after Dietrich's request to give her space. Dietrich slid along the row without a sound and settled next to stale cigarette smoke.

The little runner was in her same seat she'd been in yesterday, next to the same man Dietrich now knew was her fiancé's fellow attorney and campaign manager. Miles Marcus. A man of worth personally, professionally, and financially. But not to the degree the man considered himself. Cate's other side was empty, either seat the place her fiancé should have been. Dietrich would have been there. If he were ever to be a fiancé. Which he wouldn't.

"Stop strumming your fingers." Randall jabbed him with an elbow.

Dietrich balled his fingers. He wasn't here for the little runner with the brown hair. He was here for white hair, white hair that used to be blond.

Crawley briefly stood, before his attorney launched into his defense, the serviceman posture barely evident. Crawley did it well, not looking like a ploy for pity, just enough rigidity to claim he'd served his country as he should.

The defense cast doubt on an elderly Polish man's

ability to peg the exact tall blond in the photo of Crawley's unit after all these years. Black and white, enlarged for the judge and room to see, the picture was grainy, all the faces duplicates of each other, triplicates, a blur of expressions that looked mostly the same.

The lawyer made much of the lack of solid evidence, pointing out that hearsay and suspicion didn't count as tangible proof. Crawley's attorney pressed for truth, for black-and-white facts, hammering, without hammering into the judge his responsibility to base his verdict on irrefutable information. Even from the back of the room Dietrich saw that responsibility hit home in the judge. Pride came with his duties, an honor he wouldn't tarnish.

Crawley's attorney at last made mention of Crawley's wounds. "Fool." Dietrich shook his head. That tactic would weaken the solid points he'd made before. Nothing worse than ending on a flimsy emotional appeal. Dietrich shifted in his seat, the little runner's head making a slight turn. She was looking at her grandfather's back. This switch in strategy would work on her. It wouldn't work on the men making the decisions, though.

"In the line of duty, while serving in Poland, Crawley went to a civilian's aid in an explosion." The attorney moved from where he'd been standing near Crawley. Dietrich watched Cate, the man winding up his case as a peripheral figure. "Responding to a civil emergency was outside his duties there, a gasoline accident with a Polish tank truck. Crawley reacted purely from himself. Quick, and without even understanding the shouts around him. No translator, he acted from the sort of man he is. Not a traitor."

The little runner's face must be a mass of confusion. Dietrich couldn't tell from what he could see of her, her focus fixed on her grandfather's still form.

"Once Lieutenant McCoy was notified of Private Crawley's injuries, he came to Poland and had Crawley treated and returned to France. From there, after further treatment, Private Crawley was back on duty, not well enough to avoid a misjudgment that broke his leg. After that, McCoy sent him home to finish out what little was left of his enlistment, well before the war began, even farther ahead of any US involvement. Private Crawley never took part in any of it, never was anywhere near or involved in Berlin."

The little runner moved. The cap of brown turned to the left until the edge and then the whole of her face could be seen. Her dark eyes spotted him. A warning, a mock that he could insinuate this man was anything less than what his attorney presented. The look was there, then gone. She turned back to the front, but her face, the way it looked and the look on it, stayed.

****

Randall filed past lesser reporters and strode after the officers as they led McCoy and Crawley from the room. Dietrich stood. He should keep an eye on Randall, but then there was Cate. Miles rose and Cate stood with him, her fiancé's campaign manager's letter-perfect suit and stature whispering near her hair. There was no one for her to trust, really. Not the grandfather she used to rely on, and not the man at her side. Even less so the one who wasn't. Dietrich was trustworthy, but who confided a broken heart to the one who helped break it? She and Miles stood with their backs to Dietrich and the crowd that was filtering out. At last

Miles straightened. At Cate's nod, he slipped to the front, the direction her grandfather had been escorted, the sentry allowing Emerson's campaign manager through.

There was no hero in Cate's expression as she turned and walked Dietrich's way. She stopped when she came alongside Dietrich. He nearly reached for her hand, when she grabbed his. She slapped something rough and hard into it, something familiar, the charred wood.

"You're wrong. And you're a liar. You said romance and fiction meant nothing to you, and here you are using both so you can create a story that suits you. And them." She jerked her head toward the front. "You're just a cheap reporter looking for a sensational sale while you're here, turning a good soldier into a fickle one, saying he fell in love with his country's enemy." She squared herself. "I can tell you, without a doubt, loving an enemy is impossible."

The fire in her eyes ignited a hatred of the enemy. He tossed the lily into the air, caught it in a fist, and stuffed it into his pocket. He nodded to her empty side. "Then it seems you've become someone's enemy too."

Chapter 53

"Your prize..." She looked at his chest, at the sudden bareness of it, even his clothing, his shirt and jacket, all lacking the distinction she'd come to admire. The glitter and sheen of his victory was faded from his eyes, furtive glances instead of joy.

"You are my only prize." He took her hand and pressed it to his chest. "A treasure for always."

She watched for the light to return to his gaze, her hand squeezed tight against his bare shirt. She stared, trying to see any reflection of herself, of the two of them, of what she knew was deep in his heart.

"I will protect us. I promise. In a place we can both belong." He was uneasy as he spoke. He let go of her hand, stood, paced around where they sat in her small apartment, walked to her writing desk, and touched the stories she'd written. More stories, about them. "You are writing truth."

Of course he knew that. In the evenings when she and the other artists visited Hindenburghaus to entertain her country's visitors, she read what she'd written, a dozen soft translators she trusted relaying her heart, telling him and everyone from around the world the story of a love no fiction could capture.

"It is the same truth in your art to me." She glanced at the mirror, at the five lilies he'd carved and attached to the frame.

227

He left her desk and came to her and took her hand, bringing the two of them to that mirror to stand together, the tall and the short, the blond and the brunette, the champion and the writer—side by side.

She stared at the two of them framed by the dark wood, the flowers he'd carved like the promises he was trying to voice. But gentler. Without angst. Not so furtive. She felt his gaze on her, and she looked at their reflections, his blue eyes piercing, his image staring back out at her. His hand gripped hers, and they looked into the mirror, her apartment disappearing behind them, their faces transported to a place she'd never seen.

"Where are we?" she whispered.

"I'm taking you with me," he said. "Our home. Not what's been yours, not what's been mine. Soon."

She stared at the fast-moving background, at the almost explosive changes transforming her home to another.

"You have to trust me," he whispered at her side, her hand clenched in his. "Be ready."

I closed Amabile and stared at the cover. That couldn't be Grandpa. That wasn't the man I knew. And neither was the man being tried as a traitor. I stared across my living room at my bedroom door. I should run. Run to Non Bookends and look at the mirror hanging above Grandma's books. Over her crusade, over her belief that battles did something to a man— brought out in him what was already hidden there, be it good or bad. Good or bad, I had to see for myself the mirror I'd never paid attention to until now. Far too high for Grandma to hang, far too obvious for a guilty man to hang, also.

I stood, climbed into my running clothes, stepped outside my apartment—and ran.

Grandma was busy when I reached her store, her voice a familiar part of Non Bookends' atmosphere, the air feeling good since I'd barely broken a sweat. I threaded my way through the sounds to the back, inhaling the familiar and drinking it in. Switching to spare clothing Grandma insisted I keep in her little home-away-from-home so I wouldn't offend her flock, I stepped out of the back in real clothes and wended my way toward the front, through faded book spines, authors and their stories, Ibsen's women strong even when they were weak.

"There is Joachim." My grandmother's voice came from near where I stood. There was acquiescence in her tone, something different, something I wanted to slip around the shelving and see. "Mann wrote about a soldier becoming heroic in his defeat. Things don't always turn out as we planned. Those battlefields we imagine ourselves victorious in aren't where we truly shine…according to Mann."

I envisioned a customer taking Joachim from Grandma's hands, flipping through pages of a life turning right side up in an upside-down situation. Grandma'd never spoken of Joachim before. I frowned, listening for her to right herself from the opposite of all the characters she touted.

"You've read this?" the customer asked.

"Last night," Grandma said. "It's new. I just received it."

"You read this in one night?"

I heard Grandma nod in the silence.

"I'll take it. Thank you." Another satisfied

crusadee.

I tipped my head around the shelves, footsteps leaving and making their way to Grandma's table. I eased to where the two of them had been and scanned the spines, my finger in a race to find Mann. If only Grandma would at least put her authors in alphabetical order. Name after name ran by, everything except Mann.

"You looking for something?" Grandma asked from behind me.

I dropped my finger from her books. "I heard you…"

Grandma nodded. "Mann."

"You were up late last night…"

She nodded again. I wanted to ask her about Joachim, about Mann, about heroes in unexpected situations.

"I went to Grandpa's…"

"Maybe you could tend the store for a little bit while I run an errand? We're out of coffee. I should have bought some last night, but I read, instead."

I thought of the photos I had to take and finish for my display. Of the real running I thought I'd try again. Of Emerson and the mirror. "Of course, go ahead. I'll be happy to watch the store for you. Can you do something for me?" I asked before she walked away.

Grandma didn't offer me a "yes" just because that was what grandmothers should do. She was a "no" sort of grandma, but she looked my way.

"Come with me to the next hearing. Please." I willed Joachim into her thoughts. "They will begin questioning witnesses and bringing out evidence. It will be good for you. And for Grandpa…"

"My being there won't do him any good."

"It will. Grandpa won't even look at me, but if you were there…"

"I would make things worse."

"How can you make things worse? He has a chance. He has a case. There is no proof against him, yet. Nothing solid."

"Then I am definitely not what you want there."

"But…" It felt cliché to beg the back that walked away from me. Like a literary scene written far too many times. I watched her go, her gait rigid, and then she was gone.

I glanced up at the mirror I really didn't want to see or touch, the dark lump that looked far too much like the one Dietrich had handed me, the two of them scorched versions of the one from Grandpa's garage. It was impossible, pure foolishness, that fiction would have any merit at all. "Pure foolishness," I whispered as I retrieved Grandma's ladder from the back and set it close to the wall. "Fiction is fairy tales." One step at a time, my hands like suctions on the wall, I made my way to the top and put a foot on the final platform.

"There's no solid proof. There won't be imaginary proof, either." I stretched, inching the fingers of one hand toward the mirror's frame, my other hand bracing me.

"Can I help?"

Please, God, no.

"Are you sure you want to do that?"

I glanced down at the devil himself, blond hair and a tan corduroy jacket. *Leave us alone. This is my family's battle.* "Cleaning. I'll get back to it later." I slid my palms down the wall, feeling for each step down with my toes. *Leave us be, leave us alone.* A hand broke my descent, steadied my ankle, while another gripped the ladder. "What are you doing?"

"Just come on down."

I stared at his fingers, his blond head, the face that had dared to suggest I was my fiancé's enemy. "Let go of my foot."

There was power in looking down on him, strength even with height that made me weak. I kicked at the warmth his hand left behind as he stepped back, and I slithered down. "When are you going back to Germany?"

"Soon. My grandmother is…"

"Your grandmother? You have a grandmother, and you have the audacity to be here torturing mine? Both of my grandparents?"

He was around me and up the ladder's steps without an answer—the second step from the top—stretching and clasping the mirror's frame I'd merely touched. He lifted it from its nail and brought down to me what I'd never wanted to see.

"Is this what you wanted?"

"It needs dusted." I wanted to touch the scorched glass, the blackened frame, the lump that caused my breathing to stop. "They all need cleaned." I swiped an arm above my head. "You can just put it near the wall. I'll get to it later."

He carried the mirror to my grandmother's table, my protests mum as I followed and watched him set it on the table's edge against a stack of books. Apologies coursed through my mind as I stepped in front of the mirror. *I'm sorry, Grandpa, sorry Mama…Grandma.* Arched but rectangular, charred, with a burnt lump hanging at the side. I looked inside the frame at the broken silver that had turned coppery.

Dietrich stood beside me, the mirror a vision of the tall and the short, the blond and the brunette, the writer and the runner. Grandma's books filled the background, dull and faded colors barely visible in the glass as I studied us. And then her, Amabile, her smile, her confidence, the love she had for an enemy, the stories that still told of it behind her...along with him. Tall and blond, fine hair falling toward blue eyes. Eyes that loved fiercely from a face that looked furtive. I leaned close, the snaky fissures that turned the background into a puzzle exploding. Color flew at me, outward then inward, pages and flames filling the air. I fell back, I grasped and flailed, grabbing at pieces of our and their lives, fragments that burned as they left my hands and re-sorted themselves into something new. Grandma's books were gone when I looked again. Amabile's stories were gone also. Enemies, instead of being disfigured, were also gone. I leaned close to the glass, to just Dietrich...and me, resting against his arm.

Chapter 54

"Cate!"

I ran hard, my loafers and slacks slowing me and making real speed impossible.

"Cate, slow down!" The voice was closer, and I ran harder, my shoes clapping against my heels. A bicycle pedaled vigorously beside me as Frank pulled ahead. "Are you crazy?" He hammered his feet in a circle as he kept up with my blouse, my slacks, and my loafers.

I was crazy. There were no runners in our family. He leaned into his hand brakes as I slowed then stopped, he coming to a halt not far ahead.

"Is this how you're training now? With some crazy handicap so you can catch up?" He lifted his bicycle and turned it to face me, planting his feet at both its sides.

"I'm not training." I looked at Frank. He felt like a stranger, an enemy instead of a friend. "I'm not running the marathon."

"Because of Jill?"

"No." I sounded twelve instead of twenty-six.

"Good. You weren't supposed to quit because of her."

For her, not because of her. "I have to go. I have some pictures to take." Don't tell Jill hello. "See you later."

"When?"

I shrugged. "I don't know. After the marathon, maybe." But probably not.

"You could still run in it, even if you're not training…properly." He eyed my shoes and clothing again.

There are no runners in our family, so you shouldn't run. They need solid evidence. If it's solid evidence they need, you don't want me there. The mirror, him and Amabile, me and Dietrich…there was too much evidence, things I needed to run from, not to. I shut my eyes against tears, against the finish lines I'd never been able to run to…because I'd been running from more. Eighteen years of exhaustion roiled and began to heave in my gut.

I'd run from Non Bookends, from Dietrich, from his image and mine in the mirror. I opened my eyes and clasped both hands across my stomach. "I have to go." Not my store voice, but not the inner scream that had begun with the explosion.

"I mean it, Cate," Frank called to my back. "You could still race."

I ran. I left behind him, the army, Dietrich, and everything that looked like evidence.

Chapter 55

"What are you doing with that?"

Cate's grandmother appeared; she moved into the broken silver behind Dietrich in the mirror. Cate had been there. He'd seen her. And then she ran, her image lingering beside his until he touched the frame. He should shatter what none of them wanted to see. He should crush the vacuous wood with his hands, destroy any evidence of a love such as Amabile described.

Mavis Crawley stayed back, her image one-dimensional against a wall of books, dusty colors in rows as they had been before, her face and her hair almost ghostly.

"Someone has cleaned this recently," he said to her reflection. He watched the background, waited, wondering how long the mirror had been here and if the reflection would dissolve into something different from what it had been with Cate.

"I...I keep a neat store." Her face was fixed in the background. He turned to her, the real her, as she stared past him into the old frame.

"The pictures beside this had dust on them," he said.

"I can't be on the ladder great lengths of time. I work slowly."

"You've handled this mirror, then."

"Of course. I hung it there. Well, had it hung. I

paid a young man to hang all of these." She pointed above them with a broad sweep of her hand.

Dietrich turned back to the mirror, he in the foreground and she still in the back. "Then you've seen yourself?"

"Briefly." She came to his side, set one hand on the mirror's edge. "Now, if you're quite done, I will hang this back up. Or have it hung back up."

Dietrich let go and stepped aside. "Anything else there?" he asked.

Mavis stared at her image, her gaze traveling from her reflection to behind her, to the bookshelves and whatever else she could see in the mirror. A tiny gleam caught the light, a shiny dot traveling down her cheek.

"Nothing," she said. "When I look in this mirror, I am always alone."

Chapter 56

"I have a place."

That was what he had whispered as he walked her from Hindenburghaus back to her apartment. Berlin's streets were lit up with excitement even in the night. It was the competitions, the surge of pride and German power, the mixture of nationalities behaving as one. Her head spun. Never had her home been this way before, never had there been such brittle gaiety. Brittle yet unbreakable. That's what she had thought, surely.

She stared at the mirror now, at the five carved lilies. There were to be six, he'd said, but then he'd said, no, there would be seven. And the seventh was to be a seal, a promise larger than the one already made, one that would be forever.

"I'll admire it always," she'd told him, but he had shaken his head.

"Carvings are a path to what's more real. After the last carving, we leave this behind. We must. And then we become real. Unbreakable."

She stepped closer to the mirror, searching for what he'd meant. She stared back at herself.

"But..." Number six was their seal of what already was. He said seven would give them what she wanted, he wanted, what no one could deny them forever, even without the mirror. She studied the five lilies, recalling each word he'd spoken with them. Every promise, every

thought that had drawn her deeper and more fully into him.

"I won't leave you behind," she promised the five lilies and the mirror, recalling the words, the ties that bound them. "Even with the real, I'll hold on to you. I'll keep you with us forever. As a reminder of his promise, our love. For him."

The seventh lily—the list…

The room reeked of developing fluid. I set Amabile down and looked away from her cover, her name and its namesake embossed there. I stared instead at the faces and hands around me. Some hanging to dry, others arranged on a board. New York faces and hands, my camera capturing what wasn't visible to the eye, yet really there…like the mirror, like fiction.

I dropped Amabile into my camera bag and left the lab. I walked through the campus building until I burst through the doors to the outside. I glanced up. "Oh, that I could take wings and fly…" David. The Psalms.

"Catharine?"

I looked from the blue of the sky to black—Emerson, black hair and dark eyes four steps below where I stood. I needed warmth. Not a hand on my ankle or steadying a ladder beneath my feet. I needed Emerson's warmth…a fiancé, not an enemy.

"Where have you been?" I stopped on the next to the bottom step.

"Everywhere. I'm exhausted, Catharine." He stayed below me, hands invisible in his pockets.

"You're exhausted…"

"Didn't Miles tell you how much I wanted to be with you at the hearings? I would have been, but he told me to do double-time, spend twice as much time in the public eye, saying nothing about your grandfather but smiling and bolstering confidence in me."

"Your values."

"What?"

The distance between us was an ocean between two continents, keeping two enemies apart. If I stood in front of the mirror with Emerson, would the expanse disappear? Would he and I evolve into a couple? If I took a picture of him right now, would the truth show when I developed it?

"Miles said that customer has been there at the hearings talking to you. He's not a customer, though. He's a journalist from Germany." Emerson didn't need to say more. It was on his face, the link to Germany, the link that linked me to an enemy and severed me from him.

"I know who he is, and it's not what you think. He's not here for the investigation." Or maybe he was. Maybe Amabile linked him to the hearing. I felt cold and hot, an eruption inside, the explosion of all I'd counted on. "But at least he's there." I needed Emerson to cross the ocean between us. I wanted his hands to help me make the last step. I needed him to be at the hearing, even if he sat behind me, several rows, unwelcome but understanding what was happening... like my enemy did. I covered my face with my hands, ran them up and over my forehead, dragging my hair back with them. Dietrich was the one there. Not an ocean away—even though I'd told him to be.

"That's not fair. I would be there if I could."

I stared across the expanse, at the uneasiness in his defense.

"Let's go somewhere, Catharine, get something to

eat. We can talk. We can be seen out and about, happy together. It would take the sting out of any rumors about your grandfather and keep sketchy journalists at bay."

I saw his campaign. I saw red. I backed up the steps, no one holding onto my ankle or the ladder. "You look good in red. I'll have that dress and the other things you've bought for me...no, for you...sent to your house."

The ocean expanded between us, sending my enemy and his protests farther and farther away. At the top of the steps I opened the door and ran back into the building. This time it was Catharine I was leaving behind.

Chapter 57

I stood in the doorway of my grandparents' house. I was the enemy now. I was Judas about to betray the one I'd always thought would save me, and Grandma, the one I always thought we needed saved from. I closed the door behind me and stepped inside.

The house was undisturbed since I'd seen it last, making it easy for me to retrieve and read the unopened letters I'd returned before. I should have asked my mother. This was a crime, opening another person's mail, one more reason for Emerson to be glad he'd stayed on his own side of the sea.

Dad... I stared at my mother's handwriting. *Thank you for the note. I hope you'll send more. And say more, too, but I know that's not your way. I enjoy hearing from you, especially when it's just the two of us. You and me, a pleasant conversation and not a battle.*

I read on, my mother's words like well-placed stones in uncertain waters. I was amazed Grandpa had written her. A note was probably accurate, since the sum total of what he'd ever said would probably fit on a postcard.

I laid the letter aside and opened the next one in line, written a couple of weeks after the first. Mama begged Grandpa to write again. She didn't know he probably wasn't seeing her requests, Grandma likely whisking them away when they arrived in the mail. Mama mentioned two soldiers' names, men she claimed had served with him in France. She wondered if he'd like their addresses so he could write to them, since she'd located them nearby.

The third letter, nearly a month after the other, had her furtive cheerleader tone. She'd met with one of the two soldiers. The man remembered Grandpa, shared a couple of stories with her, and talked about how the accident in Poland made Grandpa a different man. I raced through the comments my mother shared—the hollow demeanor, the lack of Grandpa's original laugh, the haunted look at leaving Europe, and the injuries that forced that. *We called him Stilt, and boy could he make those legs move. Too bad about that broken leg. Fastest man I ever saw. Before the accident, that is.*

Chapter 58

His voice. She heard it rousing her, calling her name with an agonized shout, while other shouts barked and overpowered his. Her name from his lips was a lifeline in the darkness. She tried to respond, but she was broken. Unable to call back, unable to let go of the wood burning against what was left of the front of her dress where she pressed his mirror beneath her. She thought he called from his reflection as it lay mixed within the embers and rubble, beneath the acrid smoke forcing her awake.

She had inched like a snake through tiny flames, searching for his voice. "I'm here," she said, and lay down.

"Amabile!"

His cry was lost beneath the wail in her ears, sirens, curses. His hands touched her, so gentle, the smell of burning flesh wrapping around her own. "The mirror," she thought to herself. Unable to talk, unable to stay in arms wrenched away with threats and more cursing.

"It's too late for her," a voice snarled as she hit the floor, the mirror hot against her again. "Take him out of here. Look what he's done."

She heard him call again, his voice fading with protests, with kicking against the charred remains of what little of her home was left. The only home they'd shared, except for what lay beneath her, and even it crumbling in the heat.

A toe shoved against her leg. "She's gone." She couldn't argue, she couldn't nudge back. Only her heart was still alive as he fought against being dragged away.

She lay alone in the remains—she and the mirror, all that was left of it, of him. Voices and boots pounded around her, but still she couldn't stir. Only her heart. It listened for his call and her name amidst the German shouts and annoyance.

A mirror. She heard the request in his language, and the translation from one of her Polizei. "Nein. Nichts. Kein Spiegel," *another of her police responded. No mirror. Had he sent a friend back to ask for it? Did he want to keep her reflection as she lay dying? Dead, he'd been told. More boots kicked around her. Anger from the man who spoke his language, as "mirror" and his name and words that said surely he'd taken it were spat over and over.*

Their likenesses smoldered beneath her until the building cleared and only the rare crackling of burnt wood spoke.

"That her?" They rolled her to her back, and at last her heart spoke. She stretched her fingers toward the mirror.

"She's alive?"

She was alive where she called his name, where her fingers reached for his mirror, stretching over the charred frame and lumps. Two broken lilies, the rest ashes. Her tears told them what she couldn't, and they understood. "Gently, her and that thing she wants. That wooden and glass thing." They scooped everything, and she held on, one of the lilies burning in her fist.

Dietrich cursed and let the pages Oma had sent drop onto his lap, her revived writing tantamount to a confession, important enough she invested extra money to have it sent quickly to him here in New York. Did she know? How could she? He'd called Monika again, and she swore she hadn't contacted Oma, but said she should. He cursed again. If Oma dared to send him pages so clearly Amabile, why didn't she just say Crawley's name? Say at least one of them was guilty. Then Dietrich could put to rest for Crawley's wife what her ragged heart already knew. And show Cate… He dropped his head into his hands, his elbows on his hotel room's table. It was all true. But how could it be true? Wasn't Oma saying "he" was Crawley and Crawley hadn't left her behind after all but had been dragged away instead, told she was dead? Monika was less illegitimate, then. And Oma could be a traitor, one loving an enemy instead of just being his victim.

Dietrich tossed the letter and the beginning of Oma's new story onto the table's top. It spun as he stood and stared through the nearby window, through cool glass panes, at the piece of New York City below, where Crawley lived. Living proof of fiction.

He frowned at the tiny dots below him. Couples, people walking so close together they looked like one. Something Dietrich had never done. He'd been like the singular dots below…except for that one. One that was small and fast, jetting around the others as if needing to escape. He pressed closer to the glass, a ring of steam where he breathed. He followed the small dark dot, swiping away the fog.

He ran, then. He grabbed his corduroy jacket and

raced from his room, taking the stairs two at a time to the bottom. "Excuse me." He let the woman who'd stepped in his way pass, her fragrance and the glint of jewelry blinding him. The revolving doors spun across the lobby, and excusing himself again, he timed his dart around obstacles and across the floor so he hit an opening at just the right time. Cold air blasted against his face as he spilled out onto the sidewalk. He glanced both directions and turned toward the one the runner had gone. Small and fast.

He never ran. He did it anyway, though, through the crowd, the runner's way.

Chapter 59

I stared at the open spot in the row of framed somethings along Non Bookends' ceiling, where the mirror had been.

"You're dressed rather well. You going out with a friend?"

I turned from staring at the empty space and from the faces I didn't want to think about. "I'm supposed to meet Emerson." I ran a finger along Grandma's table and glanced up again toward the ceiling. Emerson's voice had sounded taut when he called. Apologetic, a man torn between what his heart wanted and what his heart really wanted. "He's coming here to pick me up." A place he couldn't bring my outfits back, a campaign to tie his land back to mine.

"Why here?" Her deep creases deepened even more.

"I was coming here...anyway." I glanced at the folds between her brows. "Where's the mirror that was up there?" I pointed above our heads. I waited for *How did you know it was a mirror* and *What I do in my store is none of your business.*

"It was time to take it down." Grandma lied, her own sort of fiction obvious, to hide a truth instead of divulging it.

"Where did you get it?" *Please say junk shop, antique store, someone's trash.*

"It's not really mine."

"Someone left it here?"

"No."

"Whose was it?" Asking was hard, and I braced for Amabile's, your grandfather's, someone's with blue eyes that could be trusted.

"That's what I was trying to find out." She glanced up at the vacant spot. "I'm pretty sure I know now." She looked back at me, all the furrows and ridges in her face sagging. "Oh, heck, I always knew. Just not everything."

Non Bookends' bells tinkled. Neither Grandma nor I turned. It was dark outside, but the store was open and customers still came and went. I willed them away, so Grandma and I could talk. I willed Emerson to be late, really late, which he never was.

"What did you know, Grandma?" Footsteps traveled around the store, and I willed harder that they would find a book and go sit down.

"*Through the Looking Glass*," she said, keeping her gaze on me.

"Carroll. But…"

"Right." She walked toward her room. I wanted to follow, but I wanted even more for the mirror to be there and for her to bring it to me. To us, to show both of us, together, in a reflection, the real truth.

"There you are, Catharine."

Grandma's back disappeared around the last tower of books. "You're early." I twisted Emerson's way.

"I couldn't wait." That was true. I could see it in the pinch of his brow.

"Grandma was just getting something…" I flipped a finger toward the back.

"Do you want to help her?"

"I think she's bringing it out here." I lowered my finger to the table and tapped. "It's kind of personal, if you don't…"

"Catharine…" Emerson inched closer. "I want you to know how hard this has been on me. For me, too, I mean. Not being together… Getting the clothes I bought for you back that way…"

"We should talk about this later."

"No, Catharine. Not later. Now. It's that important." He came close enough to latch his fingers onto mine. "I don't want you to give back what I've bought for you. They're yours, for always. So please, let's get this settled. Fix whatever's wrong."

He was trying to bridge the sea between us. Not just coming across the vast expanse but hoping to step onto my land. I glanced at the hand that was grasping mine instead of a bundle of hangers, and I thought of all the times I'd laced my fingers through his. "What sort of together do you want, Emerson?"

"Well, the sort we had before. You beside me at dinners, at functions, everyone seeing us as a couple."

"You beside me at my grandfather's hearing?"

The black of his eyes darkened, or maybe his skin took on a slight blanch. I watched his head dip and then rise. "Yes. If that's what you want. But understand that's why Miles was there. He went in my stead, so in a way, I've been there all along."

Grandma rounded the shelves as the front bells clattered again, the glass of the mirror against her. She slowed when she spotted Emerson, then came on, stepping to the table and propping the mirror there with one hand.

"Cate?"

Grandma turned at my name, the mirror turning with her, a panorama of images and reflections gliding past with its spin until I turned also.

"You were running just now?" Dietrich's hair was damp, waves and strands wetted to his forehead as he nearly skidded to a halt behind us.

"No, were you?" I took in the long legs built to run. Legs that were like my mother's, and my...

"I was." There was almost a smile. "I'm certainly not a runner." Long fingers combed through his hair. "But you are."

You're so small. You're not built like a runner. You're not the runner I'm looking for. I stared at my enemy, the one who had brought nothing but horror, shame, and insult to me.

"You should run," Dietrich said.

"He is running." I waved a hand toward Emerson. "And doing a good job of it...at least he was..."

"Not him," Dietrich said. "I mean you should run."

I saw it then, what he meant. Not just should run, but what I should run from. I glanced at Emerson.

"What about this mirror, Cate?" Grandma asked from behind Emerson and me.

"Just a minute, Grandma."

"I'll put it back, then. Another time, maybe."

"Sorry, Grandma." I pivoted, Emerson turning with me. Charred and streaked images stared back at us from the glass Grandma held. I was there—small, brown hair, dressed in nice clothing. But Emerson's reflection was tall and blond, dressed in a corduroy jacket. I swung to where Dietrich stood behind Emerson and me, pressed closer to Emerson, and looked again—tall, blond, corduroy, and a smile. The writer alongside the runner. Again.

Chapter 60

"You were fast. How was it you couldn't move quickly enough to get away from the accident in Poland?"

"I wasn't that fast." Grandpa sat as straight as he could in the witness's seat, the unnatural slant of a man who'd walked most of his life with a limp. McCoy's attorney pressed close with an intimidating nearness.

"Fast enough your fellow soldiers remember that in particular about you."

"Irrelevant." Grandpa's attorney stood.

"Your Honor." McCoy's attorney moved with ease in front of the military judge. "Private Crawley's integrity and character are being evaluated here as evidence. Was he the honest man his attorney presents? Or not?"

"Overruled. You may proceed." The judge leaned back in his seat.

"You ran into the exploded area, is that correct, Private Crawley? A civilian vehicle loaded with fuel."

"I did."

"To help?"

"Yes, sir."

"Explain."

"I was shocked at the initial explosion, then ran when I heard the screams. It was impulse more than thought, but I assumed the worst was past. I didn't think about another tank blowing just as I got close. I was fast in a way, but not nearly fast enough to do what needed done and get away."

"You were the first to enter the area, right?"

"I was the only one. The accident was remote."

"Remote? What were you doing in a remote place?"

"Walking, sir. I was shipping out soon. Just collecting my thoughts, and thinking about France ahead."

"So you were out walking alone. Where was Lieutenant McCoy?"

"Wrapping up in another country. He told me I'd done a good job and to go stretch my legs until it was time to go."

"You ended up breaking a leg, instead. Is that right?"

"No, sir." Grandpa stared down at his lap. I could imagine that leg, long and thin, like a cane instead of a limb. "Not then. That happened in France."

"Okay. So you witnessed the blast in Poland, heard screams, and ran toward the burning truck. A second explosion occurred, one you weren't quick enough to get away from. As a result, you were burned. Tell us about those injuries."

"The second blast burned my arms. Most of the flames from the first explosion were at the rear of the vehicle. I had just reached the cab, my arms shielding my face, when the gas tank itself caught fire. It flashed and burned the shirt off my arms and chest."

"I see. And the leg?"

"I received treatment for the burns in Poland, then further treatment in France. I was still medicated for pain and infection when I made a misjudgment behind a backing vehicle. Wasn't fast enough, again, I guess. My leg was crushed."

"I'm sorry to hear that, Private. Did you make any friends, of sorts, while in Poland? Who helped you after you were injured?"

Grandpa shook his head. "Medical people helped at some point. Then Lieutenant McCoy came to help see to my treatment and have me sent to France. No friends, though. I wasn't there long enough to form friendships, not to mention the language barrier without a constant translator. Nor was there time, with my duties."

McCoy's attorney strode back to his table, lifted a folder, and took it to the judge. "We do have records of such a blast in Poland. All of this occurring August 12, 1936. Nothing left but a charred vehicle, the rest ashes, no bodies identified. Local authorities took over."

The room was quiet. Even Grandpa was still as the judge read through the folder.

"No further questions for now."

Grandpa's attorney stood then and presented identical reports to what the judge had just read but with paperwork included that described Grandpa's stay in Poland and records of his treatment for burns.

"So what did you do during your stay in Poland?"

"I was stuck at the airport and then at a train station when I arrived. Five of us had been assigned there, each to different locations. It was a country on edge, and a US soldier wasn't completely trusted. After I received clearance, I was escorted to my barracks—a room, actually—and told to stay there. I did, until the lieutenant had me cleared for work."

"So where exactly was Lieutenant McCoy?"

Grandpa stared at his attorney. I glanced at McCoy. He didn't move. Only his attorney rolled a pencil between his fingers. "Like I said, we had men scattered all over, doing jobs, most of them in France, a few in Belgium for the elections, and some in Poland. He was working with all of us."

"Jobs designed for a possible war?"

"I wasn't privy to all that our units were doing."

"So McCoy could have been anywhere. Maybe even Berlin?"

"Objection." McCoy's attorney's pencil stopped moving. "It's not Lieutenant McCoy on trial here."

But it should have been. It was his communications those first army officers were investigating, not Grandpa's.

"Let me rephrase the question. Where was Lieutenant McCoy before coming to Poland?"

"I wasn't given that information personally. I wasn't well at that time, so I didn't ask, either."

"Did Lieutenant McCoy have friends or acquaintances in Poland? Did he already know anyone there?"

"He may have. He had at least spoken with them, if not met them before."

"Yet you had none. No further questions at this time."

I glanced at Emerson in the quiet. "Grandpa wasn't in Berlin," I whispered.

His dark brows conferenced in the middle of his forehead. He didn't understand what he needed to, that Grandpa might be freed from a mess that should have been McCoy's, or even Dietrich's, especially if he was never in Berlin.

McCoy took the stand, and his attorney spoke of the information leaked to Berlin, the supposed list that had never been recovered, and of the Aryan-looking American who allegedly relayed and was to deliver it. He spoke of Grandpa's Aryan look and his reputation for being fast, whether Grandpa could slip in and out of Germany and be quick enough to deliver a list while in Poland or Berlin without arousing suspicion.

I'm not a runner. Running's not in our family. You shouldn't run. I'm not fast enough.

"You can see from photos of him he was the Aryan ideal. And he was certainly fast."

McCoy said it like a man under oath, one who knew he was bound to the truth.

Effective if he was shifting the blame to another.

"I'd only seen him do recreational running, though, no racing. Just fun and games the men sometimes did in their off times."

"Tell us what you know about the list...how it was supposedly relayed."

"From someone in the US military, through several hands, until it was to end up in Berlin with the German army. Again, through a US military person."

"Several hands being other nationalities? All military?" The attorney paused and looked at Grandpa. "A woman, even?"

"As I said, an American soldier evidently at each end. The Germans claimed a woman may have been involved, but that was never proven."

"What was this list?"

"It was supposed to be US military names, those supporting Hitler's growing regime. Sympathizers to his Aryan army."

"Aryan. Tall, blond, above average." McCoy's attorney stared at Grandpa. "No further questions."

Chapter 61

"Hallo, Oma." Dietrich waited and listened for the tone of his grandmother's reply.

"Dietrich." Her voice carried a rich quality, courageous like she said he was. "You are home?"

"Soon," he said. "Your writing, Oma, you have done it well." Too well.

"You liked it."

"I confess, I've read some of your other books. You haven't lost your touch."

"Some of my old love stories?" Maybe there was a blush now. "You must think them foolish, a star journalist like you."

Dietrich would have smiled, writing being one of their favorite discussions. But this conversation wasn't about his grandmother's return to what they shared. It was about the one thing they shouldn't.

"This was not quite so frivolous—maybe light—as those stories."

"The story I'm writing now would be nearer to the war. A different tone."

He could hear it in her voice. The difference between comic book love and what was lived. Love that had nearly cost someone...probably her...their life.

"It felt real," he ventured. "Like the war must have felt. Innocent victims caught in danger they didn't belong in." He was putting words in her mouth, words

259

she would need if this trial exploded.

"I missed much of the war."

"You did?" He gnawed the inside of his cheek.

"I wasn't well, as you were sort of aware already."

She never spoke of that time, the same way she never spoke of her furnace injuries that were apparent.

"Your story sounds like Berlin, even if it wasn't during the war. Tell me more about it."

"It is about love. You have no interest in a woman's love story, but thank you for reading some of it."

"There was an explosion or something. I have plenty of interest in that."

There was a laugh in the silence. "The story wasn't about the explosion and what it destroyed. It was about what survived."

What might have survived—that absence beside her, the gaunt man who looked too frail to fill it— wouldn't survive the trial. "You're right, Oma, I'm a man and uninterested in romance stories. I'm curious about the damage. Humor me. Why the explosion, and what did it destroy? Give me the violence, the mystery, even if it doesn't belong in your story, and I promise I'll read the rest and do my best to suffer through the romantic parts." But don't give me the list. It couldn't be what was behind what happened. Oma was an ordinary woman, a romance writer, not a German spy falling for an American traitor, with a resultant daughter.

"Every love has an explosion, something that tries to change the way things are by destroying the way they look, but when love is real, an explosion only mars the view. What's real and important survives."

The mirror. Oma was talking about the mirror along with all the passion associated with it. She'd tried to preserve both in the explosion, coming away in the end with scars, disfigurement beneath her dress, only one burnt lily, and ashes. The mirror was in New York, though. Somehow Crawley had managed to get it out of Berlin. Through an accomplice? The English-speaking person in Oma's new writing? He wouldn't allow Oma to end this way or let that absent presence that had always been at her side come to life here in New York with a confession.

Crawley was a traitor, at the very least in love. And if it wasn't Amabile he tried to save in the explosion, it was the mirror. Where the list may have been hidden.

Chapter 62

Grandpa wasn't in Berlin. Grandpa wasn't a real runner. Grandpa wasn't fast enough—but I was.

I bent my leg back and grabbed my ankle behind me as I balanced on the other foot. I pulled, my thigh muscles protesting, already out of shape.

"Excuse me." Runners around me were doing the same thing and more, all of us nearly knocking each other over. So many, and all so tense, where the marathon was about to start. I stepped away from the start line and lowered into some squats.

"Cate?"

I looked up at Frank, standing for once without a bicycle between his legs. I wondered if he remembered how to walk the way I was remembering how to run. With a finish line in front of me. I straightened and jogged in place on my toes.

"You're running after all? Were you training on your own?"

"Only mentally." I wiped my forearm against my brow. It was a runner habit, and I did it to convince Frank more than me.

"Mentally?" He cocked his head and glanced down at my legs. I could see the concern of atrophy cross his face. "Jill's running." He nodded to the very front, where Jill's bobbing ponytail could be seen flapping above the crowd.

Overachiever. "Tell her good luck." I dropped into another squat.

"You know Jill. She doesn't need luck when it comes to this sport." Frank had that look on his face that told me he wanted to drop down to where I was, look me in the eye, and talk. His knees kept him from maneuvers like squats. I scrunched even lower but saw his face suddenly in front of mine, upside down as he bent to talk without squatting. "What do you mean mentally?"

I shot up out of my near-ground position, past Frank, who looked startled and relieved as he straightened in front of me. "Let's just say I won't be hammering the pavement with my feet anymore. I'm not running like I did." I trotted away before he could talk more or laugh at me, and moved toward the start line as far from Jill as I could get. I was done running futilely and away from things I couldn't change. Today was a race, and I had a goal—I was going to run to win.

I took my place near the start line, a hand raising in the crowd, waving as cameras pointed its way instead of mine. Emerson—his race was more important to them.

Voices amplified by megaphones roared over the excitement, but it was Emerson's voice I heard. Not what he was saying, as he spoke to a reporter who was jotting notes, but what he said when my mental training first began. *Probably good you stopped running and that your grandfather can't.*

A whistle blew and the pistol fired. Emerson's profile as he spoke to the reporter fell behind me and was gone. It was only me now, in the midst of arms and legs, grunts and measured breathing, feet hammering around me while mine lifted and flew.

We were a sea of elbows and shoes, waves of motion moving ahead and falling behind, jetting forward and lagging off to the side. One head in particular stayed above and in front of us all, a hallmark—Jill.

The crowd around me thinned as the race advanced, not just the number of runners but the spectators also as we loped into the middle miles, the long stretch where oxygen and glucose shouldn't be wasted on thinking. *Grandpa was not a runner. It's probably good you stopped running.* Jill and two others were in front of me as we entered the last quarter. *Amabile loved a runner. You're not the runner I'm looking for.* I heard the hammering of my feet as the runner in front of me pulled farther ahead. *Good thing your grandpa can't run.* But I could. I lifted my feet the way Jill's husband had taught me and left behind what I'd been told.

The crowd thickened as the finish line drew near. Voices roared. A light flashed, and then another, an immense flash close to the street. Emerson? His reporter? I glanced to the side and I saw myself. And a journalist instead of a reporter—tall, blond, the arms of his corduroy jacket holding the mirror and a sign: See Yourself—A Runner And A Winner.

Dietrich may have been smiling over the mirror, but it was me in the darkened glass. I saw myself running ahead, a runner and a winner, and...

The man in front of me fell behind, as did another one who had managed to slip past. It was just Jill and me now, and a finish line not far away. I felt the dampness of my shirt, the light yellow likely looking orange now that it was wet, the way rain enhanced otherwise nondescript clothing. It made us see what we really wanted, what we knew was probably there.

Bye, Jill. I ran harder, and Jill faded behind me. So did the finish line as I sailed over it to my own, past the cheers. Grandpa, Grandma, Emerson, and even Dietrich and the mirror, all left behind. The announcer shouted after me, but I couldn't stop. "This is a race and I want to win." From *Last one Home is a Green Pig.*

Chapter 63

My hair hung in perpetual wet, my face in a permanent smile.

I'd run beyond the noise of the throng, the shouts of the announcer, the voice that said it was good I wasn't a runner, until I'd gone far enough the afternoon sun flashed in my face. Like the sun in the mirror my enemy held and the words his sign had claimed. I stopped, then, at the truth of "See Yourself—A Runner And A Winner." I turned around and ran all the way back to where Emerson stood holding my trophy in the air, making excuses to a ring of reporters—but no journalist—why I'd kept running the way I did. He held the trophy higher as I approached. With one arm he gripped my wet waist and with the other he kept my trophy above him where everyone could see it.

I answered questions, posed for pictures, and shook Jill's hand, all the time watching for that glint of sunlight, the one in the mirror alongside the sign that saw the finish line no one else had.

Emerson drove me to my apartment afterwards, his car and the light meal we shared filled with his excited chatter. "I wish I could stay," he said as he cleared a shelf for my trophy. "You rest. And congratulations. Don't worry about being at my speech tonight." I thanked him, but I didn't rest. I showered and went to Non Bookends instead.

The store was quiet, the bells heralding my smile and slick hair, bringing an explosion of excitement when a customer spotted me and clapped her hands. Others joined, like the crowd at their finish line, as I wended my way to Grandma's table where she sat. I thanked her flock and spread my smile the way Emerson did. The way he would continue to do as he ran his race.

"Well, you did it." Grandma looked up at me. "I figured you'd be out celebrating. Or on a stretcher somewhere."

"Were you there? Did you see any of the race?" My grandparents had rarely come to any of my high school events. I hadn't seen Grandma standing near Emerson, and she would never have been near Dietrich…and her mirror. I glanced up at the empty spot where it had hung.

"I saw the most important part," Grandma said. I looked down at her. "I saw Jill eating your dust."

My smile turned to a laugh then, to an open-mouthed gale that broke all of Grandma's store-voice rules. I leaned against her table and held onto my chest, imagining Jill's face as I burst past her and the line and the accolade she ran for that chased after me instead. "Tell me. How did she look?" I wiped tears from my eyes and rubbed the happy soreness from my cheeks. I wasn't used to smiling. Or winning. I bent down and rubbed my legs.

" 'My sad heart foams at the stern.' "

I could see that. I could imagine Jill's face a mixture of misery and rage. "Who said that?"

"Rimbaud."

"I'm not familiar with him or her."

"Him. And that's probably okay. But that quote suited Jill's expression." And it suited Grandma's...in the past. Tonight she had the rare smile...very rare. A sad heart peering from beneath the gaiety, making me realize it had always been there, sad beneath angry foam.

"I'm sorry," I said to her thin smile above the rage-coated hurt. "Tell me, Grandma. Please."

She peered at me. She glanced around Non Bookends, past her books and the quotes she had attached to the shelves. "There's one love. If it's not you, you're the enemy of that love, and his enemy as well." She braced herself on the table and stood. Her hands trembled as she did, possibly for a man who may have carved wood into lilies for her enemy, and into splinters for his.

"I had to stop running, Grandma. Today I raced for the first time, and I did it to win." I glanced around Non Bookends. "Like you're doing here."

Grandma shuffled instead of marched away from her table to the back of Non Bookends. The door to her little home-away-from-home closed softly behind her.

I walked to the center of the store, where Ibsen reigned. I glanced at his plays, at Nora, at his women who were strong even when they were weak. At the questions I'd come to ask and the answers I'd come to learn, about enemies and about hearts.

The seventh lily would be hers someday. She saw it in the mirror and in his eyes. He would carve it and he would bring it, and he would run when he did. The mirror showed him running when he claimed running really wasn't what he did. It showed the lily in his hand, close and then far. And finally, her non-runner

crawling, crawling, the love still in his eyes.
Grandma—nonfiction.

Chapter 64

Dietrich had seen a runner, not his own reflection, as he lifted the mirror from Non Bookends' wall where Mrs. Crawley had had it rehung. He teetered at the top of the ladder, and he stared. He held onto the charred wood and the singular flower that framed the runner as he guided himself to the floor. Mrs. Crawley had gone to watch Cate run, and when she did, Dietrich took the mirror.

He'd snatched paper as he ran, a large piece, and a marker, hurrying to his car and toward the finish line.

Mrs. Crawley stood opposite where Dietrich was, her eyes the direction the runners would come from as he watched from behind the first layer of spectators.

Dietrich faded farther back into the crowd, found a place where he wouldn't be jostled, and worked the back off the mirror. Wood splintered around the old nails, loose nails that he worked out with his fingertips to remove the board. The back of the cracked silver was opaque and dull, blackened where the scorching had penetrated. He ran a finger over the glass. It was clean. He held the mirror to the light, studied behind the glass—nothing, no list, no hidden compartment, just empty and clean. If there had been a list there, it was gone.

The noise of the crowd intensified, and shouts and clapping hurried him as he refitted the back and worked the nails at slight angles in holes that were too large. He penned what he'd seen in the mirror, and keeping it and the poster close, he threaded himself through the crowd.

He watched where everyone watched, over their heads, stretching above them to see but not enough to catch Cate's grandmother's eye. He saw her, then. The little runner, a small dot, a growing figure, tiny but powerful, maintaining a position near the front. More than just a runner. She really was a winner. He glanced down at the mirror as the excitement grew, the noise increased, the runners neared. A runner and a writer, there they were, together in the glass, one waving to the other.

"Go! Go!" The noise was deafening, and Dietrich looked up, he broke free from the crowd's yells, slid through the wall of spectators, and held the mirror where Cate could see.

And she did. She saw something in the mirror that reflected on her face. Every muscle glistened, hardened, and transformed the tiny runner into a thing of beauty. He held onto what he saw as she sailed past. The noise was deafening, thunderous as she cleared the finish line and ran on. That thing of beauty disappeared. He stared after her, where she'd gone. A beautiful enemy.

Chapter 65

"Private Crawley was never assigned to Berlin." Lieutenant McCoy spoke without emotion, never taking his gaze from Grandpa's attorney.

I watched McCoy. I wanted to glance over my shoulder at Dietrich. I'd tried to ignore him when I entered the trial. If I turned now, would what I didn't want to hear, what was being denied on the stand, be there in his eyes…eyes that had held the mirror and the sign and smiled at me? I fidgeted with my fingers until Emerson laid his hand over mine.

"Therefore, it is your belief he was never there," Grandpa's attorney implied a conclusion.

"He was assigned to France and Poland. No other place."

Two men—one a traitor to the United States, the other a traitor to a lover. Two different countries, also, so one wasn't Grandpa. Maybe neither was. Emerson pressed harder as my fingers twitched.

Grandpa's defense attorney rehashed Grandpa's time in Poland, the evidence he was there based on work he accomplished and the explosion he suffered. McCoy affirmed everything the defense said. But the list…and its presumed trail from Poland…McCoy's stolid composure took on an air of apology for what might have happened under his watch, any tainting on the army. Yes, there was evidence information leaked from Poland and made it to Berlin, and likely through the hands of an Aryan-looking American.

I glanced at Grandpa, at his back, at the mountain ranges his shoulder blades created in the shirt he wore. I thought of Amabile's runner and of the runner in the mirror Dietrich had held. I could feel Dietrich behind me, over my left shoulder, far to the back, yet close, close enough to hold a mirror and a sign encouraging me to look and win. I slid my hand from beneath Emerson's.

It was the army officer in him that gave McCoy enough backbone to not give in to slumping as more and more evidence something had happened within his unit came out. No finger pointed at McCoy, but the invisible charge was there. Failure showed in his bearing as Grandpa's attorney drilled it in. McCoy was no match for the indications one of his soldiers had let our country down.

"Where is the proof?" Grandpa's defender charged. "The list? A direct tie from Private Crawley to this supposed channel from Poland to Berlin?"

It was McCoy's attorney who ended up answering that question with his witness who had been slow to arrive. The man from Poland who had identified Grandpa in an old photo. "Please bring Mr. Borowski to the stand," the prosecutor said when it was his turn to show evidence.

Everyone turned at the sound of the doors in the back. I turned also, as did Emerson. A beige spot to the far right had to be Dietrich as I watched the guard escort an almost slovenly, bent, older man to the front, followed by a well-dressed man I assumed to be a translator.

"What do you think about this?" Emerson leaned into me.

I looked at Emerson, the black of his hair, his concerned profile, and shook my head.

The Pole was led to the front and shown how to be sworn in, the process slow and in duplicate as his translator repeated and interpreted what we saw. *Our love story told in many tongues as I read into the night.* Once he was seated, the questioning began. I listened as McCoy's attorney created the setting, established credibility, and zeroed in on a photo different from the one we'd already seen, one of Grandpa's unit, a sea of gray with creamy-white faces, tiny circles amidst the blur of uniforms and background. The Pole was offered a magnifying glass. He took it but didn't use it as he studied the picture for a long time. At last he pointed.

"*Szybki.*" Mr. Borowski looked up, his finger on the photo. The attorney twisted as he looked where the man pointed.

"Fast," the translator said.

Fast, like a runner was. Like I was in the mirror Dietrich had held. My image had stood out, even against the sunlight's glare, even within the mottled silver. I ran as a winner, and I ran fast, someone in the crowd cheering me on. Someone like the one holding the mirror. Someone smiling, like the face above the mirror, here to write about a runner. I'd looked ahead then—saw the finish, felt the medal, heard the encouragement, and ran.

"Mr. Borowski has indicated Private Crawley." McCoy's attorney took the photo, thanked Mr. Borowski, and laid the picture in front of the judge, showing him which face was Grandpa's. "And Mr.

Borowski has referred to this person as fast." The attorney looked at Grandpa. "Fast enough he could cover a lot of ground without being missed. So fast, it was impossible for even his commanding officer to know he'd gone. So blond, you will note, that he would be admired instead of suspected in or by Germany."

"Speculation." Grandpa's attorney stood.

The judge was speculating in the silence as he stared at Grandpa's photo. I could see the deliberation in his thoughts, feel it in the pregnant pause. "Strike those comments from the record."

I couldn't. And neither could Emerson. His shoulder edged away from mine. He was running, running for the senate and running to outrun what Dietrich said he couldn't. It was me Dietrich had said should run, should run away.

McCoy's attorney fell into a litany of questions that painted a historical picture of my grandfather back then—according to this Polish man's memory, tall, quiet, blond…and *szybki*.

The runner raced across my mind, the one in the mirror.

"I need to go," Emerson whispered. "That talk I'm giving." We'd driven separate cars. The shoulder that was already far away disappeared.

The runner kept going, the glint of the medal catching the light as she did.

Chapter 66

I focused on my feet, aware of Dietrich, as I filed out of the trial. I glanced up, then down. I couldn't see it, I didn't want *I told you so* to be on his face—now that Emerson had left and my grandfather seemed a criminal. Up, then down, I looked and then didn't. Up again, until he was there. My feet stayed to the center of the aisle and moved me toward the courtroom's door, my jaw clenched, a horrid fascination at seeing what I couldn't stand to see…the man above the mirror, his smile for someone's triumph.

"I would like to speak with my grandfather." I hurried out of the courtroom and spoke to the guard.

He stared down at me. "I will check." He summoned another officer, and I was led away before Dietrich could appear behind me. I hurried after the guard's long stride, knowing I could outrun him, no matter how difficult it was to keep up with his walk. He led me through hallways, desks, and other army officers stationed at every juncture until at last I was stopped, checked, questioned, and stripped of everything except my clothing by hands and faces without warmth or life. No camera, either, but even it couldn't have penetrated the stony expressions I passed as I was led into the last fortress that kept Grandpa from the rest of the world.

This room was different from his other in location only. Otherwise it was the same as that one, and as his living room the day the army first came—square, plain, with no signs of living or life. Even Grandpa's demeanor had taken on what the walls and the soldiers outside his door had.

"Grandpa." I entered, my escort coming with me. I turned to him as he planted himself in the doorway. "Can we be alone, please?"

His gaze traveled from my empty hands to Grandpa's empty room. He yanked back his head in what looked like an armless salute, then stepped outside, closing the door behind him.

Grandpa. I only thought it this time, not trusting my voice, not knowing if it would break with tears or with violent accusations—tears at what the army said, accusations for what he may have done to Grandma…and my mother, and me, and Emerson. I glanced at the closed door behind me.

The mirror showed him running when he claimed running really wasn't what he did. It showed the lily in his hand, close and then far. And finally her non-runner crawling, crawling, the love still in his eyes.

"You didn't need to come."

I turned at Grandpa's voice, to the tall stick of a man who towered over me, the scarred hand that supported him on the cane.

"I'm here, so let's talk." I waved an arm at one chair while I took the other, both cushioned but so hard they were like fabric-covered boards. Grandpa eased himself into his, repositioning several times. He was too thin. If the bed in here was the same, he'd be a solid bruise before he got out.

If he got out.

"Grandpa…did you do this? And I want a real

answer this time."

He'd never had much life in his face, maybe none, but he had less than none now. I stared past the empty look, through the accusations and the question of guilt, beyond whatever they decided, to the man who was always on trial.

"Like I said before, that is for the judge to decide," he finally said.

"So you did, then." I kept the scream out of my voice, the slap out of my expression.

He propped the cane in front of him, anchored two scarred hands over its top, and leaned into it, repositioning himself on the hard seat. "Did what, that's the question."

"You tell me. You tell me what you did."

He stared at his hands. "I'll tell you what I didn't do, Cate. I didn't do anything like they said. I did not generate, initiate, or forward any traitorous information in or from Poland. I did what I was supposed to, and that's all. What I had to do. I'm not even sure who that man was they had on the witness stand. Of course, it's been around forty years, and he was one of hundreds of Poles, while I was a single American soldier. Much easier to notice me, I suppose." He looked up at me then, with his blue eyes, his white hair hanging straight over his forehead.

"Why, Grandpa? Why don't you stand up and make that clear?"

He could be cleared of two charges—the US Army's and Amabile's, since he was innocent in Poland and never in Germany. I scooted to the edge of my seat in a resurgence of faith in him. There could be hope. Even for Grandma, if everything everyone said was a lie, fiction, stories other people told, tales that suited them.

His face didn't change. His expression remained staid, but his eyes spoke. They whispered. Choices flitted in their glistening sheen of blue. *The love still in his eyes.* Even as he crawled. Grandpa shook his head, glimmers of life fading with his focus back on his cane and his hands, and the scars that striped their backs.

I stood. I wanted to touch those mountain ridges of shoulders beneath his shirt. I wanted to slap them, too, and jar to the surface what I'd seen in his eyes. "I'll be back, Grandpa."

In. His. Eyes. In. His. Eyes. Amabile's words marked each of my steps as I left Grandpa's room and marched down hollow tiled halls. In. His. Eyes. In. His. Eyes. I'd seen it. I'd seen something the night Grandpa told Emerson and me to make our marriage right, and now I'd seen it again, even if for only a second.

"Thank you," I muttered to the guard I passed as I stepped outdoors. It was sterile, cold, lifeless, just like the inside…except for whatever had shown itself deep inside Grandpa. I resumed my cadence down the sidewalk and to the parking lot, listening to the slap of my shoes on the pavement.

White paper, like a flag, fluttered beneath my car's wiper. Emerson, an excuse wrapped in an apology, most likely. I snatched the paper and wadded it in my fist as I climbed into my car. The engine roared as I hammered the accelerator, the growl settling to an even purr as I let off the gas. Grandpa's eyes…I had seen love. Love that hadn't died along with everything else. It was still crawling.

I dropped my head against the headrest and stared

at the bland fabric covering my car's ceiling. The fabric melted into a colorless pool of tears.

I wiped my eyes and reached for the gearshift, the white paper a ball between my palm and its handle. I leaned back in my seat again, stared at the paper, then opened the first fold. And the next, and another, until Emerson's note lay open before me.

There was the house they bought. The home she made for the two of them, but especially for him. He smiled at the way she lined his silver utensils beside his plate, thanked her for the way she organized his tools. She kept his favorite chair crowded with soft pillows and flanked by a place for his glass, his glasses, and whatever he chose to read. It was her stories he read if she laid them there, and when he did, she smiled. They lived this way, the years changing his blond strands to white, and her brown waves to silver.

That's what she saw when she looked in the mirror. It was all there. It was the looking glass to her heart. And his.

Not Emerson.

Chapter 67

There was nothing significant in the newspaper about Crawley and his trial, not even something Randall had written...yet. Randall said the real evidence hadn't made it to the courtroom yet, but he'd refused to elaborate. Dietrich rolled the paper like a club and stood up from the hotel lobby chair. The army wouldn't make their business public, even though the trial was open to anyone now. Randall wouldn't make it public, either, until the time was right. The little runner's fiancé was no doubt grateful for this silence, a silence that might be short lived. Randall was waiting with whatever it was he wasn't telling Dietrich. And he wouldn't tell. Good journalists didn't. Dietrich tapped an open palm with the tube of paper. That's what made the good ones good—they discovered things without being told.

Dietrich walked to the desk and asked that his car be brought up from the parking garage. He showed his ID and his International Driver's License. "Yes, sir," came the clerk's response. Dietrich thanked him in German and strolled to the large glass revolving door at the front and waited. Crawley surely had that list. Or had once had it. Dietrich tapped the paper on his palm again, wondering if that was what Randall knew. That list could settle almost everything for Crawley...almost. That list could also destroy him—and Oma, if she knew of it…and Cate, the little winner.

****

"Your mirror," Dietrich said. It was early enough Non Bookends was open, but still empty other than Mrs. Crawley, at a new coffeepot sending a scent into the air that blended well with words on yellowed pages. She didn't turn. He carried the mirror in one hand and her ladder with the other.

The empty space on the wall above where he set the ladder was white, a rectangle that was whiter than the rest of the wall around it. He glanced back at her, the coffeepot sputtering. She looked, but didn't have to speak. The white spot said what he wanted to know.

"I'll put it back." Holding the mirror to one side, he worked his way to the top steps, where he balanced and ran the mirror up the wall until its wire caught on the nail. "There." He came back down and glanced above them. "Good as new." And it was. Inside, where it had been cleaned, and the wall that had been protected behind it for years.

He returned the ladder and found Mrs. Crawley waiting for him near her table, a cup of coffee held in his direction.

"Thank you." He took the cup, and she held onto hers. They were enemies yet comrades, victims and warriors surrounded by the written word. "Cate did well in the race," he said through a cloud of steam.

"I saw you," she answered.

He took a swallow of too-hot coffee. He'd done it numerous times in similar situations, and he knew how to keep the wince from his eyes. "*Guter Kaffee*," he said. "Good coffee."

"I always expected someone to come. And it's you,

not them. Not the military."

Dietrich looked at her—at the bitter exhaustion, the frustrated relief. An unsteady furrow that was anxious for the final thrust of the dagger.

"I knew the moment I saw you and heard your accent. You are too much like him." She eyed Dietrich, up and down, his tall and lean form, the crown of blond hair. But someone else's waves.

"I'm not your husband's relation. I know that."

That didn't assuage her anger. The look on Mrs. Crawley's face burst into flames, the blaze in her eyes could have fired both of their cups of coffee to scorching temperatures.

"And I have nothing to do with the German military."

She set her coffee mug on the table. "He expected the military. I didn't see that, all these years." She looked at Dietrich, her question there in her look—what did he, Dietrich, want?

"The mirror..." Dietrich didn't look up.

Those two words were all it took to turn her dread to truth, fiction into fact. Steadying herself with one hand on the table, she inched around its side to the upholstered chair behind it. She backed into the seat, halting as if age had suddenly come upon her, dropped to the cushion, and looked up. "Who is Amabile?"

"She was a writer in Germany around the time of the war, and the 1936 Olympics. There is thought..." He paused. He couldn't say it even if Oma essentially had. "She may have written under another name, her real name, but then her work changed. She must have, too, because she changed her pen name to Amabile."

Mrs. Crawley slumped in her chair. "I always knew

fiction was that way. It's an honest way to write, really. Not cowardly. The only lies are the truths we wished weren't." Like her marriage. Dietrich saw that on her face. Years of rage erupting, and she was letting it. She didn't need him here. She wasn't even looking at him. Her eyes were on the life she'd lost, the years she'd been robbed of, this store no balm for the rejection she'd suffered.

Dietrich set his cup near the coffeepot, turned, and looked at the woman staring at nothing except the past. "Why did you let him hang it in here?" he asked.

Her eyes refocused for a moment from the battle she'd been fighting for years. "He didn't," she whispered.

Chapter 68

Red swollen eyes stared back at me, dried out from reading—Amabile—every word of hers I could find. I bent over the sink and splashed water across my face, sorry eyes peering back at me over my towel. Too many words.

I brought my face closer to the glass, brown eyes, not blue, not flickering like my grandfather's had for that brief moment. The outfits Emerson had returned reflected behind me, hanging over my bedroom closet door.

I left them there, showered and dressed, grabbed my purse and camera, and headed out the door. I had a deadline, one I was about to cross over like I had the finish line.

Saturday mornings were quiet in the journalism building where my photo lab was. Bleary-eyed grad students, grasping coffee cups with unsteady grips, nodded as I passed. I disappeared into my lab, tossed my bags aside, and seated myself at the large table, where an array of faces stared this way and that, everywhere except at me, in angles intended to capture what lay behind the eyes.

They were children. She saw them in the mirror, each bent over opposite sides of a puddle. Blond strands hung down from his forehead as he gazed into the water. Brown waves framed her face as she stared down also. The puddle tremored at the surface, a tiny frog diving in and streaking across the middle, finally burrowing into mud at one side, a place he thought safe from the intruders. The reflection below them shimmered and waved, a vibrating distortion of eyes and noses, mouths, and hair. She didn't look up, and neither did he, the water holding them there until at last it began to clear and features fell into place. She bent nearer the surface and the reflection that smiled back at her. Yellow hair, a faint smile, blue eyes offering a safe haven.

I shook Amabile from my head and rearranged photos, saying their names out loud to keep Amabile away.

Courtrooms, bookstores, and reflections all disappeared. I aligned Emerson's black hair and his professional demeanor with a nearly hairless older man, one whose profile I'd snapped first and afterwards asked if it was okay to use it. I paired familiar faces with unfamiliar, matching and contrasting their expressions and hands, creating a cinematic swirl of New York, its inhabitants, their lives, past and present.

I stood and stretched, looking down at the display. I stepped farther away until the photos blended and blurred, studied the shading more than the subjects, catching clusters of too-gray next to too-black, and thought how to re-sort to balance the scheme. I came back to the table and made my adjustments. I stood close, the way Amabile and "he" had stood over their puddle, looking down at the faces and hands below.

Gazes stared around the room—my grandmother's eyes, and my mother's—amidst faces that were full or empty, hopeful or hurt. And Emerson's—black holes for eyes, artificially livened by smile lines. I took a step back and panned the table's surface. My grandfather was there, a three-quarter profile, a glimmer of what would be the blue of his eyes. And above his eyes and to the left rested my enemy, the one with the mirror and the sign, a quick shot of Dietrich I'd taken outside Grandpa's courtroom, snapped straight on, without his permission, quick enough to catch what was there before realization set in. I stared at the face I wish I'd never seen—blond hair and no smile. I bent closer...in those hazel eyes, I saw something familiar—something I realized could have been blue.

Chapter 69

"If they manage to put Crawley in Berlin…"
Randall stopped talking to Dietrich the moment
Dietrich spotted me and gave his reporter friend a quick
shake of the head.

Crawley in Berlin. I looked at Dietrich from behind
his slimy companion. Amabile could put Grandpa there
if fiction became the testimony, as an illicit lover on top
of being called a traitor in Poland.

"Good morning." Randall grinned his hello,
twisting his upper half my way as he leaned against the
hallway wall outside the courtroom.

"Excuse me." Dietrich stepped around Randall. He
took me by the arm and kept me moving down the hall
away from his friend. I looked back over my shoulder
at the grin. *If they manage to…* I glanced at Dietrich's
profile. There was no "if" to him. Dietrich could seal
my grandfather's fate—a lover as well as a traitor, if he
tied Grandpa to Berlin.

"Stop." I turned to face him.

"We can't talk here." He stared down at me.

"We don't need to talk. I'm here to listen. But I
can't to you." No one engaged an enemy except in
warfare. I pivoted toward the courtroom, caught short
by long fingers and a corduroyed arm.

"I saw them, Cate." He spoke in a whisper. "I
didn't mean to. I don't even want to. At least I think it

was them." He let go of my arm. "In the mirror. They were together…he was tall. Blond. She was smaller…" His hand came toward my hair but stopped. "Hers brown. But it's silly, isn't it? Ludicrous? Living by imaginary images and silly stories?" He shook his head. He backed away, turned on his heel, and hurried down the hall.

I watched him. Fast. I'd seen it too, once in Non Bookends' window, then in the store, and again at the race. Tall and blond behind the mirror, small and brunette in what he held. A writer and a runner.

I staggered to the courtroom's door. The guard smiled, called me by name, and opened it for me. Miles was there, thread perfect next to where I always sat. I slid down a line of seats several rows behind him, choosing one where it would be too banal for him to twist and look.

The sounds of people coming in created a background of whispers, pardon me's, and creaking seats as everyone sat. I touched my hair where Dietrich almost had. *If they manage to put Crawley in Berlin.* Loving an enemy, betraying his fiancé…maybe his country. The faint fragrance Dietrich wore rose from my sleeve where he'd touched it. Loving an enemy could ruin Grandpa. Loving an enemy could ruin a fiancé… I turned, and he was there. Gazing back at me with hazel the same shade of blue Amabile saw in "his" eyes. The same shade reflecting in mine.

Chapter 70

"They got the wrong man." Randall leaned close to Dietrich as two officers led Private Crawley from the room. It wasn't Crawley Dietrich was watching, it was Crawley's granddaughter. Dietrich glanced away from her tiny back to the reporter's half-cocked smile beside him. Randall nodded his head and arched a brow toward McCoy as the lieutenant stood.

McCoy. Dietrich watched Crawley's commanding officer, ashamed he was doing it for the first time, the way he would have looked at him, or should have, had he been doing a real job instead of…he glanced again at Cate and thought of Oma…whatever he was doing. And whatever that was it had landed him on probation for refusing to come back to *Der Spiegel* when he was supposed to.

McCoy was tall, possibly brownish hair at one time…hard to tell, with age and the cap. Dietrich thought back to the photos he'd looked at when he believed this was a data situation only, not an emotional one. Years ago, it seemed, certainly too long for his employer. McCoy stood erect, shifted from one side to the other, shaking hands with both attorneys.

Cate stood. Miles did, also, a few rows ahead of her and turning as if he had known she was there all along. Miles was almost as good as Dietrich was…or used to be. There was nothing on Emerson's campaign manager's face. No regret, no false assurance, nothing to help the small runner he looked at. Dietrich counted the rows between him and the suited stick figure at the front. He could cover them before Miles knew what hit him.

Cate stepped along her row to the aisle and marched straight to the front, where the minor reporters sat. There were three of them. Hacks from local papers, just doing their jobs. Lepers, in Miles' world, untouchables he stood back from as Cate slid in beside them. Miles brushed his hands down the front of his jacket and was gone. Cate got to her feet, leaving the reporters with nothing as she walked down the aisle, past him and Randall, and disappeared through the door.

Dietrich looked back at McCoy. A commanding officer's word against his private's, meager evidence available but enough they'd led Crawley away, even without the list. If this charge stuck, Crawley could be convicted as other war criminals had.

"You go on. I've got some work to do." Dietrich slid around Randall. He threaded between the seats along his row until he hit the aisle. He turned and withdrew his journalist ID. It was time to actually meet Crawley.

Chapter 71

I needed to sit in Grandpa's chair, in his place and in his shoes, terrified that I shared his situation, his guilt.

Hazel eyes stayed with me as I drove to Grandpa's house, my heart racing along with my car, my memory of winning, the mirror, and him above it...and in it...Dietrich. My face heated as I crept over the speed limit, steering with one hand while my other slid over the warmth of my cheeks and my neck. Dietrich was the enemy. I pressed harder on the accelerator. No one could love an enemy.

Cars filled Grandpa's drive and the street in front of his house. Uniforms dotted the yard, his porch, and both doorways, another in front of his garage. Every one of them turned at the noise my tires made as I screeched to a stop. Erect postures became even more rigid. Eyes trained my direction the way rifles would have. I let off the brake and hit the gas.

Whatever they decided. I roared toward Non Bookends, hearing Grandpa in my head but with my voice. That was guilt speaking, an enemy hidden in the heart.

****

More cars surrounded Non Bookends, uniforms posted at each door. Cameras flashed on the sidewalk, and I recognized one of the reporters I'd sat briefly near after Grandpa's hearing, waiting for Miles to disappear. I gunned down the street to the first open parking space and yanked in. Crooked, like my family was, apparently. I slammed the door behind me and raced to Grandma's store.

"I'm family," I announced to the soldier at the front door. Family for better or for worse.

"ID?" He stared down at me like he would an insect.

"It's in the car." I waved an arm down the street behind me.

"She can come in," a man called from inside. "That's Private Crawley's granddaughter."

The soldier stepped aside, and I entered, brushing past a uniformed man I didn't recognize but who apparently knew me. Grandma sat at her table in a store teeming with milling men instead of customers. She waved me over with a finger. I grabbed an extra chair and dragged it next to her, and we sat.

"Grandma?" I whispered.

"You Catharine Elizabeth Hunt?" An officer stood in front of me, a notebook in his hands.

I nodded.

"I have some questions for you."

I nodded again.

"Would you like to go somewhere private?"

Grandma did what she never did. She grabbed my hand, hers icy and cold around mine below the table.

"I'm fine here."

The officer balanced his notebook on one hand and wrote with the other, taking down boring details like age, birth date, address, things I was pretty sure he already knew.

"My turn," I said, surprising him. "Who are you, and what are you doing here?" I felt Grandma's hand squeeze mine—warmer—a thank you.

"I'm asking the questions here." He glanced over his notebook at me, a face that was chiseled the way the army's buildings were. But life appeared behind his stony expression. I saw it. And he felt it when I did, a tinge of red darkening his cheeks. "But since you asked, and you will see with the rest of my questions, we're searching for evidence in your grandfather's case."

"What sort of evidence?" I thought of the mirror above us—high, ugly, ridiculously absurd in their sort of investigation. Just like the stories around him that would insinuate enough to redden all their faces.

The officer cleared his throat. "Are you aware of any correspondence your grandfather may have kept, especially from his term in the military?"

I stared at the eyes peering down at me, the notebook's bottom edge now butted against his stomach. They would find the letters I had found at Grandpa's house. "Some mail to and from my mother," I said, grasping Grandma's hand as hers loosened. "There might have been another letter or two with those." In the attic, where Grandma would be livid to realize I'd nosed around. In the garage, where the army would think it odd to store correspondence. "But they're at the house, not here. Grandpa never came here."

The officer frowned as he wrote what I'd said. "Never?"

There was a commotion near the back, and one of Grandma's authors hit the floor. The officer turned that way, but not as fast as Grandma.

"Are those men going to manhandle my books?" Grandma came to her feet. "They are old, and some are valuable, and I will certainly bill you for damages."

I came to my feet alongside her as the officer excused himself and walked to the back. Voices and words as regimented and nonsensical as they'd been that first day at Grandpa's house rose from behind shelves. "They're after a list," Grandma whispered, her head turned toward the commotion.

"I know," I whispered back. "I doubt it exists, but they sure won't find it here, if it does."

Grandma glanced at me. "No," she said, her head doing one slow shake. "They certainly won't."

Chapter 72

It was late in the day when I finally stood in front of my grandfather's chair. I had to set the cushion back in the seat...all the cushions, in fact. His home and his garage looked like a tornado had hit, quite different from the way Non Bookends looked. Grandma had insisted a reporter follow her as she dogged the men opening and closing her books, jotting notes along with the journalist, making mention of the damages the army would be responsible for. The army left Non Bookends pristine.

I dropped into his chair and into the narrow groove his thin shoulders and hips had carved. I was exhausted from the army's questions about letters I'd been asked to identify, and tools, furniture, and kitchen items I'd had to put back. *Did you find what you were looking for?* I'd asked the person in charge at Grandpa's house, the "Whatever they decide" creeping back as I faced the man. Harboring an enemy. "Confidential information," the man had said.

I levered the handle at the chair's side and leaned back. I stared at the ceiling Grandpa must have stared holes through for years. Betraying his country? Betraying his wife? Like the hazel in Dietrich's eyes calling me to betray my mother, my grandparents, and Emerson.

The yellowed white of the ceiling told me nothing,

like pages without words. Sitting in his chair didn't either. I knew what was right. I wasn't the sort of person who followed whims, who lost track of my purpose by falling for an enemy.

I righted Grandpa's chair and stood. I wasn't a traitor. After a glance around Grandpa's house, I snatched up my keys and started out. I belonged at Non Bookends...with Grandma.

****

I heard his voice before I saw him. The store was quiet except for his voice and hers. "Emerson?" He was in front of the table Grandma sat behind, she in the same chair she'd been in earlier today, the one I'd used still next to her.

"Catharine. I heard what happened here today. I came to see if you were all right."

I glanced at my watch. It was too early for the news program Grandpa's story might be on. And nothing about it would make the newspaper until tomorrow. There was the neighborhood, though, the local gossips...and Miles. "You just now heard?"

He came to where I stood, set his hand on my shoulder. "You look tired. Both of you do. Can I run out and get you some food? Coffee?" He wrapped his arm around my shoulder. I needed close. I needed it all the way to my toes.

I glanced down at my toes and waited for close to reach them. Emerson was holding on, but not to me. He was offering me coffee, but not the sort of warm I needed. Slipping from Emerson's grasp, I found "close" in the chair beside Grandma, warmth in her hand I'd held earlier. "You want anything, Grandma?"

"Oh, you know how I am," she said with more

push than I expected. "I settle things by being busy, not eating." She squeezed my hand for the second time today…for the second time in my life…and stood. "I can make some coffee here. How about the two of you?" She looked from me to Emerson, then back at me. "Well, I'll make a pot anyway, and you can have some if you like."

Grandma created background noise to our silence—water, coffee can, grounds being scooped. I crossed my legs, studied my nails. I pinched my leg where he couldn't see. *Get hold of yourself. No enemy.*

"There, that's started." Grandma came alongside Emerson, tired—more tired than the fists planted on her hips denied. "Let's see. What can I do while that's brewing?" She glanced around her store. Not a book was out of place, no evidence any had been handled by brutes. "Maybe something it takes a man to do," she said. She went to the back of the store and returned with her ladder. "I would have died today if those army men had thought to look up."

" 'The herd looked everywhere but up,' " I chimed. "*Little Hippo.*"

"That's right." Grandma smiled. She braced the ladder against the wall, holding it with one hand. "Emerson, you're nice and tall. Would you mind climbing up there and bringing down two or three of my pictures? I'll dust them off, and you can hang them back up."

"Well, I…" Emerson glanced at his watch, another "close" calling to him, then at me. "Of course. Where do you want to start?"

"Those first two above the ladder will be fine."

I watched Emerson scale the small ladder. He

really was tall, but not as tall as Dietrich. I pinched my leg again, even harder. *No enemy.*

"That's good. That's fine," Grandma coached from the floor. Her nerves must be shot. I'd never seen her so kind. "Now, Cate, you take them from him, so he can come the rest of the way down without falling."

I walked to the ladder. Emerson handed down a picture...and the mirror. I glanced at Grandma as I reached for it.

"Good, good. Now I'll grab my duster. Just take a jiffy."

I frowned after her, a picture dangling from one of my hands and the charred mirror from the other. It took more than a jiffy. Emerson dropped from the last step to the floor, and Grandma still wasn't back. I shifted my load.

"Here, I'm sorry. Let me take one of those." Emerson took the mirror, and I looked at my fingers, expecting black sooty grit, but there was nothing. I frowned at my clean hand, then at the mirror's blackened frame.

"What sort of look is that, Cate?" Grandma waved her duster at my nose.

"Are you all right, Grandma?"

"Better than you, it seems. Busy is medicinal. Here, you take this duster, and I'll get another." She shoved the feathers into my free hand. "Get that one cleaned. I'll be right back."

I toted the picture to Grandma's table and held its top with one hand. Tiny strands of feathers and dust floated in the air as I swiped at the wood and glass.

"You're probably not supposed to beat the picture. Here, let me." Emerson propped the mirror next to the picture and took the duster from my hand. He ran it over the frame I held, the glass in front, the paper behind. I was mesmerized by his slow movement, by his diligence, by his non-sweaty run. "Now this one." Emerson angled the mirror my way as he dusted the wooden back. I heard Grandma's footsteps as the reflection in the mirror caught my eye. It was a puddle, me on one side and…I frowned…Emerson on the other. He was a boy, but his black hair gave him away. The mirror shifted as Emerson worked the duster around the top and sides. "Not sure why you keep or clean something this old," he said to Grandma. I stared at the girl and boy from the new angle. The water rippled, then it cleared. Emerson ran the feathers over the glass and the two of them, wiping from top to bottom.

"Do you see them?" I asked.

He looked up at me. "See what?"

I glanced back at the mirror. I, as the girl, stayed bent over, my reflection gazing back at me. Emerson, the boy, leaned closer, staring into blank water, his face not there.

"Done with these. I'll put them back." As Emerson took the mirror away, the boy disappeared. Emerson toted only me to the ladder, me, the puddle, and my reflection.

I looked at Grandma, asking if she'd seen, without asking.

"That's probably enough." She picked Emerson's duster from the table. She had seen, in a way that said she'd seen being left behind before. "It's late. Maybe I'm more tired than I thought."

Emerson balanced on the ladder's top, stretching with the picture as a young reflection of me dangled from his other hand. "There," he said after both were returned to their places, the mirror a glare of light again. "I need to go anyway, so good timing."

The older Emerson was about to do what his young reflection had—leave me standing where I was. I listened to the clatter of the ladder as he returned it to the back, and the dusting off of his hands as he reappeared. "Catharine, did you want to go?"

I looked at Grandma, who stared up at the mirror, then at Emerson. I nodded toward Non Bookends' front.

"Goodnight, Mrs. Crawley." Emerson followed me. We wended our way through towers of novels, just like I'd been doing most of my life, except this time I took his hand and held it until we reached the front door.

"I can't go any further than this with you, Emerson. Not anymore." I was Ibsen's Nora, and I planted a kiss on his cheek and stepped back. Our fingers slid apart, my engagement ring left behind in his hand.

Chapter 73

Cate looked different in the subtle light. Dietrich stared across the table at her, studying a face that had begun as nothing more than a bookstore clerk and a woman too small to run.

Lounge noises whispered around them—the tinkling of glass, hushed conversations, people Dietrich would have been logging every detail of...before. Before Monika, and now Cate. Other faces and other conversations became a muted background to the details of the little runner's features, the graceful God-given contours framed by hair like Oma's, and the terrified expression born of shock like his.

She stared at the diminishing steam rising in the low light above her coffee cup. He twirled his cup of tea. Scotch might have done both of them a lot more good, but she had chosen a comfort drink instead of a comforting one. He did the same.

"I have to know the truth," she said at last. She looked up.

He stared at the hand he wanted to reach across the table and hold. He wanted to give instead of take for a change. He should have read more of Erika Müller's books instead of Amabile's. Maybe then he'd know how.

"I can't believe I'm coming to you for the truth." Her face scrunched. He was her enemy, no matter what.

The conflict was undeniable, he'd upset her world. "I think I have all of the pieces, but then, I don't." She grasped her head with both hands, gazed at the table, then dropped her arms back into her lap. "I've fallen into one of Grandma's stories, like in Carroll's *Through the Looking Glass*, some strange world. It's absurd. I don't want to believe it, yet it seems more real than what I was living."

Dietrich settled back in the cushioned seat, glad they had chosen a private booth far from the din, the shallow but cultured din the hotel's lounge offered. He wanted to be alone with this woman. He was as frightened of the truth as she was. But he was more frightened of the truth he felt hammering inside as he looked at her.

"So tell me. Who are you?" She stared across the table at him.

"I am Dietrich Schmidt, a journalist from Berlin. I am also grandson of Erika Schmidt, the well-known German author of romance while still Erika Müller, before she married my grandfather." He toyed with the handle of his tea cup. "Also known as Amabile, I'm afraid, the name she used for the last stories she wrote." Is writing…such as what he'd last left for Cate after the hearing.

The enemy's shock was evident as she pressed back in her seat. "And you were or are looking for Amabile's runner…"

"I was."

It was as if a ghost passed between them, taking the color from her face, the life from her body. "Because you found him…"

Dietrich spun his cup, staring at its rotation. "I

believe so."

Grandpa? The question never made it from her eyes to her mouth. He nodded, and they both sat in silence, cocooned by happy voices, suggestive tones, the cheer that came with sparkling glasses of alcohol.

She had been his enemy too. He stared at her, at the runner he had come here to deny along with her grandfather. Enemies weren't supposed to have souls, only lists of what they'd done and hadn't done, so they could be written off—by his words, by his pen.

"Are you sure?"

He heard the tremor in her voice, the last thread of hope as it mingled with his memory of her grandfather's sobs when Dietrich had spoken with him. *I'm Dietrich Schmidt, grandson of Erika Müller,* Dietrich had said when they let him into her grandfather's quarters. The old man's eyes sparked. A grasp at a lifeline like was in Cate's now. Crawley nearly fell into his chair, trembling with every move. *I'm a journalist in Berlin.* Dietrich had been honest, to temper the shock he saw in the old man, the faint feeling of knowing, like Crawley's wife had. Dietrich's words, the realization of knowing, were nothing in the dawning surge of *She's alive!* Dietrich had seen in the sobbing man's eyes.

"I don't have a confession from him, if that's what you want. Only concession. I wouldn't write an article based on concession, as a journalist. But if I were a novelist…"

A waitress appeared with fresh coffee and a new cup of hot water graced with an unopened tea bag at its side.

"Thank you," Dietrich said, and the young woman

nodded and left.

"When? How?" Cate asked.

"The Olympics. Hitler's Olympics." Dietrich had shown Crawley the copy of the photo of him with the team, the only photo out there, as far as he knew. There was probably a copy in Randall's hands, also. Randall was too keen to let any detail escape. He looked at the world through a microscope.

"He ran in the Olympics? My grandfather?" Awe, a little pride, cut through the horror on Cate's face. He felt the energy jump to her legs—the little runner, the Olympic medalist she was related to. Evidently the two had never met, even though they'd lived near each other all of her life.

"And medaled. Bronze."

"Are you sure?"

Dietrich had intentionally left all of the hard evidence in his room. Cate was too brittle to withstand a hammering of truth. "I don't know the whole story..." Yet. "But I saw a photo. It's him. With the team."

Cate fell back farther into her seat. He could see the facts spinning in her head. If Crawley was in the Olympics, then he was in Berlin...which meant he maybe wasn't in Poland the way they'd been told...it meant someone was lying. About something.

"But his scars...his leg..." She was jumping through the evidence, looking for the lie that would make all of this go away. "He was seen and injured in Poland. Isn't that harder evidence than a novel and a grainy old photo?"

"I haven't looked into your grandfather's whole military history." He kicked himself mentally. He had slipped so far from who he used to be. Randall would never have beaten him to any conclusions if Dietrich hadn't become emotionally involved. The edge that made him the best reporter in Germany felt soft around the perimeter. "If he was in Berlin, then he could still be innocent, at least based on what evidence they have. He could have just handed the Germans the list if he was there, since his looks favored their ideal."

Cate's eyes widened. "I knew it! I just knew it. Why he doesn't just tell…" It was easy to see the truth dawning in her brown eyes. Evidence that had been conjecture was cementing fast. "Grandma…" she whispered to the table. She looked up. "For her. Because of her. Because he didn't love my grandmother…"

Dietrich shook his head, a nod of sorts. A marriage of bodies, but not of hearts. Like Oma's must have been. He sank back farther into his seat. He hadn't wanted someone stealing Oma's heart, then running away. Even with her recent story where her lover came back after the explosion, it would have been more satisfying to believe it was to salvage the mirror. But it wasn't. Crawley's tears had told Dietrich that was wrong, even though the evidence hung on the wall of his wife's store.

Dietrich leaned forward, resting his elbows on the table. "You won't see me for a while."

She stared at him. He peered at and through her expression, hoping for what he wasn't sure he could see. He couldn't think around her any more than she could around him. He couldn't see the heart of Crawley because of the man's granddaughter. And Cate couldn't see her true grandfather while an enemy remained nearby to blame.

"You're leaving?"

Dietrich stood, extended a hand her way. She gazed at it, kept a steady stare on it as he wrapped her fingers in his. The warmth of her skin felt alive. He'd imagined what this would be like. He pressed her hand and helped her to her feet.

"I have work to do," he said to the face staring up at him. Without her distraction and with his rival—Randall.

The unsteady look she gave him was a goodbye. His feet remained beside the table as his heart and his promises followed her out the door.

Chapter 74

"Are you sure, Grandma?" I glanced to my right at Grandma—rigid, fixed on the road ahead, the mirror in the backseat behind us. I took her silence as the best "yes" she would give me and kept driving. To see her husband for the first time, right before the final hearing, with the one thing that could prove one of the crimes he might have committed.

Whatever they decide felt right—they, not Grandma. "Are you sure you don't want me to tell you the evidence so far?"

She shook her head. "That's none of my concern. Just drive."

She didn't flinch at the sterility of the army compound, merely extracted the mirror from the car and marched alongside me into the square building. Our footsteps echoed in the tomblike hallway, announcing a new regiment was approaching, fast.

"Private Crawley, please." I showed my ID and Grandma's, her hands full with the mirror. A nod was our answer, and a young officer stepped up to escort us to Grandpa's room.

"You have visitors." The officer knocked, opened the door, and entered. "Family." He stepped back out and looked down at us. "You can go in. Keep it short." He indicated the watch on his wrist.

I wanted to run—run the other way, and run far

without stopping. I couldn't watch the final dissolution of my grandparents, the conviction of my grandfather by army and family. I couldn't watch Grandma exact vengeance on the man who had brought war and the wrong kind of love to her door her whole adult life.

I entered ahead of her, giving her one last chance to change her mind and leave the mirror in the hall outside the door. "Grandpa? It's me." I saw the lean, bent form in the shadows arching forward, his weight supported by the cane. "And Grandma." The form straightened. I tried to stay between them, but Grandma was impossible to stop. She charged around me, into the room, flipping on a light as she did.

"You can go now," she barked at the soldier still holding the door. "This won't take long."

He nodded at Grandpa, then shut us in, us and the mirror.

I saw Amabile's story all over again as Grandpa spotted the mirror, the deep-down flicker I'd noticed before, but brighter now. Grandma and I disappeared as time took him backwards, his face transforming from old and haggard to young and alive—then to terrified, and lastly to nothing, except guilt. Grandma didn't raise the mirror as I expected her to, and shake it in his face. She let it hang in front of her, between them, the charred frame and lone lily all he could see.

I stared at the trembling finger that stretched and touched the blackened wood, scars this man probably deserved exposed at the cuff of his sleeve.

"I believe this is yours." Grandma's voice was low. I'd never seen them this close together before, never seen them face each other. But I'd seen the mirror between them forever without knowing it was there.

Grandpa withdrew his finger, leaned into the cane, and took a step back, his eyes never leaving the mirror. "I'm sorry, Mavis."

"Sorry. Not so sorry, I suppose, you'd like to look in it." She didn't lift it so he could.

He did want to. Even I could see that. The youthful passion flowered for a moment. He shook his head. "No." He stared down at the frame the way I would a coffin being lowered into the ground, a racking goodbye over the scream for resurrection. He hobbled a step back, then dropped into a chair, the cane landing in his lap.

Grandma's chest swelled and collapsed, in and out as she stared down at the man—her husband—hatred filling the room, a hatred so powerful no book, no crusade, no character's similar plight could make up for it or make it better. I braced myself, ready to snatch the mirror if she lifted it to smash over his head.

"How did you get it, Mavis?" he asked.

I watched Grandma's chest. In and out. In and out. "It came in the mail," she said, her chin high.

"The mail?" Grandpa looked up, the blue of his eyes bluer. "When? How? Who?"

"It came from Germany, years ago, when our daughter was tiny."

"Not McCoy." He shook his head. "And that young man really was...and she is...and there really is..." Color surged through his skin.

"Then you know who. He was almost who I expected." Grandma stared at Grandpa, surely seeing the same thing I did but hating it. With one last heave of wind, she marched the mirror to the door and leaned it against the wall, its back to us, so no one in the room could see what we all saw anyway. Grandma came and stood beside me, both of us watching Grandpa evolve before our eyes.

Everything he might have seen in the mirror, or maybe did at one time, flashed across his face. The past was there, the explosive rebirth igniting him from within. "Anything with it?" He looked up at his wife.

Grandma snorted, loud enough even the guard should have heard it from outside our door. The purse that had been dangling by its handle from her wrist was in both hands now, clutched against her like a life support. Grandpa evolved, while she devolved, the two of them spiraling through a silent journey of hatred. And love.

"Nothing," Grandma whispered at last. "Let's go, Cate."

Grandma didn't let go of her purse, so I grasped the mirror's charred frame and followed her through the door. Grandpa said nothing as we did. He left us to our brittle march back to the car, Grandma's shoulders drooping lower as we went.

I laid the mirror in the trunk, instead of the back seat, and slammed the lid shut. "You all right?" I came around the car to where she leaned against her door. It was a stupid question, following a war she'd been right in all along. She bore the scars of that battle, many from me.

"McCoy..." The hardness she was warranted in her eyes became glassy, shiny enough my reflection swam there.

"The enemy, in my opinion. Grandpa's commanding officer. He brought these charges." Preferred them. Over charges against himself. One set of charges Grandpa may still be innocent of. Maybe…

The sheen in Grandma's eyes deepened.

"We don't have to stay for the hearing. We can go." I put a hand on my grandmother, seeing and feeling the hot and the cold of a woman who had finally confronted her enemy. A strong woman made weak.

She released the clutch hold she had on her purse and fished around inside it. Gray and white came out, a neatly folded square she balled in her fist as she snapped her purse shut. "Let's go back in," she said. Grandma was armed for anything…even tears.

****

We slipped into a courtroom of faces familiar to me but strangers to her. The seats where Miles or Emerson would have sat were empty, freed now from us, their enemies, to stand on values of their own. I trailed Grandma past them down the aisle, letting her choose where we would sit—new seats, unmarked with memories of a fiancé who hadn't cared and his emissary who cared even less.

Randall's nod was more of a smirk as I stole a glance where Dietrich always sat—had sat. I turned my back on the leer and on Dietrich's empty seat.

Grandma and I sat without speaking, her stony coldness and my rock hardness impermeable to the hushed voices and footsteps moving behind and around us, to the opening and closing of the courtroom door. Yet I listened for him amongst them—my enemy. While we watched for the one who had destroyed the woman beside me.

The room quieted as Grandpa was led in and then McCoy from the opposite side of the front. Neither looked at the other, and neither looked at us. With minimal formality, McCoy's attorney presented his final argument on why my grandfather was a traitor, filling in as best he could around the lack of real evidence. Grandpa's attorney capitalized on that lack when he finally stood, turning Grandma's knuckles white as she clamped down on the wad she'd pulled from her purse with one hand and her purse's handle with the other. The white spread as Grandpa's attorney mentioned the missing list over and over. I glanced to my side, a half glance at Grandma's profile, at the war on her face, the lift of her chin, the set of her jaw, and her fists holding on.

"Do you need a better handkerchief?" I whispered, nodding at the off-white crumpled in her fist. It looked worn, for someone who never cried. She glanced down at her hand.

As suddenly as they had started, they were done. We looked up to Grandpa being led to the left through a door and McCoy to the right. I stared at the empty area in front of us that waited for a decision, shutting out the sounds around and behind me, refusing to hope for a German accent, German footsteps. Refusing to cry like I wanted.

"Soooo…" Stale cigarette smoke filled the air as Randall's face appeared from behind Grandma, at her far side. I nudged her with a warning elbow, pinched her sleeve, and leaned the two of us out of the smoker's encroachment. " 'I'll be a father to him and he will be a son to me, unless he breaks the laws of man…then he will undergo man's punishment…' Man's more likely harsher than God's, don't you think?"

I peered around Grandma and wished spitting was acceptable as I glared at Randall. "You read the Bible?"

I gripped Grandma's arm.

"Well read, well written." His smile morphed once again into a smirk. "I'm good at my job, so let's pray this judge is good at his."

"I doubt you ever pray." I leaned back in my seat. I held tight to Grandma and stared straight ahead. At nothing, at where the judge would eventually appear. I hated Randall. Hated the images he was creating in my head. Maybe I hated all reporters and journalists.

"I mean, without tangible evidence, a judge who tripped over his dog this morning, burnt his mouth on hot coffee, or argued with his wife might come back with any sort of retaliation…I mean judgment. Harsher than warranted."

"Excuse me." Grandma stood, her purse and the wad clutched tighter as she slid past me toward the aisle.

"Grandma?" I reached at her unsteady step as she nearly stumbled out of the row. "Grandma!" It was a whispered shout as I stood, then turned back to the snake behind us, imagining laying my purse solidly against the side of his head. "Now look what you've done." Grandma was clearing the door as I hit the aisle, leaving Randall's satisfied expression behind. Tall appeared at my side, beige corduroy, as I stopped. He stopped beside me. And I looked up.

Chapter 75

Two men led Grandpa back into the courtroom, one I'd never seen before. His attorney was not with them. I turned to Dietrich, sitting behind me, and stared at a face that knew something but told me nothing, the strength of his hand around my arm having brought me back to my seat. I ignored Randall, the smirk lounging beside Dietrich keeping the air ripe with the stench of old cigarette smoke. Randall's legs and knees extended into the back of the seat where Grandma should be. I glanced at the courtroom door—still no Grandma.

I scooted to the edge of my seat and swiveled toward the aisle. Something was wrong, and it was Randall's fault…probably Dietrich's too. I rose. A hand grasped my arm. Again.

I glanced back to where hazel eyes and a corduroy jacket shook his head at me. "Stay here." He jerked his head toward Randall, a grunt coming from him I took for agreement.

"But…"

Dietrich's hand tightened, and I sat as McCoy was led out with two men, neither his attorney.

I had no one to ask if this was military procedure, if this was how they presented the verdict, the whole progression of the case having seemed more like a novel than a procedure. Dietrich's face burned in my mind as I watched, bringing up other questions—*Where have you been? What have you been doing? When are you leaving?* Even if he'd never really be gone…

I listened to doors and focused on footsteps, anything that belonged to Grandma instead of the men behind me. The silence teemed with more questions than answers, so I stood. Enough was enough.

"All rise." Doors opened at each side of the courtroom, and I stayed where I was, Grandpa's attorney entering from the left and McCoy's from the right, Grandma trailing Grandpa's from behind.

I gasped. Grandpa surely did also as he turned Grandma's way. He stared, tightened, then looked down at his hands clasped on the table. His attorney led her past Grandpa to the small swinging gate to where we were seated. He opened it and let her through. She glanced at me, a gaze so brittle I thought she'd crack, then took a seat at the front on the aisle, and set her purse at her feet.

I sat. We all sat. The white was nearly gone from Grandma's hands as she crossed them on her lap. I looked from them to the judge as he called the room to order. "New information has come forth," the judge said. The hammer of his gavel exploded in the room. He laid it aside and reached over the front of his bench to Grandpa's attorney, who handed him a crumpled wad, white and gray…Grandma. "We have been presented with the missing list."

My eyes were too wide as I stared at Grandma's back and what little I could see of her face as the judge pried it open and flattened it. New information—Grandma's final revenge. It was the story Randall had wanted and had baited her for. I locked my hands into one solid fist. I'd pummel the slimy smoker—and his companion who'd insisted I sit instead of running out to find her.

Grandpa was called to the stand, sworn to an oath, his cane taken from him and set in front of where he sat. Pictures I'd never seen before, faces and names that meant nothing to me, smiled from an overhead above. This evidence couldn't be in Grandpa's favor with Dietrich, Randall, and Grandma behind it.

The white from Grandma's knuckles went to Grandpa's face. He paled as his attorney asked him to verify himself in the picture at Hitler's Olympics. I knotted my hands tighter. Grandpa in Berlin, at the Olympics, like Dietrich had said. He and the list, both? Grandpa muttered an answer to his hands beneath McCoy's attorney's rise to his feet, his objection the judge dismissed, and the drop back into his seat. Had this line of questioning already been discussed and the process decided? I stared at Grandma's motionless back and leaned forward, farther away from Dietrich and the snake.

Grandpa was told to answer clearly from now on. He tried. Pieces of his life dislodged as the ugly truth of his betrayals came out. We saw him with his medal, we saw him without. We saw him with the athletic team, and then we saw them without him, a man named Carlson in his place, a sick runner Grandpa had startlingly been allowed to run in place of—because of his Aryan resemblance, McCoy's attorney stood and suggested. He was dismissed again. Randall made a noise behind me.

"So you were in Berlin?" Grandpa's attorney asked.

"Yes," Grandpa conceded. Confessed. I looked at

Grandma again and thought of the mirror, of Amabile, of all the years her anger had infuriated us.

"When?"

"August first to sixteenth."

"You weren't in Poland for that time period?"

"No, I wasn't."

"Were you ever in Poland?"

"I was. August first, with the other five that went to Poland, but I was sent straight to Berlin until the sixteenth. Then I returned to Poland August seventeenth to nineteenth."

Another picture appeared where we all could see. Another gasp slipped from me, an even larger one from Dietrich behind me. Grandpa stared and Grandma's shoulders dropped as a woman not dissimilar to me smiled down at us.

"This is Erika Müller, taken before World War II began," Grandpa's attorney said. "You knew her as something else, didn't you?" He looked at Grandpa.

McCoy's attorney was the only one not staring at the lovely face looking down on us. He was frowning at Lieutenant McCoy, who didn't move beneath the woman's gaze.

"Amabile," my grandfather whispered.

As Grandpa's attorney pried, what Grandpa knew and what he didn't surfaced. He knew McCoy had shipped him to Berlin alone, telling him it was for prewar information gathering, top secret, and Grandpa was to pose as a runner because he was fast. Slipping him into the races became easy when Carlson developed food poisoning. Grandpa took his place, dressing in civilian clothing and doing whatever he was told. Except for falling in love...with Amabile, with the woman McCoy told him to woo while information was being passed through her. She was no one to Grandpa, just a job, until he met her. Then she was someone, and the mirror he'd been told to give her as a gift, carrying the list he wasn't fully aware of inside, became precious. He added his touches to the mirror, small lilies he'd carved at Hindenburghaus, the housing unit where the Olympic athletes stayed.

"And you won your race..." Grandpa's attorney stated in a question. Grandpa nodded, more of a weak shrug. "And you won Erika Müller's—I mean, Amabile's—heart."

Grandpa drew in a deep breath and turned from Amabile's face to Grandma's, the pain on his surely a reflection of what I couldn't see on hers, and of what I felt in Dietrich's taut stillness behind me. "I did."

"You were supposed to pretend to, according to McCoy. Was she a German spy? A traitor working against her own country under that pseudonym?"

Grandpa had never moved quickly except in the Olympics. And now. He was on his feet, keeping his balance with his hands on the wood railing around him. "No!" His voice thundered throughout the room. Dietrich fumbled for my shoulder, latched on to it like it was a lifeline, the way Grandpa held on to the railing in front of him.

But Grandma... I shrugged away from Dietrich as I stared at the lone woman, feeling her disgrace at the rejection being shouted from the witness stand, a testimony of her being unloved. I loved and hated all of them. Especially Dietrich, whose grip, and whose tremor, cheered only for the woman on the screen.

"You're sure of that?" Grandpa's attorney waved

him back down to his seat.

Grandpa sat. "She had no idea anything was hidden in that mirror. Neither did I understand it, until the day of the blast."

The room became liquid, dissolving around me as Amabile's stories came to life. They could have played the cinematic version on the screen above us, Grandma, Grandpa, Dietrich, and me the only ones knowing what would happen, and only Grandpa knowing why.

Broken up by thin protests from McCoy's attorney, the questions and Grandpa's answers cemented this new guilt and betrayal for all to see. McCoy had been furious when Grandpa admitted to loving Amabile. He had warned Grandpa to sever ties or risk being court martialed for his part in treason. "I never was a real runner," Grandpa whispered. But Grandpa ran then, ran faster than he had in the races. Ran for Amabile's, where she waited for him, waited for the last lily he'd carved, the promise he would take her to France, to cement forever what they'd only unofficially performed. She was in danger. He knew that much from McCoy's threats, but as hard as he ran, he was too late. She and her building exploded in front of him in the attempt to scrap the whole espionage plan, destroy the mirror Amabile had longed to keep, throwing him backwards, disorienting him, but not enough to stop him. He ran into the heat, crawled through the flames, calling for her, searching for her to drag her out.

"They told me she was dead." Grandpa stared at her smiling face above us. "I was dragged out of the building, my arms on fire from pawing through the rubble until I found her limp body. The German police treated me like a foreign thief. I didn't know their language, only the words I'd learned from her."

"Then what happened?"

"McCoy confirmed she'd been killed. It was my fault. I had not only caused her death, I'd also botched my assignment. I didn't care when he had my medal stripped away and my name obliterated from the Olympics to cover our tracks. I agreed with his lie that I'd taken money and bribes to run and win. I didn't care. He had to clean up what he could of the mess I'd made of transferring information. I had to atone for killing Amabile. Erika." I saw the regret in his eyes as he glanced behind me at Dietrich. I saw it vanish as he looked at her face again, knowing now that she'd lived. I saw something worse than regret as he looked away from Amabile and glanced at his wife. "And I made a bigger mess of things when I came home and hurt more people who didn't deserve it."

His attorney paused, appropriately, allowing Grandpa's confession to be aired for the wife Grandpa stared at. "And so the list was in the mirror."

Grandpa nodded. "I think the plan was that the mirror would be stolen. Erika meant nothing to them. She meant less when they found out I'd become involved with her."

"And the mirror was here all this time."

Grandpa looked at Grandma. He hadn't known until today. His attorney prodded him to agree, but Grandpa said nothing.

"It has been in your wife's bookstore."

Grandpa looked down at his hands. Grandma had placed Grandpa in Berlin, shown he was part of a military crime, yet he said nothing that would incriminate her.

"Tell us about Poland." As if enough shame hadn't been there for Grandpa to face.

"Orders," Grandpa whispered, staring at his lap. "I had to do my part to salvage what I'd messed up."

The attorney who had been pacing back and forth in front of Grandpa paused. I could feel the quizzical pinch of his brows. "Orders? Your part?"

Grandpa shook his head. "Erase that I had run. Remove any chance of suspicion."

"By going to Poland?"

Even from where I sat I could see the red ring around Grandpa's eyes. "McCoy staged a fake fire, showed my face around, and ran me through their hospital for burns I'd received in…" He glanced up at Amabile's face, then back down again. "That was his part. I was to break my leg."

My gut lurched.

"You what?" Even Grandpa's attorney couldn't hide his horror.

"I broke my own leg. In France."

I fell back in my seat.

"No further questions. I call Lieutenant McCoy to the stand." Grandpa's attorney held his cane for him while Grandpa struggled to his feet and stepped down. No further questions were needed. Grandpa's broken limp to his chair said it all.

Chapter 76

Dietrich watched the little runner slump. Wilt was more like it, years and years of pain she didn't understand, her grandfather's past, and a self-inflicted broken leg, insufficient atonement for all that had happened to him and all the harm he had caused.

"Not guilty." The gavel hit the judge's bench.

Crawley's attorney had summed up by reading the names on the list, one of which was McCoy's, and promising the mirror would be brought back in. Crawley was being released from the charge of betraying his country because his name wasn't there, but now the whole world knew about the other betrayal, which his wife had lived for years.

McCoy was led out of the room to await a hearing of his own. Crawley might be dragged in as an accessory—in fact he likely would—but the final decision would be far less painful than what it would be against McCoy. And far less painful than what Cate's grandparents were suffering now.

"I hope they hang him." Cate's small shoulders tightened more as the door closed behind McCoy.

People stood up around them, reporters rushing forward, the crowd filtering out. Dietrich turned to Randall and nodded at him. "You were right. Thank you."

Randall leaned close. "They were married...or

thought they were. Pretended, more like it. I spoke with your grandmother."

Dietrich felt the gape. He never gaped, and he did his best to keep from it now even though it had been there in Amabile's stories, the insinuation that a tie had been formed.

"Your grandmother's cousin did a little private ceremony. They intended to make it official in France. So you've got an aunt somewhere." Randall knew who and where, but from his cesspool of journalistic tricks, he chose an honorable tact instead.

"So you're why Oma started writing again…"

Randall grinned.

"And them?" Dietrich nodded toward the Crawleys. "Do they know about the daughter Oma had?"

"They should. I gave Crawley's attorney what I had. He just needed the list to end it, break everything loose for the army and in Crawley's life."

Dietrich appreciated the distinction Randall made between himself and the lowly hacks, who wouldn't have been so kind or so thorough. Randall had his story, though, so he was content. He'd told Dietrich the rest of it late last night, Randall's last paragraph finished once he'd baited an embittered Mrs. Crawley enough to cough up the list he was sure she must have. A list he'd concluded could save her husband. All that remained now, on top of criminal procedures, was watching McCoy be exposed for contriving to poison an Olympian's food, destroying a private Polish gas tanker—along with Amabile's apartment—to cover up his own military crimes, falsifying dates and records in Poland, and endangering soldiers as well as civilians.

Randall ferreted out dirt for the sheer pleasure of being able to, making a show of being smirkingly disappointed when something wholesome came with it.

Cate remained in her seat, alert, intent on the cluster of newsmen around her grandfather while still watching the back of her grandmother. Dietrich heard Cate sniffle, fished a handkerchief from inside his jacket, and extended it toward her.

"He really did love an enemy," she whispered. She turned to Dietrich, stared at him.

"He loved two, actually, but in very different ways." Dietrich moved the handkerchief closer, a white flag. "Enemies surrender sometimes," he said. She stared at the white, then at him as she took it.

"Grandma?" Cate rose to her feet, Mavis Crawley on hers, maneuvering down the aisle. She stopped at their row, stared at her granddaughter, then nodded at Dietrich. He rose with them, saying what he could in a look before she continued down the aisle and out the door. She'd just given her husband over to Dietrich's family while giving the man freedom from all charges at the same time.

"She's the real story," Randall said. He stood, bringing his aroma of reporter's smoke with him.

"Don't you dare," Dietrich warned.

Randall smirked. "Journalist's honor. But her story tells it all. It's what novels are made of—heroines that save the hero, even when he's barely been heroic for them." He smirked again and walked out the back.

"I don't know what he means by that, but he's wrong to speak of my grandparents that way—or in any way." Cate glared where Randall had gone.

"He's right, actually, but he won't talk ill of them

in whatever he publishes."

Cate whirled.

Dietrich raised a hand. "Listen to me. Your grandmother has finally written herself into her own story, and she's a real heroine...an enemy surrendered." Like Oma, who surrendered her heart to write a final chapter to show Dietrich the truth that she cherished and set her lover—all of them, actually—free.

"Surrendered?" Cate shook her head. "And heroine? The only thing she got out of today was shame. Public shame."

"And she wore it well." Dietrich stared down at Cate. "She gave up revenge and took the shame. A last heroic effort after years of wrong. Even more wrong than she'd thought."

Cate dropped back in her seat. Her grandfather was being taken out of the courtroom. He would be a free man before long. "I don't understand," she whispered as Crawley disappeared behind the door.

Dietrich walked to the aisle and stepped into Cate's row. He sidled between the seats until he stood above her. "The one thing my grandmother held onto in the explosion was the mirror, even though it was little more than charred ash. It was part of him. By the time they moved her, no one was around who would know what it was, and they felt sorry for her and brought it to the hospital along with her, probably figuring she would die anyway. Your grandfather meant to take her to France, where he would marry her, even though in his and my Oma's eyes they already were married. But he intended to confess to your grandmother first that he'd fallen in love with another, and break off that engagement to free her."

He gauged the little runner, the fragile power he didn't want thrown off course again. Details about the mock wedding and the daughter that resulted might be too much. He'd save it for later when her finish lines were clear again.

"Your grandfather thought Amabile was dead after the explosion, and my grandmother knew nothing about what had happened to him. Much later, when she was well enough, she found an address for him here in New York and sent him the one thing she believed he could look into and come back to her. The mirror.

"Your grandmother received it. She was actually right all along when she said your grandfather was different. He was. And the mirror seemed like a piece of the puzzle he'd never told her. He couldn't because of McCoy's threats, and the guilt your grandfather carried. Tracking the sender, your grandmother eventually put a literary name on the mirror and began to seek out my grandmother's books. It took time, but she found Amabile, and they told what she had suspected and feared.

"By the time the army came around, something she didn't expect, she began to figure out what no one else did, except for Randall—the mirror was part of another plot, too. She removed the back and found the list. McCoy had it put there and used your grandfather to carry it to my grandmother, telling him to pretend to woo her so she'd hold on to it, and then the German army would steal it from her. Roughly, if they had to. Your grandfather figured that out and ran to save her, but failed.

"Your grandmother held onto the mirror, waiting until she was sure she could use it as her final blow to your grandfather. The army investigation baffled her at first, but then she realized it doubled her chances for revenge because of the list. Except it didn't have your grandfather's name on it. It had McCoy's. If she'd held onto it, your grandfather would have ended up court martialed."

"But she didn't." Cate stared at him. "She could have, but she…"

"Took all of the pain on herself instead, even after being told how deep his relationship had gone with my grandmother. Your grandmother turned in the list knowing it would help him, even though she had to sit there and be publicly disgraced."

"She forgave him? After seeing what I saw in his face in his room before the trial, and everything else she found out today, she forgave him?" She looked at Dietrich. "My mother won't believe this. For all her efforts to fix our family, she never understood this one thing. None of us did…until Grandma."

Dietrich lowered into the seat beside her, reached for her hand, and pried the handkerchief free. He waved it in front of her face. "Your grandmother." The white came close. "And your grandfather. He loved two enemies, and she loved one. They both faced that today and they both let go."

"But the seventh lily…he still had it, I think…"

Dietrich dropped the handkerchief and took Cate in his arms. She was so small. The little runner. "The seventh lily won't go to waste. It survived your grandfather's splinters and the ashes of my Oma's mirror for a reason." Like Monika had. "That lily is ours now, and it comes with a promise." He drew her closer. "Do you like Germany?"

He didn't wait for her answer. He never heard what she said. He buried what felt and sounded like a yes deep in an enemy's kiss.

A word about the author…

Colleen L Donnelly put her science education to use for years, and then put it behind her to pursue other passions. Her first love is writing and her second is hunting—hunting for that next good story, hunting for shed antlers or mushrooms in the woods, hunting for the next good author to read.

An avid believer in work hard/play hard, Colleen splits her time between indoors and out, always busy at something.

Find her at: http://www.colleenldonnelly.com/

Thank you for purchasing
this publication of The Wild Rose Press, Inc.

If you enjoyed the story, we would appreciate your
letting others know by leaving a review.

For other wonderful stories,
please visit our on-line bookstore at
www.thewildrosepress.com.

For questions or more information
contact us at
info@thewildrosepress.com.

The Wild Rose Press, Inc.
www.thewildrosepress.com

Stay current with The Wild Rose Press, Inc.

Like us on Facebook

https://www.facebook.com/TheWildRosePress

And Follow us on Twitter
https://twitter.com/WildRosePress